PENGUIN BOOKS
THE TENTH RASA

Michael Heyman is a scholar and writer of nonsense and children's literature. He is an associate professor of English at Berklee College of Music in Boston, where he teaches courses partly, if not wholly, nonsensical. He has published articles and reviews in various children's literature journals and volumes and is currently working on a textbook on children's poetry.

Sumanyu Satpathy is a professor of English at Delhi University and one of the only nonsense scholars in India. He specializes in modernism, post-colonial theory and queer theory, among other topics. He has written and edited several books, including *Re-viewing Reviewing: The Reception of Modernist Poetry in the TLS (1912–1932)* and *Conrad's Heart of Darkness*, and has published papers in various scholarly journals. He has been awarded international fellowships from the USA, Canada and Great Britain.

Anushka Ravishankar is the only Indian nonsense writer published in English in India. Originally a mathematics graduate, she has written numerous plays and works of verse, fiction and non-fiction for children. Anushka's *Tiger on a Tree* has won several awards, including the Andersen Award in Italy, and has been included in the 2005 Notable Children's Book List by the American Library Association. She lives in Delhi with her husband Ravi and daughter Akshara.

The Tenth Rasa

an anthology of indian nonsense

Edited by
MICHAEL HEYMAN
with
Sumanyu Satpathy and Anushka Ravishankar

PENGUIN BOOKS
An imprint of Penguin Random House

PENGUIN BOOKS

USA | Canada | UK | Ireland | Australia
New Zealand | India | South Africa | China | Singapore

Penguin Books is part of the Penguin Random House group of companies
whose addresses can be found at global.penguinrandomhouse.com

Published by Penguin Random House India Pvt. Ltd
4th Floor, Capital Tower 1, MG Road,
Gurugram 122 002, Haryana, India

Penguin
Random House
India

First published by Penguin Books India 2007

Illustrations on pages 10, 11, 17, 18, 23, 28, 30, 35, 36 by Sukumar Ray
Illustrations on pages 55, 56, 57, 60, 61, 63 by Anushka Ravishankar
Illustrations on pages 67, 98, 116, 133, 142, 147, 174 and those used as separators by
Vinayak Varma
Illustrations on pages 200, 202, 205, 206 by Edward Lear

10 9 8 7 6 5 4 3 2

ISBN 9780143100867

Typeset by Eleven Arts, Keshav Puram, Delhi 110035

Printed at Repro India Limited

www.penguin.co.in

FSC
www.fsc.org
MIX
Paper from
responsible sources
FSC® C047271

This is a legitimate digitally printed version of the book and therefore might not
have certain extra finishing on the cover.

Contents

Acknowledgements

This book is the result of a Herculean effort on the part of many people. We would like to thank everyone involved for their generosity, their hospitality, their time, and for putting up with our nonsense.

Many thanks to Berklee College of Music for the Faculty Development Grant, Karen Zorn, Charles Combs, Larry McClellan, Ravi Singh, Poulomi Chatterjee, Devika, Narendra and Vasudha Jadhav, the children from Sampurna's nonsense workshop, Dileep Chandan, Rajib Baruah and the Brahmaputra, Kishore Choudhury, Nabin Chandra Sarma, Nirupama Dutt, Punita Singh, Elchuri Muralidhara Rao, J.P. Das, Niranjan Behera, Preeti Sampat, M.D. Muthukumaraswamy, T. Govindaraju, the staff of Tara Books in Chennai and especially V. Geetha, Sushama Sonak, Usha Mehta, Vinda Karandikar, Mangesh Padgavkar, Esther David, Ranjit Hoskoté, Prathibha Nandakumar, Sukanta Chaudhuri, Gouri Patwardhan, Paul Kumar, Rajeeva Verma, Abu Bakar Abbad, Sanjoy Hazarika, Punkaj Chaturvedi, Manohar Shetty, Lakhan Gusain, Jerry Pinto, Arjumand Ara, Pushpesh Pant, the Children's Book Trust Library, Balvantsinh M. Parmar, Aradhana Bisht, Chad Reynolds, Kathy Rooney, Kevin Shortsleeve, other Freds and Applehead.

Special thanks to Sayoni Q. Basu, without whom this would never have happened; Anita Vaccharajani, for tireless translation and note-writing in the face of babies and wonky eyes; Sampurna Chattarji, for her wonderful translations and notes and for saving this book; and Gloria Machlis Heyman, for versatile and voluptuous versification of 'Raven, O Raven', the Urdu nursery rhymes, 'Ninepur', 'The Jamun', 'The Yellow Bear' and 'The Shadow-Catching Baiya'.

A Note on the Translations

'Do you know Languages? What's the French for fiddle-de-dee?'
'Fiddle-de-dee's not English,' Alice replied gravely.
'Whoever said it was?' said the Red Queen.

Lewis Carroll, *Through the Looking-Glass* (1871)

In Carroll's *Through the Looking-Glass*, Alice may be saying something here that we have heard more than a few times: 'You can't translate nonsense!' This statement is often made before our well-meaning friends understand what literary nonsense really is. Because it is not *absolute* non-sense, folk and literary texts are certainly translatable, even if they do present some special challenges. In this, nonsense translation is not unlike any other kind. Even 'fiddle-de-dee', the translation challenge posed by the Red Queen, is not meaningless and might very well have an equivalent in other languages.

The translations in this volume were done by an army of hardy, generous folk who put in enormous effort not only in creating the translations but also in helping with notes and dealing with one persnickety, pickity, pedantic editor. Credit for the notes should go mostly to the translators, authors and collectors of the individual pieces. The process of translation has varied with each piece. Some were translated by one person directly from an original language, while others went through a more lengthy process. For the sake of accuracy we have tried to get literal translations first. From the literal translation, meetings with translators and copious notes on language issues, rhythm, rhyme, form and context, more polished versions were created. In the case of poetry, Anushka Ravishankar, Michael Heyman and Gloria Machlis Heyman worked at transforming many pieces into some semblance of the original form. The acknowledgement for each piece reflects only the original translator. The titles given here for folk texts are often our own; for literary texts, we have given a translation of the original title. All the folk rhymes, unless otherwise noted, are available in oral form. While some are printed in collections, those which we have used are mostly from people's recollections. No definitive published versions are available for them. For the Bhojpuri texts, the editors gratefully acknowledge the help of Professor Rajeeva Verma of the Department of English, University of Delhi, and, for the Urdu nursery rhymes, the help of Dr Arjumand Ara and Abu Bakar Abbad, of the Department of Urdu, University of Delhi.

Our goal in these translations was to keep as much original meaning as possible and in poetry to retain the original verse form, including rhyme scheme, rhythm and formatting. Because the sound of nonsense is often at least as important as the sense, we have made extra effort to retain the play and music of the original languages. Of course, as with all translation, but particularly in nonsense translation, we have had to make heartbreaking choices—to cut some wordplay, to approximate, substitute, or simply lose some phonetic effects. We have debated over the funniest way to parody Sanskrit and how to deal with the rich vocabulary of family relations that does not exist in English. Whenever such issues have arisen, we have also included translation notes to help explain our choices and the specific issues at hand. The resulting translations never entirely capture the genius of the originals, but we hope they are reasonably accurate and have a charm of their own. As Sukanta Chaudhuri writes in his translation of Sukumar Ray, people 'might debate whether nonsense can be translated; but I reassure myself that at worst the result will still be nonsense'.

Uncovering the Tenth Rasa

An Introduction

AN INDIAN NONSENSE NAISSANCE

Why nonsense?

Through the murky December day, the auto-rickshaw bumped and wove along Delhi streets. I sat on my hands to keep warm, speeding past figures draped in shawls huddled around small fires. Hauz Khas to Hazrat Nizamuddin, the railway station, a half-hour stretch through wide-laned streets, around the endless roundabouts clogged with the day's traffic and the occasional contemplative cow. After a few weeks of the clinging Delhi fog, of scrabbling for nonsense scraps, I was finally on my way to Chennai, on yet another Rajdhani Express. As we rolled out, the city scenes slipped into suburban sprawl, all seen through the train window typically scratched and mucked and tinted into near opacity. A middle-aged Punjabi couple sat across from me, opening tiffins and occasionally peeking over at me. I sat cross-legged, headphones on, peering through the windows at a passing blob that could have been a man, or a lamp post, or a giant asparagus. Once we had settled in and exchanged a shy hello, they asked what I was doing in India.

'I'm collecting nonsense.'

A blank stare. After further explanation I was faced with the same lecture, the same question, I had encountered many times before.

'Why are you doing this?' the man said with genuine concern in his eyes, as if I had told him I had devoted my life to painting the toenails of cats. 'In a world of such trouble, such pain and struggle . . . What is your goal? Why *nonsense?*'

In over four years of peripatetic nonsense hunting and gathering, this is perhaps the question most asked of me—on trains, in lectures, in the classroom; by librarians, scholars, urchins and curious cows. Asking me 'Why nonsense?' is like asking a doctor 'Why medicine?', or a lawyer 'Why law?' The answers explore fundamental issues of humanity not easily discussed so casually, on a train rolling through the hills and paddies of eastern India.

The simplest answer I can give, you hold in your hands. I invite you to skip the introduction for now—explore the poems, songs and stories that, I hope, speak for themselves. If you are still not convinced then this introductory essay may help explain at least our motivation for embarking on this fool-worthy task in addition to one or two other useful titbits, such as the definition of the nonsense genre, the history of Indian nonsense, its characteristics and how it might just possibly save the world.

Let me begin, then, in answering the above question in more detail. There is no better place to start evaluating the importance of nonsense than to recognize that it is inherently *pleasurable*. Nonsense is an artistic expression of play and that, I would argue, is valuable simply for its own sake. If nothing else, these texts present a cultural exuberance—a sense of *joy* in language, work, spiritual matters, politics—all the things that make up our daily lives. Observe tabla players recite their *bols*—*dha tire kita taka tin na kite taka*—and watch the joy in their eyes, hear it in their voices, a pure joy in rhythm, sound and structure, born of nonsense.

Play, however, is much more than some structured, joyful activity. It is fundamental to our nature and shows that serious business need not always be serious, nor deprive us of joy. Play creates the parent–child bond, it teaches rules even in the very breaking of them, it is a source of community and a weapon against tyranny, a comforter and an instrument of ridicule, a reminder of youth and an initiation into adulthood. It expresses our humanity, and, just as all people around the world play, so all cultures create variants of nonsense which is, after all, a structured play with language and logic.

The urge to play is natural in children, but it is quite rare that they are able to create good literary nonsense (though we have some strong efforts in this volume). Likewise, in my classroom I teach nonsense, but when my students try to write it, it often ends up being either perfect sense, or worse: stylized, boring gibberish. The reason for this is that nonsense is a particular *kind* of play, one that is not pure exuberance, not unrestrained joy and, above all, not gibberish (though all of these are often elements of it). Rather, it is an art form rooted in sophisticated aesthetics, linguistics and play with logic, and it is the *art* of nonsense that is one of its most appealing aspects.

Another considerable aspect of this volume is what it can show us about Indian culture and history. Nonsense veins run through all of Indian culture, touching on spirituality, politics, gender issues, class, conceptions of childhood, education and linguistics. Nonsense appears promiscuously in all strata of culture, from formal medieval court poetry to Bollywood film. It reveals tantalizing connections between Indian regions and cultures along with striking differences. Indian readers, I hope, will make many discoveries here, not only in the nonsense of their own languages and culture but also, and even more important, in seeing material from so many regions and languages to which they would otherwise have had little or no access. Non-Indian readers are given a glimpse not only of the vastness of India but of aspects of its culture that are usually unknown outside India (let alone within!).

Lastly, this volume is only a beginning in the field of Indian nonsense. I hope it will recognize and foster nonsense as an accepted Indian genre and encourage further research, scholarship and development of the genre by providing a good, if not complete, variety of sources. Already, as a result of our research, nonsense workshops are happening, articles are being written, books have been published—many are discovering their nonsense heritage while also initiating a nonsense naissance.

Challenges

Before I get into a more detailed discussion of the texts, let me first relate some of the challenges and flaws inherent in the project. To begin with, the very qualifier 'Indian' is misleading, for in a nation that is a relatively recent conglomeration of ancient, shifting kingdoms, the term 'Indian' begins to lose a practical meaning. With eighteen main languages, around 100 minor ones, over 1000 documented dialects, twenty-eight culturally distinct states, seven territories, a significant north–south-east–west divide and over a billion people, India is far too complex for easy generalization. Because of such diversity, we have had to deal with a surprising lack of cross-state and cross-language knowledge. Yet, within this incredible diversity are some shared cultural and linguistic ties that justify this kind of endeavour.

Another significant stumbling block has been the attitude we often encountered concerning children's literature, and especially nonsense. Indian art tends to be quite formal and traditional—steeped in theory, endless classification, rules and serious goals. Nonsense does not seem to fit easily into such conservative ideas. Despite the efforts of a few government agencies like the Children's Book Trust and the National Book Trust, nonsense and children's literature in general still do not have much respect in India, as is evidenced by the lack of libraries that carry significant children's book collections and the overall poor quality of these books.[1] Things have started to change recently, but the Indian children's book market still has a long way to go.

One of the most challenging aspects of our research has been to get as wide a range of nonsense as possible, in terms of language, region and genre. With seventeen languages represented and most major geographical regions covered, with a striking variety of nonsense types, of both folk and literary variety, I still must recognize that this volume is far from fully representative of Indian languages, regions, or of the wealth of nonsense within India. Such a goal would take perhaps a lifetime of research. My only hope is that if you do not see yourself represented in this volume, if your language or region or favourite flavour of nonsense song is not here, then you should consider it your responsibility to carry on the nonsense torch, to use this first volume to ignite more Indian nonsense creation, collection and scholarship.

Definitions of nonsense

Anushka Ravishankar and I arrived at the Mumbai residence of Mangesh Padgavkar on 8 January 2004. It was a private flat within a nursing home, and we were shown in by a young woman and told to sit and wait. After a few minutes, a stooped man in white shuffled out and slowly settled on the couch nearby, blinking at us from behind thick, soda-bottle lenses. We

[1] For a good introduction to Indian children's literature, see Meena Khorana's introductory essay in her annotated bibliography, *The Indian Subcontinent in Literature for Children and Young Adults* (1991).

reminded him briefly why we were there and he asked, somewhat testily, what we wanted from *him*.

'We want you to tell us about nonsense,' we said.

His whole demeanour changed. He smiled and leaned forward, looking back and forth at us with a sparkle magnified by his massive lenses. In a strong voice he recited the Marathi nursery rhyme, 'Adgul-madgul' (tr. Anita Vachharajani),

Adgul-madgul
Lovely gold bangles!
Silver anklets so shiny,
A baby so tiny,
On its forehead,
A dot so pretty!

He then launched into a full-blown lecture on the nature of nonsense. Over the next hour or so, Mangesh Padgavkar expressed the deep relationship he had with nonsense. He told us, first, that nonsense should ideally be intuitive rather than intellectual. He said that if he wrote ten poems, six would be intellectual and only four intuitive, or to use his word, 'genuine'. Then he grinned, rethought for a moment and revised his claim. Out of ten poems, perhaps only *one* was genuine, the remainder intellectual. A moment later he threw his hands in the air: 'No! Maybe of these ten, or of *all* my poems, *none* is genuine!'

We all laughed at this, but it revealed some truths about the genre. Padgavkar sees it as a fundamental part of us, but also believes that access to its mystical source is limited for adults, if not completely impossible. One of the sources he mentioned was the mother–child bond, indicating that nonsense verse works on a spiritual level ingrained in us from birth. He claims that we respond to nonsense with our 'being', that it exists without effort, without 'intellect', like a tree that simply '*is*'. It reminded me of John Keats's letter[2] claiming that poetry should 'come as naturally as leaves to a tree' (70). No coincidence, as well, that Keats invented the

[2] *Letters of John Keats*, ed. Robert Gittings, Oxford: OUP, 1992.

term 'negative capability', the poet's ability to remain 'in uncertainties, Mysteries, doubts, without any irritable reaching after fact & reason' (43)—a sentiment which Padgavkar would certainly approve of in terms of nonsense. During his lecture, he would occasionally burst out in one of his own nonsense pieces, or in other folk rhymes. When his exuberance overflowed, when he was getting to the spiritual significance of the genre, he could not help but pitch his body forward, reach out across the end table and grab my arm, as if pleading with me to understand him.

I would like to expand on Mangesh Padgavkar's passionate take on the genre by looking at some other definitions that encompass the wide variety of texts considered to be in the nonsense family. We may begin by classifying literary nonsense texts as those where there is a type of balance between 'sense' and 'non-sense'. Such balance is necessary if the text is not to become either plain sense, as in a best-selling crime novel, or utter gibberish, as in a baby's babbling. The former is unremarkable, the latter, unintelligible. Good nonsense engages the reader; it must 'invite interpretation' (Tigges, *An Anatomy of Literary Nonsense*, 255), implying that sense can be made, but at the same time it must foil attempts to make sense in many of the traditional ways.

In order to keep the balance, the 'sense' side of the scale must weigh heavily: Nonsense thus tends to be written in tight structures, that is, with strict poetic form or within the bounds of formal prose. It also usually follows meticulously many rules of language, like grammar, syntax and phonetics. Nonsense stories are about identifiable characters and the usually simple plots are understandable. In short, there is much that actually makes sense in quite an ordinary way. On the nonsense side of the scale are all the ways in which the text fights against sense, primarily on the semantic and logical levels. The specific methods by which the genre does this are outlined below, but it is important to recognize that nonsense operates not by ignoring the rules of sense but by subversively playing with them—stretching, squeezing, flipping upside down, yet, in the end, still depending on their existence. Indeed, nonsense usually emerges from an *excess* of sense rather than a lack of it, or as Tigges states, through a 'multiplicity of meaning [balanced] with a simultaneous absence of meaning' (255). With such a simultaneous multiplicity of levels of meaning, there is no way of saying, as many critics do, 'Ah, it is *this* one, not *those*.'

Seen this way, nonsense thus becomes a genre that is at least as creative as it is destructive (as meaning*ful* as it is meaning*less*), a reflection of the god Shiva in his iconic manifestation as Nataraja, performing *ananda tandava*, literally the 'dance of bliss'.[3] In this dance, Shiva executes the eternal, cyclical destruction and creation of the world. Nonsense also engages in a joyful dance of destruction, although how much is destroyed, how much is subverted and how much is untouched are debatable. From the wreckage of such destruction, though, comes the creation of new kinds of sense and new ways of making it.

To use one more metaphor, nonsense leads us down a path of sense, only to turn aside from the expected destination at the last moment; in the end, we find we keep walking in circles—or beautiful, infinite fractals—and that the joy and the *meaning* is in the journey, not the destination. 'Meaning' in nonsense thus has less to do with our interpretation of conventions like plot, theme and character, and more to do with how these are subverted, with *how* the text clashes with various kinds of sense. What we gather from the struggle reflects both ourselves and the world. The genre, as T.S. Eliot puts it, is a careful parody of sense (*On Poetry and Poets*, 29), and as such it questions logic and language, our usually unquestioned, fundamental ways of making meaning of the world. We not only laugh at the absurd creations within the text, but also at our own imaginations' courageous attempts to grapple with them, and, most significantly, at our inability to escape our fundamental nature as meaning-making machines. These self-reflexive doubts can lead, in turn, to the questioning of the world we have created, including, particularly, social and political power structures fabricated under the untrustworthy aegis of 'sense'. In such a wider context, nonsense can be seen as a force for social change, linguistic exploration, political satire, religious expression and philosophical inquiry. Yet, nonsense is the opposite of some dreary, didactic tome. Despite the tension, the

[3] The idea of nonsense *creation* was developed in part in conversation with Kevin Shortsleeve, in a meeting of the Society for the Prevention of Sense (SFPS).

frustration of expectation and transgression of the sacred, it is *funny*, somehow. In such laughter, such meta-awareness, we briefly stand outside of our habitual selves, question everything—ourselves included—and in doing so face the potentially frightening consequences through the dance of nonsense, our own *ananda tandava*.[4]

If we come down from these lofty clouds of numinous nonsense, we can see that perhaps the easiest way to identify nonsense is by the common techniques found in it. There seem to be certain universal nonsense techniques in both English and Indian nonsense, as well as a few more culturally specific ones that are a set of tools used to work upon geographically specific cultural and literary raw material. As a rule of thumb, the more of these techniques used, the more we consider the text to be in the genre. They can be roughly divided into two groups, the first being more strictly linguistic, the second more logical, though most of these have aspects of the other.[5] Linguistic techniques include neologism, portmanteau, reduplication and sound-over-sense. Neologism (the invention of new words) and portmanteau (smashing together two real words to create a third nonsensical one) are perhaps the most widely known devices of nonsense, yet they are used surprisingly little. Such invented and cobbled words appear in many texts, particularly in Sukumar Ray's pieces—words such as 'Gorgondola' or the 'whalephant' (both translation-approximations that mirror the original language fairly accurately). These make good nonsense because they are suggestive without dictating exact meaning. One predominantly Indian linguistic technique comes from the propensity of Indian languages to use reduplicative patterns. In English, we use a few of these, such as 'chit-chat' or 'go-go', but Indian languages make much more use of such

[4] These mystical senses also touch on Alan Watts's definition of nonsense as a representation of Zen philosophy, or G.K. Chesterton's claim that the appreciation of nonsense is the closest approximation to religious faith we can find in literature. For details on these definitions, see Alan Watts, *Nonsense* (1967) and G.K. Chesterton, 'A Defence of Nonsense', in *The Defendant* (1914). See also Aldous Huxley, 'Edward Lear' in *On the Margin* (1923).

[5] The basis of this list of techniques comes from Wim Tigges, *An Anatomy of Literary Nonsense*, *passim*.

formations and the nonsense reflects it. In the Oriya piece 'Ickity-Sickity' (whose title alone is a translation of this), for instance, the Oriya reduplicative phrase, *puturu-puturu* is used to describe soil. This phrase has no solid definition, yet it is onomatopoeically evocative of the softness of mud.

One nearly universal characteristic of nonsense is a sheer joy in the musicality of language, its sound and rhythm. Nonsense writers are often more concerned with the sound than the sense and pull out all the tools of euphony. Sampurna Chattarji's brilliant translations of Sukumar Ray offer a glimpse of his flights of phonological fancy. A few lines from Sukumar Ray's 'Glibberish-Gibberish' should demonstrate this:

Come happy fool whimsical cool
    come dreaming dancing fancy-free,
Come mad musician glad glusician
    beating your drum with glee. (1–4)

But language functions in more ways than just as word-music. A nonsense world emerges because of the *nature* and *sound* of the language used, rather than language simply being used to describe a world. Thus, in the poem 'No' by Padgavkar, the word 'rip' has everything to do with the word 'ripple' (though we do not exactly know what this relationship is), mostly because it physically exists within the word. In these pieces, language functions less as a signifier and more as raw material. Words *as* words have as much substance as 'things' and the nonsense world's laws are dictated more by alliteration than litigation, more by resonance than reference.

While language is of course a system of meaning based in part on logic, the following nonsense techniques can be said to lean more towards logical manipulation and they include, to begin with, paradoxical simultaneity of meaning. Simultaneity generally refers to the simultaneous existence of two or more, usually contradictory, meanings. In Ravishankar's 'Lost and Found', for instance, the word 'contra-rily' functions in two contradictory ways:

I lost it
I lost it
my mantra
on a contra
rily judged
word (1–6)

The word root 'contra' functions here, but then we see it is just the first part of 'contrarily', yet to make consistent meaning and pronunciation we cannot have both. In Indian nonsense there is an even more particular kind of simultaneity that rarely occurs in English nonsense. This I would call nonsense tautology and it occurs when two different words or phrases are used side by side, implying a *different* meaning but actually having the *same* meaning. This is the dominant technique used in the 'thorn' verses/stories found in many folk traditions.

There was once a ber tree
It had an eighteen-and-a-half foot thorn.
On its tip were three villages,
Two were empty and no one lived in the third at all.
In it lived three Brahmins,
Two were fasting and one ate nothing at all.
('A Story about a Story', 2–7)

The language and structure imply a distinction between the two described states, yet it becomes clear that in the whole series there really are only three identical things. To arrive at this conclusion, however, we must fight *against* the language; the implication of distinction cannot be completely forgotten and we find ourselves looking for slight distinctions, which do indeed sometimes exist. Fasting, for instance, has a slightly different meaning from simply not eating.[6]

Other kinds of logical manipulation are non sequitur and arbitrariness,

[6] Tautology is also used in British nonsense, though it was more popular in the seventeenth century (and before).

absurd precision and imprecision, faulty cause and effect, and the use of infinity. Non sequitur and arbitrariness are ubiquitous in nonsense, yet they must be used sparingly. Much folk nonsense is full of them and thus fails to elicit any concerted effort to make sense. These are only effective as nonsense when they challenge us to *make* sense of them, even though, in the end, we cannot. A particular kind of arbitrariness, absurd precision, is the inclusion of detail, often numbers, which are so precise as to imply some significance in that precision. Of course, there is none. This also includes the mention of obvious detail, like the grand revelation of Ravishankar's Brother Marbel, who cogitates on the Taj Mahal being 'very white'. More common in Indian nonsense, though, is the use of imprecision. Ravishankar revels in the incomplete thought, the deficiency of meaning, as with cousin Nibboo: 'At Parur he was very pleased/He said, "I am—"/And then he sneezed' (4–6). Faulty cause and effect is another pervasive method of nonsense. One example will suffice, from Kunjunni's 'Because':

Because the poppadum is round
So the cow's milk is white
Because the cow's milk is white
So the milk pot's made of clay. (1–4)

Why are these things so? Surely there is some connection? Notice that these are not always completely unconnected logically. The poppadum may not be related to milk, but milk is certainly related to the milk pot. Even in the first two lines the very syntax implies connections with which we must struggle. After all this cognitive effort, we know, of course, that this is nonsense—yet we played the game, a sure sign of *successful* nonsense.

The last method to be treated here is the use of infinity. Nonsense writers, both Western and Indian, have found that the concept of infinity is yet another device that teases our intellect. It is a concept we have a word for though we cannot comprehend it. Infinity appears in Indian nonsense in various ways, starting with the folk form of nonsense series, such as in the Assamese 'Where is that mango?':

Where is that mango?—It fell into the wood.
What became of the wood?—The fire consumed it.
Where are the ashes?—The washerman carried them away.
What did the washerman do?—Washed the king's clothes . . . (3–6)

This kind of accretion is a common method of constructing nonsense and it can go on and on. In fact, that is part of the fun of it, for it becomes a game of invention between nonsense-makers, both adult and child. A more concrete sense of infinity appears in 'Never-Ending Tale', a bedtime tale in which the parent always answers the child's question of 'what happened next?' with 'Another sparrow came, took one grain and flew off', until the child sleeps.

For the sake of this anthology, I have tried to keep all the definitions, both Indian and Western, in mind, not only to mitigate any potential imperialist tendencies of trying to fit Indian writing into a form defined by the Western model, but also to be as inclusive as possible without relaxing standards to such an extent that *everything* is considered nonsense, as sometimes happens in nonsense anthologies. Jokes, riddles, light verse, fantasy, fables—none of these forms is in itself nonsense. A joke is funny because it makes sense; nonsense is funny because it does not. A riddle is clever because, eventually, it makes sense; nonsense is clever in how it suggestively does not. Light verse, fantasy, fables . . . nonsense can live in any of these forms and more. Indeed, it thrives on some overarching form that gives it some recognizable shape and meaning—something to make sure the nonsense techniques do not make the text explode into boring gibberish—yet the form itself provides only such (necessary) restraints; it does not equal nonsense. Thus, nonsense is a kind of parasite inhabiting a host form, yet it has a life of its own.

In this anthology we include a vast array of nonsense texts, some of which we might consider perfect examples of the nonsense form, while others only use certain nonsense techniques without falling into the category itself. Writers like Sukumar Ray, Mangesh Padgavkar and Anushka Ravishankar all frequently exemplify classic, formal literary nonsense. But this is just the beginning of what is in this volume. For instance, we have many folk texts which tend to veer towards the gibberish side of the sense array. Because of their nature and our assumptions about folk texts, there is therefore less expectation that they make sense. Without the formal restrictions of literary nonsense, and without the expectation of sense, we are less inclined to play with meaning, yet the nonsensical nature of these texts is undeniable. Folk material is thus important as a precursor to literary nonsense. Of course, the 'meaning' of a text can come from many sources, and as Lalita Handoo, a Kashmiri folklorist, reminded me, folk texts are never truly non-sense; quite the contrary, they are windows into cultural and historical study. Other texts related to literary nonsense include some political/cultural satires by Annada Sankar Ray that use nonsense as a *device* but are otherwise quite obviously direct satire. Post-modernism is a grandchild of nonsense, and you will find the story by M.D. Muthukumaraswamy, which is a contemporary example of stream-of-consciousness writing, a genre that borrows from nonsense but is quite distinct in other ways. Our goal has been to make sure that everything in this volume has *some* relation to nonsense.

The origins of Indian nonsense

Into the mystic

We may look back as far as certain holy scriptures or mystical texts, such as the Vedas, the Upanishads, or medieval poet-saints like Kabir, for the paradoxes that later appear in modern nonsense.[7] One distinctive example of this 'mystical' nature is the ubiquitous 'thorn' texts, already mentioned. As we did research on these enigmatic verses, we were told that they had some kind of spiritual significance, yet no one knew exactly what it was. Eventually, we were able to get one particularly ancient version by Sant Namdev, a medieval poet-saint, that is probably less corrupt than the more recent folk rhyme descendants. In this version, after the list of nonsense tautologies, we get a 'message': 'Namdev says that being without a guru/Leaves you incapable of seeing the truth at all!' ('Three Villages', 7–8). Thus the 'nonsense' in the text represents our experience of the world without spiritual guidance.

[7] See Satpathy's introduction for more on these mystical texts.

Having observed this, though, we must also factor in the prose piece by Khwaja Banda Nawaz that is only slightly newer and has no such apparent didactic intent. Did Sant Namdev invent nonsense tautologies to teach his lesson, or did he create a moral for an already existing nonsensical folk verse? Regardless, the serious moral does enter the field, even though it does not exist in all other manifestations of the text that we have found. This may be due to the exuberance and irreverence of the folk tradition that often does not allow such seriousness to remain. The various retellings, contortions and expansions of this basic form in the folk tradition leave behind the message, assuming it was there initially, and build on the amusing sense of absurdity found in the un-'enlightened' form.[8]

Perhaps we enjoy not having all the answers. Indeed, this may be the whole point. The successful reading of nonsense could be seen, in a way, as learning how to live with such apparent opposing dualities, even to enjoy them. In order to proceed through a nonsense text, we have to rely on more, or less, than our default sense-making strategies and ride with it, so to speak, or, to use Keats's term, exert our 'negative capability'. As Hess and Singh suggest[9] in reference to Kabir's 'upside-down language', in order to read *with*, rather than *against* these texts, we must let go of our tendency to think in the usual two-dimensional, linear way that leads to only one correct answer; rather, we are invited to think beyond two dimensions to embrace multiple, contradictory truths which, after all, better reflect reality.

The folk

The folk tradition is perhaps the strongest influence on the formation of literary nonsense. The subcontinent is rich in nonsense-like folk material, some being for or by children, some quite adult. The former includes lullaby, game rhyme, counting rhyme, nursery rhyme and song. If we look back to the folk rhyme 'Adgul-madgul' that Mangesh Padgavkar recited to us, we see such a nursery rhyme—one that, while not strong as nonsense, does begin with a completely nonsensical reduplicative

[8] See the 'Thorn' Texts section in this volume for a wide variety of such texts.
[9] *The Bijak of Kabir*, trans. Linda Hess and Sukhdeo Singh, Oxford: OUP, 2002, 146.

form. Another example from the multitude of folk nonsense is this Bengali nursery rhyme, or *chhoda*:

Nitter-natter
Son-in-law's chatter
A spider fell down splitter-splatter.
The spider fought all arms and legs
Seven pumpkins laid seven eggs.

This piece, which could indeed be composed by adults or children, may not have the overarching structural continuity or sophistication of literary nonsense, but it is typical of the fun, the arbitrariness and sheer absurdity of the child-like folk imagination.

But folk nonsense is not just for young children. 'Adult' nonsense appears in religious festivals, as in the 'Onam Song', and weddings, as in 'A Mocking Wedding Song'. In a Punjabi celebration, adolescents play a nonsense game in which they must carry on a 'conversation' with each other. However, each line they say must have no logical relation to the line spoken immediately prior to it by the other party. The end result is a conversation of nonsense—contextually chaotic, yet serving a practical social purpose in bringing together shy boys and girls who do not know what to say to one another.[10] Spoken by a 'fool' figure, nonsense rhymes also appear as short performance pieces in the intervals of the lengthy folk drama productions (usually Indian epics) in different parts of India.

Not only the spirit of folk nonsense but also its forms, methods and themes find their way into modern literary incarnations. New Oriya operas (a form of folk drama once, like all folk material, transmitted orally), for instance, are now written by playwrights like K.C. Pattnaik. The reversals so often found in folk text, like the sun shining at night, reappear in many modern texts, such as Gulzar's 'The One-Eyed Town', where the 'rivers flowed on bridges' and 'trains ran on water not land' (9–10). Dash Benhur's 'The Shadow-Catching Baiya' follows different folk methods, in using the accretion form found in many other folk

[10] Pushpesh Pant, in conversation with the author on 24 June 2001 in New Delhi.

texts where a word or idea from one line is then used in the next (see 'Let's Tell a Tale II'). Likewise, in Benhur's text a word or idea from the last line of the section is used in the next stanza. Benhur also shows a thematic movement from the traditional, mythical *baiya* (a boogeyman-like figure), to the regular folk, to the police and finally to modern civil engineers and ministers—a progression of sorts from the traditional to the modern.

English influence

The influence of the English on Indian nonsense is undeniable. Ever since the mid-nineteenth century, and possibly even before, English works of nonsense have found their way into the particularly English-influenced areas of India, especially West Bengal and Maharashtra. Rabindranath Tagore, Sukumar Ray and other figures of Indian nonsense read Lear and Carroll and wrote with them in mind. Little surprise, then, that Ray's prose *Haw-Jaw-Baw-Raw-Law* is strikingly similar to Carroll's Alice books in plot, writing style, use of illustration and characterization. From the eminent nonsense figures like Tagore and Ray came a host of imitators and this style of English-influenced nonsense was disseminated even more widely. In Assam, for instance, Navakanta Barua wrote quite derivative nonsense twice removed from English sources (via Ray), such as in his poem 'Ninepur', which is strikingly similar to Ray's 'Article Twenty-One'. Nowadays it is difficult, if not impossible, to separate the English influence from the native and in most cases the genre develops as a hybrid.

One significant shared characteristic of English and Indian nonsense is the complex sense of subject matter and audience. Nonsense writers in English like Lear, Carroll and Edward Gorey have often been accused of covertly writing for adults, due variously to their technical brilliance and what is considered subject matter too sophisticated, philosophical, or otherwise 'adult'. Some Indian nonsense literature has been considered too sophisticated for children, but therein lies much of its appeal. It deals with difficult, and what many consider 'adult', issues in ways that can be handled by children—implying, with great respect, that children can and should be given such material. Lear, Carroll and Gorey toy with death, dissolution and melancholy, and Indian nonsense is no different. Sukumar Ray's 'Tomcat's Song', for instance, evokes nothing less than an existential crisis. It describes a treasured cake being stolen by a cat and the narrator's ensuing, obviously exaggerated, philosophical funk. While the cause here is, of course, absurd, the philosophical ruminations are less so, implying a dual audience, or, indeed, that the adult and child may not be so far apart after all.

Concerning the English influence, I should mention that some of the 'influences' mentioned here may not be so much directly borrowed from the English as simply characteristic of the genre overall. While Ray's similarity to Carroll cannot be denied, many of the nonsense techniques and qualities that some might see as 'English' may in fact just be a result of the universal nature of nonsense mentioned earlier in this introduction. Indeed, the 'adult' subject matter we have seen may just be a fundamental part of nonsense in any culture. As Edward Gorey, perhaps the greatest American nonsense writer, said, 'If you're doing nonsense it *has* to be rather awful, because there'd be no point. I'm trying to think if there is sunny nonsense. Sunny, funny nonsense for children—oh, how boring, boring, boring. As Schubert said, there is no happy music. And that's true, there really isn't. And there's probably no happy nonsense either' (Schiff, 89). Gorey might exaggerate a little, but perhaps in play, nonsense, regardless of the language, not only allows children to engage safely with the 'awful', but also takes away their fear of it.

How to be Indian . . .

While we may question certain aspects of the English influence, it is still in many ways fundamental to the creation of modern Indian nonsense. Because of this, Indian artists have often rebelled. One of the more insidious appearances of English culture in India has been in the nursery, through nursery rhyme, English-style education and textbooks, and high-quality English children's books against which Indian children's books have trouble competing. Indians, however, through nonsense, use these English forms subversively. In traditional Tamil verse, for instance, we encounter a rat taking a plane to see Queen Elizabeth:

You will get hungry on the way
Pray, what will you eat?
I'll buy bajjis and vadas, hot
And give myself a treat. ('Mister Rat', 9–12)

Here the Indian rat takes his culture with him, the *bajjis* and *vadas* (both Indian foods), but the poem is perhaps a reference to expatriate Indians, the 'rats' who have abandoned India in her time of need for the promise of wealth in foreign countries.

A well-known Bengali political satirist, Annada Sankar Ray, whose writing, though not pure nonsense, is often nonsensical, gives us a verse called 'What the Little Girl Learnt':

Baa baa black sheep
    Have you any wool?
No ma! No ma!
    That's all bull.
Not black, not a sheep,
    Not at all woolly . . . (3–8)

This piece, an obvious dig at omnipresent English nursery rhyme, reveals the depth to which Indians are immersed in English culture, and how, through verse, they rebel. One might also look at this verse in light of colonial race issues, as the British did (and still do) sometimes refer to Indians as 'blacks'. The Indian child would then be denying not only the offensive label (to an Indian) of 'black' but also the ovine obedience expected of an inferior, savage colonist.

The anti-colonial streak also runs in the open satire of Sukumar Ray's '*Tyash Goru*' (Limey Cow), whose 'eyes are droopy-woopy, its face is very vast/Its neat and tidy hair is combed to the last' (*Abol Tabol*, 40, 3–4). In an email dated 4 April 2005, Sampurna Chattarji wrote, 'Even today when you use the word "*tyash*" for someone, it is derogatory and means overly and unpleasantly westernized—Ray originally used it to refer to Anglo-Indians.' Other examples abound, including Amitabh Bachchan's imitation of the English in the film *Amar Akbar Anthony*.

While some Indian nonsense texts rebel against their English models, most assume a unique Indian identity not through reaction but, rather, through assimilation. Indian writers take the form, in some ways dictated by the English and make it their own by applying the general tools of nonsense to distinctly Indian material. They revel in all things Indian, from the sound of the languages to their distinctive foods. The cultural material in the 'thorn' texts, for instance, is very much an Indian affair: it includes drought, clay pots, rice, buffalo, rupees, the devaluation of money and Indian village life. Such domesticity has been noted by Satyajit Ray, who claims it to be one of the distinguishing features between the nonsense of Lear and Carroll and that of Sukumar Ray (and, by extension, other Indians). He observes that English nonsense characters are kept at a certain distance from 'our familiar world' (Introduction, *The Select Nonsense of Sukumar Ray*) while Indian nonsense places its characters closer to real Indian life. Although Satyajit Ray may be ignoring such quintessentially domestic characters as Lear's Nutcrackers and Sugar-tongs, his point still stands overall. This obsession with Indian domesticity, in addition to all things Indian, creates a distinct brand of nonsense.

The obsession with food is well documented in Indian arts, from pop music to novels, and nonsense, usually intensely gastronomic in any culture, is no exception. To give only one of many possible examples, Sampurna Chattarji's collection of macaronic verse, *The Food Finagle*, is particularly interesting in its syncretic attempt to play with various food names from different regions of India. In 'Explained', for instance, Chattarji exploits the similar sounds of Indian foods and English words: 'Idiyappam keeps yapping/Puttu plays golf' (1–2). She plays off of the sounds 'yap' and 'putt' to give quite a Humpty-Dumptian version of naming theory, one that considers the signifier somehow intrinsically linked with the signified's physical characteristics and, regarding 'yapping', the physical characteristics of the *word* itself.

Another particular Indian obsession is with large families. In a culture where numerous members of one's extended, and often quirky, family live in the same space, and where marriage matches involve massive family scrutiny, many literary works, as well as movies and TV, revolve around family issues such as obedience to parents and conflicts with in-laws. Overly gregarious in-laws turn up in the Bengali *chhoda* (nursery rhyme) 'Nitter-Natter' and in Sukumar Ray's 'Indirections' which makes fun of the complex familial relationships that Indians must constantly juggle:

Here's Jagmohan! Splendid! I'm all in a mess
In looking for Adyanath's uncle's address.
You couldn't have met him, but Khagen you know—
Well, Shyam Bagchi, Khagen's own uncle-in-law,
Has married his daughter to Kesto, you see,
Whose landlord's wife's cousin, whoever he be,
Has Adyanath's uncle as aunt's brother's son.
D'you know where he lives? For I simply must run . . .

(*SNSR*, 8, 1–8)

Other Indian cultural obsessions are with the extreme weather and indigenous flora and fauna. Sukumar Ray's 'Where Do They Go on a Wild Goose Chase?' for instance, describes a king who endures the afternoon summer sun, which 'drills holes into his head so dry' (*Abol Tabol*, 18). Anyone who has spent a summer in India can surely feel for the king and knows the value of the monsoon rain that 'falls like sleet/ And then—I've tasted it myself—it's absolutely sweet' (*Abol Tabol*, 3–4). The heat and the rain also bring about the country's lush, tropical flora, as seen in Shreekumar Varma's 'Ghost Office', where we see the 'local village post office which is situated in the middle of a stream in a small compound surrounded by trees bursting with grey mangoes and pink jackfruit and vines of jasmine oozing out of the earth like night-worms'. Indian nonsense is abundantly supplied with such overflowing plants, fruits, and generally all things natural and indigenous. Rather than Carroll's very English forests and sculpted gardens, Indian nonsense quite naturally follows its own path.

The nonsense carnival

The next few points I will address are also quintessentially 'Indian' topics, yet their treatment in nonsense calls for a more specific approach. One revealing way of looking at nonsense is through the lens of Mikhail Bakhtin's book *Rabelais and His World*, which defines the 'carnivalesque', the wild spirit of a Renaissance carnival that mocks and upturns any given society's sacred cultural conventions, like religion, class and sexuality (*Rabelais and His World*, 10). At the carnival, lay folk dress in wimples, collars and saffron robes and disport themselves in a distinctly irreligious manner; kings and slaves, depending on which masks they wear, can reverse roles; and sexual mores, like strategic bits of clothing, are thrown to the wind. Likewise, nonsense literature in all cultures tends to make everything it touches stand on its head. Indian nonsense, in particular, takes a carnivalesque approach to Indian aesthetics, politics, religion, class/caste issues, respect for elders and the guru–disciple relationship, all topics that are normally treated with the utmost respect.

The carnival begins with medieval Indian poetry. In the sixteenth-century Vijayanagara court of Krishnadeva Raya, the poets would have contests to test their skills of literary analysis of complex poetic forms. The legendary court jester and poet Tenali Ramalinga is said to have created some verses that, on the one hand, were executed in a perfect formal style but, on the other, were sheer absurdity and nonsensical wordplay. The poem 'Goat's Tail', that uses only the words '*meka*' (goat) and '*toka*' (tail), is an example of this. An English equivalent might be to write a villanelle, a devilishly complex form, using only 'goat' and 'tail' and a few connecting words. The result turns what is usually a serious poetic form on its head, making the form and any inherent spiritual or aesthetic associations ridiculous.

Annada Sankar Ray, as we have already seen, uses nonsense techniques to take advantage of the liberties that the carnivalesque allows. In his verse entitled 'Ballyhoo', he mocks some of India's most revered political and literary figures, even the beloved Rabindranath Tagore, a national icon. This kind of mockery by a Bengali is simply unheard of, yet Ray's use of nonsense gives him such licence. Some of his other verses, like 'Outside In' and 'Let's to Delhi' comment on political corruption and cry out for a truly democratic process in the new Indian government.

Religion, all-pervasive in Indian culture, gets its turn in the carnival, as well. In one Bengali *chhoda* we see class, religion and religious music, all taboo topics for mockery, mocked:

What's up? Frog in a cup.
What sorta frog? A musical frog.
What sorta music? Brahmin music.
What sorta Brahmin? Eulogic Brahmin.
What's eulogic? A horse's kick. (1–5)

The Brahmin, the highest Indian caste and that from which priests must come, is ridiculed, along with his religious authority and his music. Such class criticism pervades Indian nonsense and can also be seen in the Hindi verses that make fun of 'Fat Cat', the typical fat, lazy, upper-class man. Sukumar Ray has the most developed carnivalesque nonsense, as seen in the court scenes of *Haw-Jaw-Baw-Raw-Law*.

The tenth rasa

So far, we have seen in Indian nonsense the more universal nonsense characteristics, the influence of English culture and language and some of what makes Indian nonsense truly 'Indian'. Yet, despite its roots in the history and culture of India, and despite its skilful practitioners, it has not been given the respect it deserves. This may be because it needed to be recognized as independent from British as well as from other Indian literary forms and it needed to be accepted as a serious Indian art—no small tasks for a genre derived in part from the British, in a country replete with endless literary forms, both folk and formal, and ancient, conservative concepts of the nature of art. Sukumar Ray, however, was fit for the task and came up with an ingenious solution to all of these problems.

In his Preface to *Abol Tabol* (1923), his famous collection of nonsense, he included an apologia: 'This book was conceived in the spirit of whimsy.

It is not meant for those who do not enjoy that spirit.' Part of the function of this was to warn the more serious-minded public and critics away from such a strange literary product. But there is far more meaning to this simple statement, owing to the Bengali words that cannot be directly translated. The 'spirit of whimsy' in this passage is, in Bengali, '*kheyaal rawsh*' and refers to a fundamental classification of Indian aesthetic theory, that of the *rawsh*, or *rasas*, as they are more commonly known (a word which also has the meanings of taste, the 'essence' of something, as well as living liquids like sap and juice). All Indian arts are designed to produce complex emotional effects on the audience. These effects are strictly delineated and classified according to Bharata's *Natyasastra* (c. AD 200), an ancient treatise on the arts, and include nine *rasas*.[11] Each *rasa* corresponds to one emotional effect: love, anger, the comic/happy, disgust, heroism, compassion, fear, wonder and peace. All serious art must evoke combinations of these *rasas*.

The result of Ray's inventing the tenth *rasa* is twofold. First, it helps to distinguish the nonsense form from other Indian literary forms. As Satpathy has discussed, Tagore initiated this distinction by recognizing that children's *chhoda* represented a separate rasa: 'There are nine rasas in our aesthetic theory. But, the *chada* (or *chhoda*), meant for children, contains a kind of rasa which does not fit into any of the nine rasas. The beauty of this rhyme can be called, *baalras* [children's *rasa*]. It is neither thick nor pungent. It is, rather, clear, innocent, beautiful, and that which cannot be related to anything.'[12] Tagore was the first to recognize such value in folk rhymes and stories and, according to Chaudhuri, 'it was largely owing to his efforts that these began to be recorded and studied seriously'.[13] Having folk material taken seriously was an important step for Indian scholarship and paved the way for Sukumar Ray to distinguish further the genre of nonsense from folk and other forms of literature.

[11] Bharata's treatise includes eight rasas. The ninth, corresponding to 'peace', was later extrapolated.
[12] 'Lok Sahitya' (Folk Literature), in *The Works of Rabindranath Tagore*, Vol. 3, Calcutta: Bishyobharati University Press, 1986, 3.
[13] Rabindranath Tagore, *Selected Writings for Children*, ed. Sukanta Chaudhuri, New Delhi: OUP, 2002, 2.

Ray's new *rasa* is not restricted to children, as Tagore's is. Rather, it represents the complexity of literary nonsense. As Satyajit Ray, Sukumar Ray's son, claims in his introduction to his father's volume, 'There are traces of such whimsy in the folk poetry of any nation. But authentic literary nonsense masks its caprice beneath an apparent gravity in an urbane and sophisticated manner unknown in popular rhyme.' By creating a tenth *rasa*, and designating it the prime *rasa* of nonsense, Ray was thus distinguishing nonsense, the essence of whimsy, from folk material, which only has 'traces of such whimsy'. He was also giving it respectability as a genre that includes an adult audience.

More significantly, though, the creation of the *rasa* of whimsy revises about 1800 years of fundamental aesthetic theory, necessitating that nonsense be considered a serious, even conservative, art form. Long before Bharata's treatise on art, Indian aesthetic theory was well developed, codified, directly related to religion and therefore mostly, if not exclusively, serious. Bharata recognized that the 'comic' mode existed but marginalized it (at best) by making it share a *rasa* with 'happiness', a conjunction any modern theory of comedy, such as Freud's on jokes, would cast doubt upon. The creation of this tenth *rasa* thus has some quite revolutionary and revisionary effects. Incorporating 'whimsy' into the pantheon of *rasas* and claiming it to be the primary characteristic of nonsense legitimizes the genre in the eyes of even the most aesthetically and culturally conservative judges. Furthermore, including the concept of whimsy with the other *rasas* introduces a rebellious, potentially dangerous concept. 'Whimsy', which is a good translation of the Bengali '*kheyaal*', is an 'odd fancy; idle notion; whim', or alternatively a 'curious, quaint, or fanciful humour' (*Webster's New World*). But the Bengali word, even more than the English word, has a pejorative meaning, especially in the adjectival form. Thus, to sanction that which is odd, idle, contrary, fanciful—all partially in a pejorative sense—is dangerous; it could potentially disrupt the seriousness, the discipline and the sanctity of the others. In particular, it distinguishes itself from the combined 'comedy/happiness' *rasa*, perhaps showing the inherent rebellion or at least the sheer absurdity of nonsense that Gorey referred to, a mode that is often problematically comic. As French absurdists like Ionesco show, nonsense can be comic, absurd, disquieting and terrifying all at once.

As *rasas* are not temporal creations but eternal qualities, Ray's inclusion of 'whimsy' implies that is has *always* been there, unrecognized yet affecting the other *rasas* (especially the comic/happy). One would have to go back to reconsider the other *rasas* in light of the newest 'discovery' and completely revise the ways they are used in the arts. Of course, one has to believe in the *rasa* for the revolution to occur. If the aesthetic pundits of Sukumar Ray's time had accepted his concept, then he would have succeeded not only in the ultimate 'Indianization' of literary nonsense, but in potentially revolutionizing Indian art. His nonsense, not surprisingly, was not taken as seriously as he would have liked, though it did become wildly popular and continues to be to this day. West Bengal is also one of the few areas in India where nonsense is taken seriously by adults. His was but a beginning for this still nascent art form in India.

Michael Heyman

TRADITION AND MODERNITY IN INDIAN NONSENSE

This anthology celebrates not only the universal spirit of whimsy but also the hybrid genre called Indian nonsense. But can one speak of the category 'Indian nonsense'? Is there anything identifiably 'Indian' about the nonsense written in different Indian languages? Such questions can be attended to in two ways. First, by thinking about how the form or genre of nonsense accommodates the Indian reality, for nonsense draws and thrives on reality though often by poking fun at if not totally denying or distorting it. Second, by examining in what form it already existed before colonization and how it changed when it came in contact with foreign cultures, especially the tradition of English nonsense in the nineteenth century.

What is Indian reality is itself a difficult question. For ages quotidian reality in India has been dismissed as *maya*, the illusion or appearance of the phenomenal world (*OED*). The unseen world of the gods, heaven, hell, fairies and ghosts is as much real (or unreal) as the practical world of earth and sky, the seasons, wilderness, animals, royalty, social and caste hierarchies, priests and cowherds. The oil-man (*teli*), the potter and his pots, and the crow would coexist alongside the sacred thread, the tiger, the raja and the Brahmin. It is these signifieds which typify pre- and postmodern subcontinental realities and invite the description 'Indian'. Beginning with the earliest times, the dominant worldview shaped the cultures of different regions, and as the so-called modern Indian languages emerged between the eleventh and thirteenth centuries, the dominant view was regionally modified and shaped with local traditions and historical circumstances. This common source explains the similarities which can be discerned in both modern and traditional nonsense across linguistic and cultural regions.

That which we call modern or literary nonsense in India is a hybrid product that arose from colonial contact. Though Edward Lear noted that his works were already known in northern and western Indian towns when he visited India (1873–75), it was Bengali literary culture that responded to the foreign brand of nonsense first. After all, Lear had dubbed Calcutta 'hustlefussabad' (*Indian Journal*, 2 January 1874). It was only a matter of time before the rest of India too reacted to the call of literary nonsense. In the case of neighbouring Orissa and Assam, which were part of undivided Bengal for many years, modern nonsense came about not so much through English as through Bengali influence. The nature of the influence of English nonsense on Bengali has been well researched; but the same cannot be said of the other Indian linguistic cultures.

The English tradition would not have been so easily accommodated in India if the latter did not have its own indigenous traditions of nonsense, though no specific term was in circulation. Beginning with Rabindranath Tagore, many Indian artists and scholars have invoked various ancient forms when they attempt to theorize or even write nonsense. From the Vedas and Upanishads to the work of the medieval poet-saints paradoxes and puns abound and one may notice how they anticipate the genre of nonsense, even though read as philosophy or mysticism. From oral and mnemonic folk tales, lullabies and game rhymes to folk theatre and modern films, nonsense has been an integral part of the Indian consciousness. As would be evident from the third section of the present anthology, India had a strong tradition of folk nonsense. Sukumar Ray himself hints at the connection between the native Indian tradition and its modern counterpart when he calls nonsense the '*rasa* of whimsy'.

How does one identify traditional Indian nonsense, given the fact that the category is being applied ex post facto to a kind of culture in which the modern sense of nonsense was non-existent? To begin with, we should recognize that it exists in intersecting matrices: oral/folk and literary; religious and secular. Thus, during the course of research on this volume, when we asked people about literary nonsense in their respective languages they would invariably deny its existence in their language. But when asked more specifically, they would recall traditional children's rhymes, and folk or game rhymes, many of which we have used in the present volume.

The tradition we are speaking of is the tradition of children's rhyme variously designated across linguistic cultures. In Bengal, Tagore is one of the first to recognize this fact and see a link between the traditional *chhoda* and Indian literary nonsense. In an essay entitled, '*Chhele Bhulano Chhoda*' (1893) he writes:

> Ancient rigveda was composed as panegyric to Indra, Chandra and Varuna; but *chhoda* has emerged from the panegyric meant for the twin gods enshrined in the mother's breast—little boys and girls. Neither of these can claim precedence over the other; the *chhoda* may not be historically old, but is so intrinsically. On account of its primitive simplicity it is one of the most ancient of all human compositions.

Less easily seen as precursor to modern Indian nonsense is what can be found in the religious domain. Commonly used terms in Indian-Hindu *tantra shastra* (texts that deal with esoteric aspects of religious teaching) are often meaningless. '*Om hring cling*' is one such set of gibberish. After the Persian influence, expressions like '*gilli, gilli, golla*' became common.

Though these are in themselves meaningless, they may make sense in specific contexts. For example, when a street magician performs a trick and uses these terms, they are taken to be essential to the show as they are addressed to the supposed master of charms, who alone would understand them. When used in secular and workaday contexts, as they frequently are by writers of modern Indian nonsense, the same expressions become genuine nonsense. Similarly, in some regional cultures, *tantriks* used *sandhyabhasa* or *sandigdhabhasa*, meaning 'twilight language' and 'doubtful/equivocal language' respectively. This is a language that the practitioners of the twilight knowledge zone used in order to deliberately keep the system beyond the reach of the common man. The language of mystification is called *ulti bhasa* (inverted language) in Hindi.[14] In Kannada, the literary form or style of producing apparent nonsense is called *bedagu* or *mundige*. The following is one example of hermetically sealed *bedagu*:

Gangadevi became a widow
Gowridevi took off her ear-rings
The wind-god carried the bier
Basudeva set it on fire
Then on the news spread
Lord Guheswara is dead.[15]

A reader who understands at least the basic plot and names would still wonder: How can the eternal goddesses, the two paramours (Ganga and Gowri) of Lord Guheswar (Shiva), be widowed? How can, for that matter, the great and immortal Shiva die? Through their inner paradox these lines anticipate the modern tradition of nonsense. Since this verse is part of a mystic epistemology, it has received different hermeneutic exegeses. One of the explanations is that it captures the attempt to articulate the shift from dualistic experience to monism.

[14] For an alternative perspective on the function of this inverted language, see Hess and Singh's analysis, outlined in Heyman's introduction in this volume.
[15] From the *vachanas* of Allama Prabhu (a twelfth-century Kannada mystic). I am grateful to H. Shiva Prakash for directing my attention to these *vachanas*.

Some other interpretations are so far-fetched as to invite the description of nonsense themselves.

Some verses attributed to Kabir, a medieval mystic poet, belong to a similar but more recent tradition. Kabir puns on words and writes the following mock lament about the vagaries of language:

Chalti ka naam gaadi
Maal ko kehtey hain khoya
Rangeen ka naam narangi
Dekh Kabira roya.

[What moves is called interred/vehicle
Commodity is called lost/desiccated milk
What is colourful is called colourless/orange
On observing these, weeps Kabir!]

The words *gaadi*, *khoya* and *narangi* signify a vehicle, desiccated milk and orange respectively; but Kabir alludes to the alternative connotations (interred, lost, colourless) which are literal meanings but are antithetical to the other meanings. In these lines Kabir illustrates the imprecision of language, its inability to capture reality. The statements make sense but the words allude to that which they are not.

In the context of intralinguistic obscurities, one might refer to Ramakrushna Nanda who says,

> Unintelligibility or irrelevance does not reduce the value of *nanabaya*. The rhythm and style is unique. Sometimes the meanings are unclear or impossible to ascertain. In English some of these children's rhymes are called 'nonsense' or meaningless rhymes. By defying the metrical prescriptions and grammatical conventions the spontaneity of these rhymes endear themselves to children.[16]

[16] Ramakrushna Nanda, ed. *Odiya Shishusangit Samkalan*, Bhubaneswar: Orissa Sahitya Akademi, 1981, 3.

Nanda further refers to the limerick form of Lear in the context of humour in nursery rhymes. After providing the Oriya reader with some metrical details regarding the form and quoting Lear's 'Old Man with a Beard' as an example of the form, he says, 'Lear's humorous rhymes are enjoyed by both children and adults. In Oriya no such accepted forms or purely humorous compositions exist' (Nanda, 11).

The term 'nonsense' itself has had many equivalents or near equivalents in various modern Indian languages which were applied to whatever was ontologically, conceptually, empirically and realistically untenable. The Sanskrit word '*udbhat*' ('absurd' or 'bizarre') has been widely prevalent. There have been other etymologically intractable words which themselves are therefore nonsense terms to designate common utterance/speech acts which are non-connotative or are inflected by connotative as well as denotative (semantic) confusion/imprecision. In Bangla they could be *ja-ta* or *ajgubi*, in Hindi and Punjabi *und-sund* or *be-matlab*. In Malayalam the word for nonsense is *asambandham* or *aprasangika*. Vaikom Muhammad Basheer uses the nonsense word *hunbusato* as the title of a story. In one of his essays in *Literature and Culture*, U.R. Anantamurthy refers to the fifteenth-century mystic poet Purandara's use of the word *lolalotte*. In Kannada *lotte* refers to the unintelligible children's dialect and *lola* further emphasizes the word. Anantamurthy says that the Kannada term refers to whatever is 'childishly nonsensical'. 'The very sound conveys the sense [that it is nonsense].'[17]

But in the specific context of the modern literary genre, Indian writers of nonsense are still at a loss to attach a respectable name for their compositions. In Bangla, following Sukumar Ray, the term *abol tabol* has come to signify nonsense. But in most other Indian languages there does not seem to be a widely accepted term for nonsense, and often the English word is used freely. In Oriya many alternatives have been offered. Following Nandakishore Bala, the term *nanabaiya* has gained popularity. It covers a wide range from sensible nursery or game rhymes to nonsense 'pure and simple'. More recent and better-informed

[17] Anantamurthy, 'Tradition and Creativity' in *Literature and Culture*, Calcutta: Papyrus, 2002, 111.

writers have offered such terms as *asangata shaitya* (Panigrahi), *alukuchi-malukuchi* (J.P. Das), *ana-bana* (Dash Benhur, J.P. Das). According to Niranjan Behera, the Bathudi tribe of Mayurbhanj call naughty and obstinate boys and girls '*bai-jhaia*'. He also suggests that the word *bai* refers to madness or whim, and tagged to an alliterative nonsense, the resulting term, *bai-jhaia*, is indeed closest to the idea of nonsense.[18]

Some Indian formulations of nonsense make interesting reading. Somehow, the term is seen as pejorative and as a genre some established writers consider it infra dig to experiment with nonsense. Sometimes an apologia is also pressed into service. Tagore, for example, offered not one but two elaborate explanations, when his nonsense collection, *Khapchhada* (1937) was published. The title means incongruity/mismatch, but it is also a pun on *chhoda*. Imagining an audience who had purportedly urged him to write non-serious verse, he says,

> You urge me to write simply
> but it isn't simple at all to write simply.
> . . . It is difficult to write nonsense . . .

The term that I translate here as 'nonsense' is '*jaa-taa*', which literally means balderdash but is not being used here pejoratively. It is an equivalent of *abol tabol*. If he is equivocating here about his attempt to write nonsense, it may have been because such poetry was seen as childish, not behoving—in his own self-image—a writer of his stature. In 1937 he writes equally apologetically in his second prefatory verse addressed to Rajshekhar Basu whose knowledge of Sanskrit was legendary. Tagore invokes the high canonical traditions with numerous allusions to Puranic myths and justifies the high status of nonsense.

> Should you see that the outer covering
> has come off the old man.
> ....
> If his utterances do not have any bearing on sense,
> and his mind is crazy,

[18] Behera's letters to the author dated 2 February 2004 and 1 November 2004.

Or, that it has reached the furthest limits of caprice,
and you blame it all on his education,
Then shall I speak of why Brahma has four faces.

Then he goes on to recount the function of the four faces of Brahma, and concludes,

In the fourth, waves of excitement
break the dam of sanity.
From such an impact, p'haps nonsense swirls up.
Thus, the disciple of Brahma, the poet says,
'No matter how much you laugh at me
It will be on record
That imagination plays with creativity
But it is no less crazy about miscreation!'[19]

This shows how Tagore infuses an element of high seriousness into nonsense, even if his admirers do not take these efforts seriously. His *Khapchhada* is not very often talked about and it has remained untranslated as a whole.

In his autobiography, Kalindi Charan Panigrahi, a major Indian poet who wrote in Oriya, recalls how he along with some friends like Annada Sankar Ray (who as a Bengali must have borrowed the concept from Sukumar Ray) formed the 'Nonsense Club' in Cuttack in the 1920s. He thinks of nonsense as that which 'pleases us by a sequence of sweet sounding word patterns or syntax but through contradiction and paradox, or incongruity or absurdity'. He calls those literary creations 'Nonsense' which draw their inspiration from the traditional Oriya '*nanabaya geeta*' or those children's rhymes and folk tales which fill the young and old alike with the kind of *rasa* described above (Panigrahi, 369). More recently, Bengali poets and critics like Sankho Ghosh and Shivaji Bandopadhyay have dealt with the subject of nonsense in book-length studies. Ghosh entitles his book *Kalpanar Hysteria* (The Hysteria of

[19] Rabindranath Tagore, *Rabindra Rachanabali Janma Shatabarshiki Edition*, Vol. 3, Calcutta: Government of West Bengal, 1960, 439–40.

Imagination), which in itself offers a view of nonsense as imagination run wild, not very different from Tagore's interpretation of the source of nonsense as the torrential eloquence of 'miscreation'.

Traditional Indian nonsense has now been collected and printed in book form in different Indian languages. But they are not museum pieces. They survive to this day mainly through regional oral and folk traditions and continue to be part of the living tradition in rural India. They have also mutated through their appropriation by the stage, modern and postmodern arts, as well as FM radio, advertisement and TV. As the inclusion of dialogues and songs from Bollywood shows, Indian nonsense is alive and well. The process started by Sukumar Ray when he adopted nonsense for the stage plays *Jhalapala* and *Lakshmaner Shaktisel* has progressed to reach Indian theatre, cinema, and beyond. With the Indianization of MTV, the ultimate symbol of postmodernist culture, nonsense has returned to its rightful position in mass consciousness.

I would like to conclude by invoking here Adi Sankaracharya's formulation in his Sanskrit treatise I: '*Artham anartham bhabaya nityam*'. It is taken usually as an indictment of materialist aspirations: 'Remember always that *artha* (money) is the source of all *anartha* (calamity).' But it also could mean '*artha* (meaning) is the source of all *anartham* (trouble)', '*artha* (meaning) is the source of all *anartham* (non-meaning)', or, even, 'meaning is contrary to its own self'. The saying takes us back to what we started with about the category 'Indian nonsense'—that it is part of India's traditional epistemology, and second, nonsense, like parody, is caused as much through authorial intention as through readerly intervention.

Sumanyu Satpathy

IS NONSENSE?

What is nonsense? One answer to this perennially and frequently asked question is that nonsense is a genre of literature that is much maligned and yet much enjoyed. It is easy to spot, given a little intelligence, that this is no answer at all, since it could just as easily be a definition of hard-boiled detective fiction, pornography or period romance. As a practitioner of the art, I have often felt the need for a definition of nonsense which will once and for all end confoundment, silence dissent and serve as a foolproof defence of nonsense against solemn sceptics and carping critics. Hence, although my colleagues have already waxed as eloquent as candles about the genre and its many subtleties, I will attempt once again to define it for the confused reader, and defend it for the honour and glory of nonsense and its many practitioners.

As with all philosophical inquiry, we must begin this exploration into nonsense with the fundamental question: is it? To answer this question, the questioner has to first ask himself or herself another fundamental question: am I? If the answer to the latter question is in the affirmative, then we must select a random sample of such questioners, who will then proceed to ask each other: are you? Once the incontrovertible fact of the questioners' respective existences is established, the question the questioners must ask themselves, each other, and anyone else who might care to listen is: does it automatically follow that genres of literature exist? In other words: are they? If this is answered in the affirmative, then and only then do we have necessary and sufficient conditions for the existence of nonsense as a genre.

After this is proved beyond doubt, we can go to the next, self-evident step, the question of what nonsense is. Because if it is not, then it is nothing. However, since nonsense is a negation of reality, its nothingness is of great significance, and defines it with precision. Whereas if it is, then it is something else. This is the quintessential nature of nonsense—the ability to be nothing and something at the same time. The Hamletian dilemma does not apply to nonsense, because there is a simultaneity of is-ness and is-not-ness in it which is unparalleled in any other field of human endeavour. In fact, even in the world of plants, famous botanists have been known to have commented again and again on the impossibility of finding a parallel to the non-Hamletian nature of nonsense. Besides, nonsense also defies Aristotelian dialectics, Darwinian evolution, Hitchcockian suspense and Heisenbergian uncertainty. It does, however, find a resonance in Godell's formulation of the Unprovable Proposition.

The moment Godell's famous theorem is understood, it is easy to comprehend that nonsense is the unprovable axiom upon which the whole epistemological system, that is to say, all of literature, philosophy, carpentry, zoology, pottery and even some parts of meteorology and cosmetology stand. Nonsense, therefore, is the very foundation upon which the edifice of modern knowledge has been painstakingly built over the centuries. Remove nonsense and you are left with nothing. Which is to say, more nonsense.

Hence it would not be an exaggeration to state that without nonsense, life as we know it would cease to exist, and nobody could doubt the tautology that life as we do not know it is no life at all. Thus, with meticulous logic and careful analytical inference, we have established that nonsense is the very stuff of which life is made. No further defence of the genre is required.

If you are still not convinced of the crying need for the appreciation and pursuit of nonsense, then, dear reader, you need to read this book, because your education has, as it is wont to do, addled your brain with too many facts and too little wisdom. If you are convinced, then you hardly need encouragement. Pursue nonsense as assiduously as Lewis Carroll's Baker pursued the Snark and you will softly and suddenly vanish away. But you will leave in your place a wiser, happier and more enlightened human being.

Anushka Ravishankar

WORKS CITED

AN INDIAN NONSENSE NAISSANCE by Michael Heyman

Bakhtin, Mikhail, *Rabelais and His World*, 1965, trans. Helene Iswolsky, Indiana: IUP, 1984.

Chesterton, G.K., 'A Defence of Nonsense' in *The Defendant*, London: J.M. Dent & Sons, 1914: 42–50.

Eliot, T.S., 'The Music of Poetry' in *On Poetry and Poets*, London: Faber & Faber, 1957.

Huxley, Aldous, 'Edward Lear' in *On the Margin*, London: Chatto & Windus, 1923: 167–172.
Kabir, *The Bijak of Kabir*, trans. Linda Hess and Shukdeo Singh, Oxford: OUP, 2002.
Keats, John, Letter to John Taylor, 27 February 1818, in *Letters of John Keats*, ed. Robert Gittings, Oxford: OUP, 1992, 70.
———, Letter to George and Tom Keats, 21, 27(?) December 1817, in *Letters of John Keats*, ed. Robert Gittings, Oxford: OUP, 1992, 43.
Khorana, Meena, *The Indian Subcontinent in Literature for Children and Young Adults*, New York: Greenwood, 1991.
Lear, Edward, *Edward Lear: The Complete Verse and Other Nonsense*, ed. Vivien Noakes, New York: Penguin, 2002.
———, *Indian Journal: Watercolours and Extracts from the Diary of Edward Lear*, 1873–1875, ed. Ray Murphy, London: Jarrolds, 1953.
Pant, Pushpesh, conversation with author on 24 June 2001 in New Delhi.
Ray, Sukumar, *The Select Nonsense of Sukumar Ray* (*SNSR*), trans. Sukanta Chaudhuri, Calcutta: OUP, 1987.
———, *Abol Tabol: The Nonsense World of Sukumar Ray* (*AT*), trans. Sampurna Chattarji, New Delhi: Puffin, 2004.
Schiff, Stephen, 'Edward Gorey and the Tao of Nonsense' in *The New Yorker*, 9 November 1992: 84–94.
Tagore, Rabindranath, *Selected Writings for Children*, ed. Sukanta Chaudhuri, New Delhi: OUP, 2002.
———, *Khapchhada*, 1937.
———, 'Lok Sahitya' (Folk Literature) in *The Works of Rabindranath Tagore*, Vol. 3, Calcutta: Bishyobharati University Press, 1986.
Tigges, Wim, *An Anatomy of Literary Nonsense*, Amsterdam: Rodopi, 1988.
Watts, Alan, *Nonsense*, 1967, Dutton: New York, 1977.

TRADITION AND MODERNITY IN INDIAN NONSENSE
by Sumanyu Satpathy

Das, J.P., *Alukuchi Malukuchi*, Bhubaneswar: Lark, 1993.
———, *Alimalika* 1993, New Delhi: Publication Division, 1993.
Ghosh, Sankho, *Kalpanar Hysteria*, Cacutta: Papyrus, 1984.

Lear, Edward, *Complete Nonsense*, Hertfordshire: Wordsworth Editions, 1994.

———, *Indian Journal: Water Colors and Extracts from the Diary of Edward Lear*, 1873–1875, ed. Ray Murphy, London: Jarroldes, 1953.

Lehmann, John, *Edward Lear and His World*, New York & London: Thames and Hudson, 1977.

Nanda, Ramakrushna, ed., *Odiya Shishusangit Samkalan*, Bhubaneswar: Orissa Sahitya Akademi, 1981.

Panigrahi, Kalindi Charan, *Ange Jaha Livaichi* (1901–1972), Cuttack: Cuttack Student's Store, 1973.

Tagore, Rabindranath, *Rabinrda Rachanabalijanma Shatabarshiki Edition*, Vol. 3, Calcutta: Government of West Bengal, 1960.

Literary Nonsense

KABIR

Kabir, a famed fifteenth-century illiterate poet and teacher, created many verses which were written down by his disciples. Some of these are called *ulatbamsi*, or 'upside-down language'. These absurd, paradoxical, opaque and possibly symbolic texts have usually been seen as either deep, meaningful puzzles to be solved, or pure nonsense. Perhaps they are, in a way, both. They turn on Kabir's conception that the mystery of reality is ineffable and can never be communicated; that it is the 'untellable tale', the '*akatha katha*'. In poem after poem, Kabir rejects the possibility that formal, linear discourse can lead to enlightenment. In his view, only the abrupt leaps and seismic shocks of the 'upside-down language' can provoke such transformative shifts of consciousness. This is the cornerstone of his teaching method. See the Introduction for more on this form of language and the potential 'meaning' therein.

FROM BIJAK

SABDA 62

Translated by Ranjit Hoskoté from the Hindi original

Mother, see what splendour I've rained on both families!
Twelve husbands I devoured at my father's house
and sixteen more at my in-laws'.
Sister-in-law and mother-in-law
I strapped to the bed,
brother-in-law I abused.
I set fire to the hair of that crone
who harassed me.
My womb swelled up with five,
then two, then four more.
I had the woman next door for breakfast,
and the mother of wisdom too.
Poor little things! Then I laid out the bedroll
of ease and slept, my feet sticking out.
Now I neither come nor go,

neither live nor die.
The Master has wiped away all shame.
I grasped the Name and threw the world away.
I grasped the Name—so close, so close!
Sings Kabir: I saw the Name!

Sabda 2

Translated by Ranjit Hoskoté from the Hindi original

O saints, don't sleep with your eyes open!
Time can't consume you,
the years can't tire you,
the four ages can't bring you to ruin.

The Ganga whips round and drinks up the ocean,
gobbles up the moon and the sun.
A sick man gets tough, knocks down the nine planets.
Reflections scorch the water that holds them.

A legless man runs in all directions.
A blind man surveys the world.
The rabbit whips round and swallows the lion.
Such marvels! Who knows what they mean?

A jar knocked upside down will float,
a jar standing upright will sink.
A man may be as stubborn as hell
But the Master's grace will take him to heaven.

A man in a cave thinks that is his world,
of the world outside he knows nothing.
The arrow swivels in its arc and strikes its archer.
Only the fearless know what this means.

They call him a singer, but he never sings.
That other, the mute, he can't stop singing.
A listener tolerates the soloist on stage
out of boundless love for the Unheard Sound.

They talk and talk, but the one who listens
knows that the real story can never be told.
The earth rears up and goes clean through the sky.
Listen to the Great One speaking.

A man with no cup drinks the nectar of eternal life.
A swollen river refuses to flood.
Whoever gets drunk on Rama,
says Kabir, will live for ever.

Sabda 52

Translated by Ranjit Hoskoté from the Hindi original

Give it a thought, Dr Know-It-All!
It's pouring sheets, the thunder's deafening
but not a single raindrop's fallen!

An elephant's chained to the foot of an ant,
a sheep has pounced on a wolf.
A fish has leaped from the tide
to build a hut on the shore.

Frog and snake share a bed,
a cat brings forth a dog,
the lion's hiding from the jackal.
Such marvels! They're beyond words.

Who can follow the antelope of doubt
through the jungle?
The archer takes aim, trees catch fire
in the water, the fish go hunting today.

The wonder of such knowledge!
Whoever hears it will go flying
wingless to heaven, says Kabir, and never die.

TENALI RAMALINGA

When an excessively proud writer once entered the Vijayanagara court of Sri Krishnadeva Raya (1509–30) and invited the pandits to a contest of deciphering the meaning of his poems, Tenali Ramalinga, the court jester and poet, is said to have challenged him to first assign a meaning to the following impromptu verse.

The poem (an *utpalamala*, a popular poetic form borrowed from Sanskrit), only ostensible nonsense, can be explained by means of gestures making the following ideas apparent: a heroic man agreeing to take part in a duel when challenged, his prompt refusal to the overtures of a lady and his charitableness towards the needy. The next stanza portrays the pauper as showing signs of fear when confronted, his longing for an illicit relationship and his tendency to repel the poor when manhandled.

A Man of Mettle

Translated by Dr E.M. Rao from the Telugu original 'Tejamu, saadhuvrittamunu'[1]

A man of mettle having courage,
Strength of character and readiness to dare
Says thus to his challenger,
To another's wife thus,
And thus to the almsman;

A pauper lacking in courage,
Strength of character and readiness to dare
Says thus to his challenger,
To another's wife thus,
And thus to the almsman!

[1] 'A Man of Mettle' and 'Goat's Tail' based on *Chatupadya Ratnakaramu*, ed. Deepala Picchayya Sastry, 2nd edition, Guntur: Welcome Press, 1927, 25, 18–23.

Goat's Tail

Translated by Dr E.M. Rao from the Telugu original 'Mekatokaku meka toka mekaku toka'

On another occasion, a little-known poet came to the court of Krishnadeva Raya and challenged the scholars to explain the meaning of a complex, language-bending composition of Srinatha (1350–1450) in praise of Allaya Vema Reddi, a royal chieftain. Tenali Ramalinga must have been miffed at the poet's impudence and asked him to first explain the following impromptu creation. The original Telugu is transliterated here, to make the sound and wordplay more apparent.

The poem has nothing but a play on the words *meka* (goat) and *toka* (tail). The visitor was so afraid to enter into a debate with a poet of Ramalinga's calibre that he chose to concede victory to him and remained quiet. Moreover, as the challenge verse is in the same *sisa* metre (a derivative from the S'irshaka metre in Sanskrit) as the original, and given the ductility of the language, the poet must have feared that it was entirely possible for Ramalinga to even create a new meaning and build a case against him. The sense of the nonsense was too formidable for him.

Mekatokaku meka toka mekaku toka,
Meka tokaa meka? toka meka
Mekatokaku meka toka mekaku toka,
Meka tokaa? meka toka meka
Mekatokaku meka toka mekaku toka,
Meka tokaa meka? toka meka
Mekatokaku meka toka mekaku toka,
Meka tokaa? meka toka meka

Meka tokatoka mekameka meka toka
Meka tokatoka mekameka meka toka
Meka tokatoka mekameka meka toka
Meka tokatoka mekameka meka toka.

To a goat's tail the goat is the tail, O Goat and O Tail,
Can a goat's tail be the tail of a goat?

To a goat's tail the goat's tail is the tail of a goat,
Can a goat be the tail? O Goat, is the tail a goat?
To a goat the goat's tail is the tail of a goat,
Is the tail a goat or the goat a tail?
To a goat's tail the goat is the tail, O Tail and O Goat,
Can the tail of a goat be the goat's tail?

Goat ta-tail go-goat goat tail
Goat ta-tail go-goat goat tail
Goat ta-tail go-goat goat tail
Goat ta-tail go-goat goat tail.

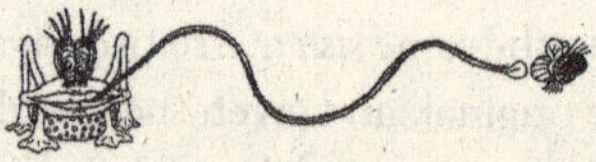

SUKUMAR RAY

GLIBBERISH–GIBBERISH

Translated by Sampurna Chattarji from the Bengali original 'Abol Tabol'

Come happy fool whimsical cool
come dreaming dancing fancy-free,
Come mad musician glad glusician
beating your drum with glee.
Come O come where mad songs are sung
without any meaning or tune,
Come to the place where without a trace
your mind floats off like a loon.
Come scatterbrain up tidy lane
wake, shake and rattle 'n roll,
Come lawless creatures with wilful features
each unbound and clueless soul.
Nonsensical ways topsy-turvy gaze
stay delirious all the time,

So come you travellers to the world of babblers
  and the beat of impossible rhyme.

Mister Owl and Missus

Translated by Sampurna Chattarji from the Bengali original 'Payncha aar Paynchani'

Mister says to Missus Owl,
  I just love it when you howl,
Listening absent-mindedly
  My soul dances blindedly!
That rubbed voice and scrubbed croon
  That upswelling happy swoon!
Just one of your ear-splitting hoots
  Rips the trees out of their roots,
A twist, a turn in every note
  Crescendos creaking from that throat!
All my fears all my woes
  All my throbby sobby lows,
Are all forgotten thanks to you
  My darling singing Owleroo,[2]
Moonbright beauty, sweet as sleep,
  Your nightly songs, they make me weep.

Pumpkin-Grumpkin

Translated by Sampurna Chattarji from the Bengali original 'Kumdo Potaash'

(If) Pumpkin-Grumpkin dances—
Don't for heaven's sake go where the stable horse prances;

[2] Owleroo: A coined word to convey the endearment latent in the original Bengali '*penchi rey*'.

Don't look left, don't look right, don't take no silly chances.
Instead cling with all four legs to the holler-radish branches.[3]

(If) Pumpkin-Grumpkin cries—
Beware! Beware! Don't sit on rooftops high up in the skies;
Crouch down low on a machan bundled to the eyes,
Sing 'Radhé Krishno Radhé' till your lusty throat dries.

(If) Pumpkin-Grumpkin laughs—
Stand next to the kitchen poised on straight and skinny calves;
Speak Persian in a misty voice and breathe through silken scarves;
Sleep on the grass, skip all three meals, no doing things by halves!

(If) Pumpkin-Grumpkin runs—
Make sure you scramble up the windows all at once;

[3] holler-radish branches: In the original the word '*hotto-mula*' is a portmanteau word formed by combining two separate 'sense' words: '*hotto*' meaning market or village fair, and '*mula*' being the colloquial way of saying '*mulo*', which means radish. However, the word '*hotto*' in this hyphenated form also suggests a related word, '*hotto-gol*', meaning noise and pandemonium. The attempt was to convey some of the associative and literal meanings of the original phrase as well as retain its syllabic structure.

Mix rouge with hookah water and on your face smear tons;
And don't dare look up at the sky, thinking you're great guns!

(If) Pumpkin-Grumpkin calls—
Clap legal hats on to your heads, float in basins down the halls;
Pound spinach into healing paste and smear your forehead walls;
And with a red-hot pumice-stone rub your nose until it crawls.

Those of you who find this foolish and dare to laugh it off,
When Pumpkin-Grumpkin gets to know you won't want to scoff.
Then you'll see which words of mine are full of truth, and how,
Don't come running to me *then*, I'm telling you right now.

JOLLYCODDLED

Translated by Sampurna Chattarji from the Bengali original 'Ahladi'

Look we're laughing lookit us laugh, we're the laughing lads,
A tribe of three, toothlessly, laughing louder than our dads.
Big brother's laughing, so am I and so's the little one,

Dunno why we're laughing, so we're laughing just for fun.
Why laugh at all, we think, let's not laugh till after,
But thinking makes us break into a bubbling bout of laughter.
We feel like laughing open-eyed or when they droop 'n close,
Or when we've pinched a person or stuck a finger up our nose.
We laugh to see an oar an ant a weaver's loom a yellow moon
An oil can a grown man a train a boat a gas balloon.
As we try to learn our ABC each of us a whiz—
Laughter gushes noisily like soda with a fizz.

Ooby Dooby Doom![4]

Translated by Sampurna Chattarji from the Bengali original 'Dadey dadey droom!'

Vroom vroom the cars zoom, carriages and cabs,
People hurrying, ever-scurrying, in fevered dribs and drabs;
Run like mad and then *begad!* run over, die like flies,
The English billy with his filly 'Help me Mama!'[5] cries.
Without a care with total flair we beat a drum and play
'Ooby dooby doom! Dooway dooway dooway!'

The muddy streets of storm and sleet, wear your trousers rolled,
On gusty nights a gouty blight, why catch your death of cold?
Let evening come let morning go let afternoon drift on,
Forget the stress forget the mess skip work and feel reborn—
Catch instead this snatch of song our moonlit tune hurray,
'Ooby dooby doom! Dooway dooway dooway!'

All the fools go by the rules, sit with their books all fussed,
Some look frazzle-hazzled, some others look nonplussed.
Some strain their brains with thinking, faces turning ashen
Some sit and nod incessantly in a stupid fashion.
Don't rack your head my friend instead sing out loud and gay
'Ooby dooby doom! Dooway dooway dooway!'

Each one of you all glum and blue, wasting so much time,
Toiling so and moiling so on this painful onward climb!

---

[4] The refrain of the song, which gives the poem its original title, is not merely excellent nonsense but could also very well be used in an actual song. The inspiration for the English equivalent is the sixties' 'doo-wop'. In fact, in the garb of this nonsense poem, Ray critiques many things, from the frenzied pace of modern life to the dunderheaded studiousness of schoolboys determined to study hard and get ahead. (A malaise that continues to plague middle-class Bengali homes!)

[5] 'Help me Mama!': Ray uses the English words 'Mama' and 'Papa' in his quiet mockery of English gents and ladies horrified out of their genteel skins by the unruly Indian traffic roaring by.

What matters most you're missing, you're getting it all wrong,
Can't you hear loud and clear the drumming in the song?
    Pick up the tune and start to croon with derring-do, we say,
    'Ooby dooby doom! Dooway dooway dooway!'

WORDYGURDYBOOM![6]

Translated by Sampurna Chattarji from the Bengali original 'Shobdo Kolpo Droom!'

Whack-thwack boom-bam, oh what a rackers
Flowers blooming? I see! I thought they were crackers!
Whoosh-swoosh ping-pong my ears clench with fear
You mean that's just a pretty smell getting out of here?
Hurry-scurry clunk-thunk—what's that dreadful sound?
Can't you see—the dew is falling, you better stay housebound!
Hush-shush listen! Slip-slop-sper-lash!
Oh no the moon's sunk—glub-glub-glubbash!
Rustle-bustle slip-slide the night just passed me by[7]
Smash-crash my dreams just shattered,[8] who can tell me why?
Rumble-tumble buzz-buzz I'm in such a tizzy!
My mind's dancing round and round making me so dizzy!

---

[6] The title attempts to convey the tonality and rhythm (rather than the exact meaning) of the original 'Shobdo Kolpo Droom!'. '*Shobdo*' means 'word' as well as 'sound' and '*kolpo droom*' signifies a wishing-tree (myth.) as well as a liberal, generous person (fig.). In the poem, Ray seems to depict a fantastical world where words have lives of their own and phrases act out their meanings in very physical and literal (not to mention dramatic) ways.

[7] Rustle-bustle slip-slide the night just passed me by: The original Bengali makes literal a phrase in common use—*raat kaate*, using scissor-sounds to dramatize the literal 'cutting away', or passing, of the night. However, in English, the 'scissoring effect' would not work, hence the similarly common phrase in English 'the night passes' is used here and made literal with the appropriate sound effects.

[8] Smash-crash my dreams just shattered: The Bengali phrase '*ghoom bhangey*' (literally, 'sleep breaks') becomes 'dreams shattered' in English to enable the use of the relevant 'smash-crash' sounds.

Cling-clang ding-dong my aches ring like bells—
Ow ow pop pop oh my heart it bursts and swells!
Helter-skelter bang-bang '*help! help!*' they're screeching—
Itching for a fight, they said? Quick! Run out of reaching!

Stand-Alones Together

Translated by Sampurna Chattarji from the Bengali originals

i

Come come sit down, tell me why in that town
The doctors each and every one are boiled-potato haters.
It says in the paper, the brain turns to vapour
And grey cells don't grow, now you know why no 'taters!

ii

Did you hear what he said, the old fool?
The sky, it seems, smells sour as a rule!
But the sour smell vanishes when rain falls like sleet
And then—I've tasted it myself—it's absolutely sweet.

Article Twenty-One

Translated by Sampurna Chattarji from the Bengali original 'Ekushey Aain'

This poem can be seen as a satirical take on the draconian and often meaningless laws prevalent in British India. The nonsensical notion of punitive action ruled by the number 21 is perhaps a jibe at both the arbitrariness of the legal system and the unfairness of punishment disproportionate to the 'crime'.

Disastrous laws rule the land
Blessed by Shiva's loving hand!

If by chance you slip and fall
Guards appear grim and tall,
Drag you to court at a run—
    And fine you rupees twenty-one.

To sneeze before six is a crime,
You need a ticket all the time;
Ticketless sneezing spells trouble—
For cops arrive on the double,
Punish you with a pinch of snuff—
    Twenty-one sneezes are just enough.

If someone has a shaky tooth,
You're taxed four rupees in truth,
And if by chance a moustache grows,
You're fined a hundred annas on the nose—
And prodded till you execute,
    A twenty-one-times salute.

If while walking you should chance,
Left or right to idly glance,
News rushes straight off to the king,
Platoons dash out with a spring,
Put you in the sun to make you hotter
    And give you twenty-one cups of water.

All poets who've ever versified,
Are caught and caged quite mortified,
While a hundred chanters all off-key[9]

---

[9] a hundred chanters all off-key: The 'chanters' in the original are clearly specified as being '*Udey*', a derogatory term for people from the state of Orissa. While Bengalis tend to consider themselves culturally superior to those from Orissa, Ray's intent is probably to mock the very notion of that superiority by putting the phrase '*Naamta shonaye eksho Udey*' within a nonsensical framework.

Chant the tables in medley,
They write not poetry by the ounce
But twenty-one pages of accounts.[10]

In that land at midnight deep,
If you snore while fast asleep,
Up they charge and on your head,
Rub cowdung mixed with molten lead,
Twenty-one times you're twirled and flung
Then, for twenty-one hours you're hung.

One Off Into Two

Translated by Sampurna Chattarji from the Bengali originals

i

The moment a rainbow appears in the sky,
Countless folk look up, drop their work and sigh,
Seeing this a nitpicky old man gets so very furious,
He says, 'Can't you see, the colours are all spurious?'

ii

Bong-bong go the drums tweet-tweet the flutes
Yik-yak phew-spew the cough of old coots
Hip-hurray omigosh goggle-gape go green
The master's son's first tooth has only just been seen.

[10] twenty-one pages of accounts: What adds another layer to this line in the original Bengali is the image of the *mudir khata*, literally 'grocery book', or the book in which your grocery bills for the month would be carefully noted down.

Mish-Mash

Translated by Sampurna Chattarji from the Bengali 'Khichudi'

A duck and a porcupine, no one knows how,
(Contrary to grammar) are a duckupine now.

The stork told the tortoise, 'Isn't this fun!
As the storkoise we're second to none!'

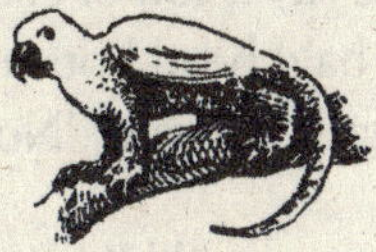

The parrot-faced lizard felt rather silly—
Instead of insects must he now eat green chilli?

The goat charged the scorpion at a rapid run
Jumped on his back so now head and tail are one.

The giraffe lost his taste for roaming far and wide,
Instead, like a grasshopper, he'd rather jump and glide.

The cow said, 'Am I sick, too, from this disease?
Or why should the rooster chase *me*, if you please?'

And oh the poor whalephant—that was a bungle,
While Whale yearns for the sea, Eli wants the jungle.

The hornbill was desperate because it had no horns,[11]
Merged with a deer now, it no longer mourns.

[11] To echo the wordplay inherent in Ray's original '*Shingher shing nei mone bhari koshto*' (which, literally translated, would read 'The lion was desperate to own a pair of horns'), the hornbill, which has the word 'horn' (*shing*) embedded in it, has been used here.

Wise Old Woody

Translated by Sampurna Chattarji from the Bengali 'Kaathburo'

Black pots white beard an old man sits
Enjoying the sun, eating boiled wooden bits.
Shakes his head and hums and sings a merry song
You'd think he's a sage, but you would be wrong!

Mutter-mutter he utters words that make no sense—
'The sky is full of cobwebs, wood has holes hence.'
His bald head hots up his body pours sweat,
Angrily, he yells, 'No one understands this yet!

Those stupid blind fools have not a grain of sense in stock
Donkeys! Morons! All they know is how to run amok.
Which wood has what juice, they can't even guess,
Or why new moonlight makes holes in *wood*, no less.'

Round-about scritchy-scratchy he does many sums
Split wood splat wood he calculates on all his thumbs:
Which crack tastes good, which like hell,
Which crack has *exactly* what kind of smell.

Rat-a-tat knock-knock one against the other
Says he, 'I know how to stop wood being a bother.
After all this messing around with wooden sticks,
I know just *how* to put an end to all their tricks!

Which one can be tamed, which one is quiet,
Which one keeps flickering, which one's a riot.
Which one knows nothing, neither truth nor lies,
I know why wood has holes you see, because I am wise.'

Tomcat's Song[12]

Translated by Sampurna Chattarji from the Bengali original 'Hulor Gaan'

Dark-sprawl creep-crawl a nasty empty night,
Trees softly covered by a velvet lack of light.
The tangled knot the sooty clot under the banyan tree
Glitter-throbs with glow-worm mobs fancy as can be.
In the shivery-shrubbery hush of the spook-silent city
Come come my brother tom let's rum-pum a ditty.

Let's whisper sweet songs in shrieks to each other
The one humming in my head do start strumming brother.
Half-broken sleep-woken a night-blind slice of moon
Rises scarlet-bright at midnight not a second too soon.
Reminds me in a jiffy-jot by the earthen pot I say
A half-broken sweetmeat's been lying for a day.

Off we dash when in a flash the cruel cut of the knife
A catty dame devoid of shame sits gobbling for dear life.

---

[12] The original with its use of snappily paced internal rhymes has an almost sing-song, tripping tone which becomes necessarily more formal in English. The use of invented compound words 'creep-crawl', 'glitter-throbs', 'sleep-woken', 'jiffy-jot' and so on aim at duplicating that effect as far as possible.

Her sly-puss cheeks with sweet treats are so clearly stuffed,
With a snicker our last flicker of hope gets rudely snuffed.
What's the point of living on, brother tom, we think,
When all we see seems to be a conjurer's hoodwink.

It all seems dreadful empty it all seems dreadful cheap,
The wife alack seems as black as a chimney sweep.[13]
Our broken-hearted woe come let us pour into a song
In melody soul-splittingly let us sing it all night long.

Nonsense Gone-sense

Translated by Sampurna Chattarji from the Bengali original 'Abol Tabol'

There once was a king—(snitch,
Wasn't a king but a wicked witch!)
He had pet peacocks—(go eat oats,
Why peacocks? They were baby goats.)
In the courtyard lived his grandsons—
(Without a house what courtyard, dunce?)
Apparently a brother on his father's side—
(Not a brother, silly, mother's uncle's bride.)
Kind of his protégé you could say—
(Born dumb, what could he say pray?)
Anyway, there they were the three souls—
(Five, your counting's full of holes!)
O can't you stop sniping for a second—
(Okay, if your tale's better than I reckoned.)

[13] black as a chimney sweep: Interestingly, Ray uses the English word 'chimney' in the original. It is not uncommon to find English words/phrases cropping up from time to time in other verses.

Well then, as soon as evening fell
As soon as the pills went down like hell,
He charged up, flinging his matted hair—
(Hair? But the poor man's pate was bare!)
So he's bald, so what, you little grouch?
You sullen-faced stupid slouch!
I'll throttle you by your scrawny neck
And pound your head—now what the heck?
O so now you'd rather run away?
I told you, storytelling is no child's play!

For Better or for Verse

Translated by Sampurna Chattarji from the Bengali original
'Jongla boney pagla budo aamaye eshe boley'

In a dank forest an old crank asked if I would know
'In half an acre of ocean how many jackfruit grow?'
I estimated roughly and said, 'Begging your pardon—
Just as many as the prawns growing in your garden.'

Why?

Translated by Sampurna Chattarji from the Bengali original
'Keno shob kukurgulo khamokha chaynchaye raatey?'

Why do dogs bark all night without any reason?
Why are there no cavities in a toothless gum all season?
Why does the earth have a flat head, tell me who's at fault?
Let us sit under a tree and bring these queries to a halt.

Gorgondola[14]

Translated by Sampurna Chattarji from the Bengali original 'Drighangchu'

Once there was a King.

One day he was at court—which was as usual swarming with friends and flatterers, rich men and revellers, sepoys and sentries—when out of nowhere a jungle crow flew in, perched on a high pillar to the right of the throne, bent his head, looked all about him, and in an extremely serious voice said, 'Caw.'

Such a deep and serious voice in the midst of all that revelry was unheard of—the entire court fell silent; round-eyed and open-mouthed, the assembly stood and stared. The Minister, who was about to explain something important from an impressive stack of papers, lost the thread of his argument and looked on with a vacant expression. A little boy who was sitting near the doors suddenly went 'boohoohoo', and the man who was pulling the punkha lost his grip on the rope, which fell on the King's head with an unceremonious plonk. The King, who had been falling into a nice little doze, got up with a start and said, 'Call the executioner.'

The executioner arrived. The King said, 'Chop off his head.'

Horror! Heavens! Whose head did he mean? Trembling with fear, every single person in the assembly began stroking his head tenderly, as if to protect it from the executioner's axe.

The King dozed some more, and then suddenly shooting a sharp glance about him, said, 'Where's the head?'

The executioner, poor wretch, folded his hands and asked, 'O King, whose head?'

The King said, 'You illiterate lout! The one who made that abominable sound, *his* head.'

Hearing this, everyone in the court let out such a tremendous sigh of relief that the crow gave a nervous flutter and flew away.

[14] Title: A nonsense word, as is the original Bengali, with the aim of echoing the slightly guttural and ominous sound of the original.

It was only then that the Minister explained to the King that it was a crow who was the cause of that monstrous sound. The King listened carefully and then ordered, 'Let all the pandits be summoned.' In five minutes flat, all the pandits in the kingdom were summoned.

The King asked them, 'A crow just appeared in my court, made a terrible sound and went away. Could you learned men tell me why?'

What reason could there be for a crow to caw! The pandits were at a loss; they looked at each other uneasily. A very young pandit finally said in a small and embarrassed voice, 'Maybe he was hungry.'

The King exploded, 'What brains! If he was hungry, why did he have to come to court? Is the court a snack shop? Minister, get rid of him.' Immediately everyone took up the blustering chant, 'Yes, yes, get rid of him.'

When the chant died down, another pandit spoke up, 'O King, every effect has a cause—if it rains you know there are clouds, if you see a light you know there's a lamp, therefore that there should be some cause behind the beauteous mellifluous sound effects issuing from the corvine throat of the avian crow—what's surprising about that?'

The King said, 'What's surprising is that fatheads like you get paid fat salaries for spouting nonsense like that. Minister, stop this man's salary from today.'

Immediately everyone shouted, 'Stop this man's salary!'

After seeing two pandits dispatched in this ruthless way, the rest were too scared to offer any suggestions. Minutes went by, but no one said a word.

The King, as is customary in such cases, blew his top. He bellowed—'No one must leave the court till an answer to my question is found!'

The King's command—who dared resist it? They all sat, stiff and silent as statues. Some thought so hard, rivers of sweat poured down their brows. Others scratched their heads so hard they went completely bald. They all started feeling hungry—but not the King. The King was interested in neither food nor rest—he sat on his throne and drowsed.

It was hopeless. Everyone in the court started cursing the pandits, secretly calling them 'oafs, buffoons, nincompoops'.

Suddenly a thin dried-up looking man gave a terrible shout and fell down flat on his face. The King, his Minister, friends, flatterers, wazirs, wazoos, all got agitated at once and said, 'What happened? What happened?'

They splashed water on his face, fanned him frantically, coaxed and cajoled him, till finally, still shaking like a leaf, the man stood up and said, 'O King, was it a jungle crow?'

Everyone said, 'Yes yes yes, why why why?'

The man continued, 'O King, did he sit on that pillar with his face to the north—and did he bend his head, roll his eyes and make a sound that went "Caw"?'

Everyone got terribly excited and said, 'Yes yes yes—it happened just like that!'

Hearing this, the man began howling and weeping and saying, 'Alas, alas, why did no one inform me at that very moment?'

The King said, 'Indeed, why did no one inform him at that very moment?'

Nobody knew the man, but nobody had the guts to say so, so instead they said, 'Yes, we should have informed him'—even though not one of them understood what information they should have given him, and why.

When the man had finally finished crying, he screwed up his face and said, 'Gorgondola.'

What?! Everyone thought the man had lost his mind.

The Minister said, 'What's Gorbondola?'

The man said, 'Not Gorbondola, Gorgondola.'

That explained nothing to nobody—but they still nodded their heads and said, 'O!'

The King asked, 'And what is that like, my man?'

The man said, 'Sire, I am an unlettered man, what do I know. I have just been hearing about Gorgondola from my childhood, which is why I know that when Gorgondola appears before a king, he puts on the appearance of a jungle crow. And that when he enters the court, he heads for a pillar to the right of the throne, sits on it with his head bent and his face towards the north, rolls his eyes and makes a sound that goes "Caw". I know nothing more—but perhaps the pandits might.'

The pandits quickly and vehemently denied this, 'No, no, we know nothing about this matter.'

The King said, 'You were crying because you hadn't been informed. If you had arrived in time, what would you have done?'

The man said, 'I'm afraid to say, Sire, because people may not believe me.'

The King said, 'Anyone who does not believe you—his head will be chopped off, so speak without fear.' The crowd clamoured in agreement.

The man said, 'Sire, I have a mantra, which I have been waiting to use on Gorgondola for aeons. If I could only say it to him, who knows what amazing occurrences might take place. Nobody has written of this in any books. Alas, will I ever get such an opportunity again?'

The King said, 'Tell me the mantra.'

The man said, 'Heaven forbid! That mantra must not be uttered in front of anyone but Gorgondola. I'll write it on a piece of paper instead—

and after fasting for two days you can read it on the morning of the third day. If you see a jungle crow in front of you, you can utter the mantra, but under no circumstance must anyone else overhear it—because in case the jungle crow is not Gorgondola at all, and someone else hears the mantra while you're reciting it, then the results will be truly catastrophic!'

At last the court was dismissed. All those who had been holding their breaths all this time now breathed freely and chattering nineteen to the dozen about Gorgondola, the mantra and its astonishing unknown effects, they all went home.

After fasting for two days as instructed, on the third morning the King opened the piece of paper and read it. This is what he read—

An orang-utan of yellowish green,
Bricks and bats turn turtle unseen
Tough made easy the gardener's blatant,
In Dharmatala the situation's vacant.[15]

The King learnt it by heart. From then on, whenever he saw a jungle crow, he shooed everyone else away, recited the mantra, and then waited for some astonishing occurrence. To this day he is still waiting.

[15] An orang-utan of yellowish green: The English word 'orang-utan' is used in the original verse. A ten-line version of this rhyme appeared in the play *Shabdakalpadruma*. Here it is, translated by Satyajit Ray (Introduction to Sukumar Ray's *The Select Nonsense of Sukumar Ray*, trans. Sukanta Chaudhuri, New Delhi: OUP, 1987).

A green and gold orang-outang,
Rocks and stones that jolt and bang,
A smelly skunk and izzy tizzy,
No admission, very busy.
Ghost and ghoul, do re mi fa
And half a loaf is better far.
Coughs and colds and peanut plants,
Pussies are the tiger's aunts,
Trouble-shooters, blotted blobs,
City centre vacant jobs.

FROM HAW-JAW-BAW-RAW-LAW[16]

Translated by Sampurna Chattarji from the Bengali original Haw-Jaw-Baw-Raw-Law

It was awfully hot. There I was lying quietly in the shade of a tree, hot, bothered and sweaty. Next to me on the grass was my handkerchief. Just as I was about to pick it up to wipe my face, it went 'Miaow!' How utterly weird! Why on earth would my hanky say 'Miaow'?

I turned my head. My hanky wasn't a hanky any more. No, in its place there sat a bright red roly-poly cat, twirling its whiskers and staring at me with big blinky eyes.

'How annoying!' I exclaimed. 'A hanky one minute, a cat the next!'

Without batting an eyelid, the Cat retorted, 'What's annoying about that? One minute an egg, the next minute a lovely quacky-whacky duck! It happens all the time.'

I thought a bit. Then I said, 'In that case what shall I call you now? You look like a cat but you're not; in actual fact you're a hanky.'

The Cat said, 'You can call me Cat, you can call me Hanky, you can even call me Emperor.'[17]

I said, 'Why Emperor?'

The Cat sniggered. 'You mean you don't even know that?' and closing one eye he began laughing in a nasty, knowing way.

I felt a complete fool. Obviously, this Emperor nonsense was something I should have understood at once. To cover up, I hurriedly blurted out, 'I know! Of course I know what it means.'

Pleased as punch, the Cat purred, 'Yes, it's really very simple—the

[16] Title: This is the original (transliterated) title, which is literally an alphabet string comprising the 33rd, 26th, 23rd, 27th and 28th consonants of the Bengali alphabet. But the resonance that this 'string' has in the Bengali language gives it the wholeness of a word; in fact, 'Haw-Jaw-Baw-Raw-Law' has entered the Bengali lexicon as a synonym for nonsense. A literal English approximation (such as 'el-em-en-o-pee') does not have such a 'meaningful' resonance, yet the transliterated Bengali has its own interesting semantic resonances in English.

[17] You can even call me Emperor: In the original the word is '*chondrobindu*', which is the diacritical mark that appears on top of certain letters to indicate a nasal intonation. This word then leads into the Cat's nonsensical word-making. Hence the choice of the word in English had to be one which would lend itself to a similar exercise.

Emperor's M, the Cat's "is", the handkerchief's "chief"—and what does it make? Mischief. Got it, I hope?'[18]

I didn't get it. At all. But out of sheer fear that the Cat would burst into its nasty spluttering laugh again, I nodded and said 'oh yes' as quickly and brightly as I could.

There was a lull in the conversation. The Cat was gazing intently at the sky. Suddenly he said, 'If you're feeling that hot, you might as well go to Tibet.'

I said, 'That's easy to say and hard to do.'

The Cat said, 'Why? Why is it hard?'

I said, 'Do you even know how to get there?'

The Cat gave a belly laugh and said, 'Me not know! Calcutta, Diamond Harbour, Ranaghat, Tibet—simple! It's a straight road, one hour fifteen minutes long. You might as well just get up and go.'

I said, 'Well then, if it's that easy, why don't you show me the way?'

The Cat suddenly became serious. He shook his head and said,

---

[18] The Emperor's M, the Cat's 'is', the handkerchief's 'chief'—and what does it make? Mischief: The key to this is the method of the original, where the first part of the new word (in this case 'mischief', in the original, '*choshma*', meaning 'spectacles') derived from the sound (em), the second part from a word-within-a-word that is not really there ('is'), and the third part from a word-within-a-word that is really there ('chief'). While one could have translated the Bengali to arrive at the English word 'spectacles', the nonsense element here was not so much the meaning of the word derived but the method by which one derived it.

'Uh-huh. I'm afraid that's not my job. If TreeCat were here, he could tell you precisely.'

I said, 'Who's TreeCat? And where does he live?'

The Cat said, 'In a tree, where else?'

I said, 'Where can I meet him?'

The Cat shook his head vigorously and said, 'No, no, that can't happen, that's impossible.'

I said, 'How come?'

The Cat said, 'I'll tell you how come. Say you've gone to Uluberia to meet him, by then he'll be in Motihari. By the time you reach Motihari, he'll be in Ramkishtopur. And by the time you arrive at Ramkishtopur, he'll be off to Kashimbazaar. Now do you see why it's impossible?'

I said, 'In that case, how do *you* meet him?'

The Cat said, 'It's a big bother. First I have to figure out all the places he won't be in; then I have to figure out all the places he *could* be in; then I have to figure out where he is right now. Then I have to figure out, by the time I get to the place he is in right now, where will he be next? Then I have to figure out—'

Before he could carry on, I butted in, 'How do you figure all this out anyway?'

The Cat said, 'It's very tough. Want to see how tough?' Picking up a stick, he drew a long line in the grass, and said, 'Imagine that's TreeCat.' This statement was followed by a long and gloomy silence.

At last he drew another identical line and said, 'Imagine this is you,' and hunching over, fell silent again.

Suddenly he drew another line and said, 'Imagine this is the Emperor.' Every few minutes he thought gravely, drew a line and announced, 'Imagine this is Tibet'—'Imagine TreeCat's wife is cooking'—'Imagine there's a hole in the tree trunk'—

Finally, I couldn't bear it any more. I lost my temper. 'What rubbish!' I snapped. 'He's talking utter nonsense and I refuse to listen to another word he says!'

The Cat said, 'In that case, I'll make it a little simpler. Close your eyes, and whatever I tell you, calculate it in your head.'

I closed my eyes.

Eyes closed, I waited. And I waited. Not a peep out of the Cat.

Suddenly I had a feeling I had been tricked. I opened my eyes and there he was, escaping over the garden fence with his tail in the air, laughing that nasty spluttering laugh. [. . .]

I [. . .] turned away in a huff, when who should I see but a man with a smoothly-shaven head smiling coyly at me, looking like something out of a play in his long robes and pyjamas. Just looking at him made my blood boil.

As soon as he realized I'd noticed him, he bowed his head in an ingratiating manner and rubbing his hands smarmily began saying, 'Oh no please I beg of you, do not ask me to sing. Really, I mean it, my voice isn't in good shape today.'

I said, 'What a pest! Nobody's asking you to sing!'

The man was so shameless, he still kept nagging into my ear, 'Have I upset you? O brother, have I upset you? It's okay, I'll sing a few songs for you, you needn't lose your cool.'

Before I could say anything, Old Goat and Gobbledygook raised their voices and shouted in chorus, 'Yes yes yes, let there be songs, let there be songs.'

As if on cue, Smoothie took out two massive sheaves of music from his pocket, held them close to his eyes, hummed a few snatches and launched into a song in a reedy voice—'Red songs sung to a blue tune, giggly-wiggly smell.' He sang this once, twice, five times and then ten.

I said, 'This is a disaster! Aren't there any more verses to that song?'

Smoothie said, 'Of course there are more verses, but in another song. That other song goes—'In and out the alleys run, the pavements are so full of fun, use ink to get your whitewash done.' I don't sing that song any more. Then there's another song—'New Potatoes from Nainital'—that has to be sung in a very soft voice. That's another one I can't sing these days. The one that I do sing, however, is 'The Peacockwing Song'. Saying this he launched forth—

Searocksting peacockwing heard up in the sky
Bottlehoppers jarstoppers sing so fine and high
Bright light bent light babbling all the way
Black white fat slight in teary shadowplay.

I said, 'You call that a song? Can't make out head or tail of it.'

Gobbledygook said, 'Yes, the song is indeed very hard.'

Old Goat said, 'Where's it hard? The bit about bottles and jars was a bit hard, yes, but otherwise I don't see anything hard about it.'

In a tone of injured pride, Smoothie said, 'In that case why don't you just tell me you want an easy song, instead of giving me an earful? You think I can't sing easy songs?' Saying which he began—

The bat said to the porcupine,
Tonight you'll see a funtomime.

I said, 'Funtomime's not a word!'

Smoothie said, 'Says who? If porcupine, elephantine and columbine are all words, then why not funtomime?'

Old Goat said, 'Why don't you keep singing, and we'll settle that later on, okay?'

Instantly Smoothie began again—

The bat said to the porcupine,
Tonight you'll see a funtomime.
Titmice and owls will come tonight—
The poor mice will die of fright,
Frogs and frogesses will shake with fear,
And burst into rashes from nose to ear,
Maddened moles will run amok
Snapping sniping their jaws will lock.

I was about to object again, but I restrained myself. The song continued—

The porcupine said, what, here, but how?
Can't you see my wife's napping now?

Tell Mr Owl and also his missus
If they wake her with raucous hisses
I'll poke them with all my strength
Make sure you tell them this at length.
The bat said, the owl's entire family
Will simply hoot at your sad homily.
Whoever sleeps in the pitch-black night?
Your wife's a dingbat and a dwight.
And you my friend are getting loony
A chimney-chuffing muffing moony.

I don't know how much longer the song would have carried on, because right then a big brouhaha broke out. Looking around, I realized a crowd had gathered. A porcupine was sitting and sniffling and snuffling on its own tears and a crocodile in an official hat was slapping it on the back with a massive book and whispering, 'Don't cry, don't cry, I'll make everything all right.'

Just then a turbaned and uniformed bullfrog lifted a ruler and shouted, 'Libel suit.'

At once a big black ugly owl in a loose robe appeared and, perching on a high stone, shut his eyes and started dozing, while an enormous mole began fanning him with an awfully dirty fan.

The Owl opened his bleary eyes, looked all around him, closed his eyes and pronounced, 'Let the complaint be made.'

With great effort and astonishing speed, the Crocodile put on a weepy expression and digging his nails into his face, produced a few measly crocodile tears. Then, in a hoarse voice, he said, 'Your Honour Justice Incarnate! This is a libel suit. Therefore first we must understand what a suit is. A suit is a case. Cases are very useful things. You get them in different kinds—suitcases, briefcases, glass cases, spectacle cases, bookcases, etcetera! Suits are kept at the bottom of a suitcase; therefore it is essential that we get to the bottom of this case.'[19]

[19] This is a libel suit . . . the bottom of this case: The Bengali for 'libel suit' (*maanhanir mukkodoma*) leads into some intricate word-spinning revolving around the *maan-kochu* (literally an edible root, figuratively a mere trifle). Choosing to stay faithful to the

He had only got this far when a turbaned jackal leapt up and said, 'Your Grace, suits are useless things. Eat a woollen suit and your throat tickles, tell someone "suit yourself" and they get offended. Whoever eats a suit? Only pigs and porcupines. Ugh and ewww.'

The Porcupine was about to start sniffling and snuffling again, but the Crocodile hit him on the head with his gigantic book and asked, 'Got any documents evidence witnesses?'

The Porcupine glared at Smoothie and said, 'There—all the documents are in his hand.'

The Crocodile snatched the sheaf of songs from Smoothie's hand and started reading at random—

Two on one did leap
Lie on the bed and sleep
Wrap the bundle and keep
Roses and jasmines reap
Fish that swim so deep
Spinach leaves in a heap
Pavements dare not peep
Clean and wash and sweep—
Tell me, why d'you weep?
[. . .]

The Porcupine began to wail piteously, 'I am lost! All my money down the drain! God knows where I got such a foolish lawyer, he can't even find the right documents!'

Smoothie had been standing aside rather bashfully all this time. Now suddenly he spoke up, 'Which one do you want to hear? "The bat said to the porcupine"—that one?'

The Porcupine looked important and said, 'Yes, yes, that one.' Immediately the Jackal charged up again, 'What *did* the bat say? Your Honour, may we have permission to present Batty the Bat as witness!'

---

meaning of '*kochu*' would have severely limited the comical wordplay which is the basic point of this section. Hence the word used here enables a free flow of associations, that is, the suit, the suitcase, the case, types of cases.

The Bullfrog puffed out his cheeks and chest and hollered, 'Calling Batty the Bat!'

Everyone looked around expectantly, but no sign of Batty the Bat. The Jackal said, 'In that case, Your Honour, let them all be sentenced to death by hanging.'

The Crocodile said, 'And why pray? We have an appeal left yet.'

The Owl closed his eyes and said, 'Make your appeal. Present your witness.'

The Crocodile looked around desperately and then asked Gobbledygook, 'Will you be my witness? I'll give you four annas.'

At the very mention of money, Gobbledygook leapt to his feet and began laughing his disgusting laugh.

The Jackal said, 'Why are you laughing?'

Gobbledygook said, 'There was this person who had been told that when you get up to be a witness, there'll be this book with a green cover, blue leather ears and a red seal on its spine. So when the lawyer asked him, do you know the defendant, he said, yes I do, he is covered in green, has blue leather ears and a red seal on his spine. Ho ho hee hee hee—' [. . .]

The Jackal said, 'What's funny this time?'

Gobbledygook said, 'There was a person who was weak in the head, he liked to go around naming everything. His shoes were named Impropriety, his umbrella Alacrity, his drinking cup Pomposity, but when he went so far as to name his house Bamboozlement, a great earthquake knocked his house and everything in it to the ground. Ho ho ho ho—'

The Jackal said, 'Indeed? When you're done laughing, may I have the pleasure of knowing your name?'

Gobbledygook said, 'Right now, it's Gobbledygook.'

The Jackal said, 'What do you mean right now?'

Gobbledygook said, 'You mean you don't even know that? In the mornings, my name is Potato Pie and then as soon as evening falls it's Spoonerism.' [. . .]

The Jackal said, 'Your Honour, they're all out of their minds, they're worthless as witnesses.'

The Crocodile lashed his tail angrily and said, 'Who said they're worthless? In keeping with convention, I have paid a good four annas

for this witness.' And saying this, he pressed sixteen coins one after the other into Gobbledygook's palm.

A voice rang out from above, 'No.1 Witness, total calculation worth four annas.'

I looked up. It was Graven Raven sitting on a branch and scribbling accounts on his slate. [. . .]

The rumour that witnesses were being paid good money had by now led to a tremendous commotion as everyone clamoured to be a witness. While people in the crowd pushed and shoved to be first, I noticed Graven Raven swoop down from his perch on the tree straight into the witness stand.

Before anyone asked him anything, he started off, 'In the name of the most Revered Ravenology, Rt. Hon. Graven Raven, No. 41, Tree Mart, Raven Colony. Come to us for all manner of calculated and extravagant, retail and wholesale, and all other known types—'

The Jackal said, 'Don't talk drivel. Just answer my questions. What's your name?'

The Raven said, 'How annoying! I just told you—Right Honourable Graven Raven.'

The Jackal said, 'Home?'

The Raven said, 'I just told you—Raven Colony.'

The Jackal said, 'How far is it from here?'

The Raven said, 'That's very hard to explain. Per hour it's four annas. Per mile it's ten paise, if you pay in cash there's a discount of two paise. By addition it comes to ten annas, by subtraction three annas, by division seven paise, and by multiplication twenty-one rupees.' [. . .]

The Jackal said, 'I must say you're an impudent rascal! I ask you, having arrived as a witness, what do you know about the libel suit, or is that too much to ask?'

The Raven said, 'I like that! Who's been sitting here all this while doing the accounts? Whatever you want to know is at my fingertips. Firstly, what is a suit? A suit is a garment. Garments come in four kinds—inner, outer, summer, winter. What happens if you eat them? Jackals feel a bit tickly in their throats, but crows feel nothing. Then there was a witness, worth four annas, his ear had turned blue—and was known as the Plague. Then there was a man who used to give everything a name—he called the Jackal Oil-thief, the Crocodile Carbuncle, the Owl Horrendipitous—'

Chaos broke out in the court. The Crocodile ate up the Bullfrog in one lightning gulp, seeing which the Mole began whimpering shrilly, and the Jackal began shooing away Graven Raven with an umbrella.

The Owl said ponderously, 'Quiet, everyone. I'm going to declare the verdict.' He summoned a rabbit with a pen behind its ear and said, 'Write down all I say. Libel Suit, No. 24. Prosecutor—the Porcupine. Defendant—Wait! Who's the defendant?'

At once everyone exclaimed, 'Oh no! There's no defendant.'

Hastily, Smoothie was coaxed into becoming the defendant. Being the fool that he was, Smoothie thought even defendants would get paid good money, so he didn't make the slightest fuss.

The verdict was pronounced. Three months' jail for Smoothie and seven days of hanging.

I was just thinking that I ought to object to such an unfair verdict,

when Grammarian Old Goat BA charged at me yelling 'go-go-go-goat', butted me in the back and bit my ear.

Everything became fuzzy. Grammarian's face began increasingly to look like my Mejomama's. Completely befuddled, I peered at it closely. It was my Mejomama, who was tweaking my ear and saying, 'Aha, so that's your game! Dozing under the pretext of studying your grammar, are you?'

I was aghast! At first I thought I must have dreamt it all. But then—though you may not believe it—when I looked around for my hanky, it wasn't there, and a cat was sitting on the fence, smugly trimming its whiskers. The minute it saw me it jumped down and ran off. And exactly at that moment, from the back of the garden, a goat bleated.

I told my Boromama the whole story, but Boromama said, 'Be off with you, turning a whole lot of outlandish dreams into a story.'

That's what happens when people grow old—they become so dull, they refuse to believe anything. That's why, seeing that you at least are not that old, I thought I'd take you into confidence and tell you the whole story instead.

RABINDRANATH TAGORE

FROM KHAPCHHADA

THE OLD WOMAN'S GRANDMA-IN-LAW'S FIVE SISTERS

Translated by Sampurna Chattarji from the Bengali original 'Khantobudir Didishashudi'

The old woman's grandma-in-law's
        Five sisters live in Brick-a-Brac,
Their saris hang upon the stove,
        Their pots upon the clothes rack.
Prying fault-finding eyes they fox

By living in a cast-iron box,
        For a spot of air their money
They by open windows stack,
        And put in every limeless betel leaf
The salt their curries lack.

Desperate to Hear an Elephant Sneeze

Translated by Sampurna Chattarji from the Bengali original 'Shunbo Haatir Hanchi'

Desperate to hear
        an elephant sneeze—
Keshta began combing
        Nepal's many trees.

To tickle its trunk
        took a bamboo twig,
and seven jars of snuff
        each fat and big;

Trawling through slush,
        How hard he tried,
Two thousand sneezes
        Later, he died.

On the Floor of the Hall

Translated by Sampurna Chattarji from the Bengali original 'Shobhatoley Bhunye'

        On the floor of the Hall
        Reclining and all
The snoring Sultan in his boots,
        His grey beard wagging

His loud voice bragging
The Minister singing in toots.
The singer's excitement
Was the perfect incitement—
With a shawl round his hips
The General dances to admiring hoots.
And dropping all work
The footmen berserk
Play tunelessly now on their flutes.

ANNADA SANKAR RAY

WHAT THE LITTLE GIRL LEARNT[20]

Translated by Sampurna Chattarji from the Bengali original
'Meye Kemon Shikchhen'

A-ha!
Yes ma!
Baa baa black sheep
Have you any wool?
No ma! No ma!
That's all bull.
Not black, not a sheep,
Not at all woolly.
So where'll I get wool?
You're wrong, fully.

[20] This seems, among other things, to spoof the irrelevance of English nursery rhymes that are religiously taught to Indian children. See the Introduction for more on this piece.

Let's to Delhi[21]

Translated by Sampurna Chattarji from the Bengali original 'Dilli Cholo'

Let's to Delhi let's to Delhi
Dogs on the walk cats on the belly.
Come elephants and horses
Come lame one-eyed forces.
Come mutes and muggers
Come crooks and thuggers.
Come saints and sages
Come head priests of ages.
Come film stars and starlets
Come jobless needy varlets
Come bigwigs and fat pigs
Come all who can dance jigs.
Delhi's where we'll decide
Exactly who's on which side.
Then every vote that becomes ours
Will put us in the seat of power.

Clerihew

Translated by Sampurna Chattarji from the Bengali original 'Clerihew'

The poem is a humorous deflation of the almost reverential status granted to scientific, literary, political and cultural icons of Bengal and India. Acharya Jagdish Bose (1858–1937), the Bengali scientist known for his theory that plants were capable of reacting to certain stimuli, as an animal would; Sarat Chandra Chatterjee (1876–1938), the Bengali novelist whose reformist, socially relevant novels made him more popular than either Bankim Chandra

[21] A satiric take-off on the political slogan '*Chalo Dilli*' issued as a clarion call in 1944 by Netaji Subhas Chandra Bose, firebrand freedom fighter and founder of the Indian National Army.

or Tagore; Pandit Jawaharlal Nehru (1889–1964), India's first prime minister, whose daughter Indira Gandhi and grandson Rajiv went on to become prime ministers of India, thereby taking on the role of India's 'first family' both loved and criticized for its 'dynastic ambitions'; Samaresh Sen, a contemporary leftist poet; Anamika Dey, an unknown dancer (Anamika literally means 'nameless', also the name given to the little finger). After all the 'heavyweights', Ray adds a sting in the tale by talking of someone unfamiliar, giving the poem a downward spiral.

It was Acharya Jagdish Bose who
Declared plants to be animals too.
The only thing surprising about that
Would be getting surprised by such old hat.

Rabindranath Tagore in his dreams
Is off to the Land of Figs it seems.[22]
No not to Peru and not China either
The sad part is he's going to neither.

As for Sarat Chandra Chatterjee
He's as sweetly silent as can be.
And speechlessly the world has seen
His words light up the silver screen.[23]

Pandit Jawaharlal Nehru was so wise
That blue was red[24] in his eyes.

---

[22] the Land of Figs: In the original, the place mentioned is Pakur, a very small town in rural Bengal. Ray's intention seems to be to gently deride Tagore's sudden interest in his own land as opposed to his much-lauded travels and lecture tours to the West.

[23] words light up the silver screen: Chatterjee's accessible writing led to his works being adapted not only for the stage but also for the screen. In fact, one of the most adapted books of his continues to be *Devdas* (1917) which saw a Bengali version in 1935; two Hindi versions in 1936 and 1955; two Telugu versions in 1953 and 1974 and a Malayalam version in 1989. The most recent screen adaptation was in 2002, starring Bollywood icons Shah Rukh Khan and Aishwarya Rai, a testament to Chatterjee's cross-cultural and multilingual appeal.

[24] blue was red: Here Ray is probably commenting on the notion of the Nehru family as the 'blue-blooded' ruling family of India.

Hearing this, blue got red in the face
And a kite flew his ear to another place.

Mister Samaresh Sen has written plenty
I've read all he's written one-and-twenty.
But looks like Mister Samaresh Sen
Has written only what he's read, I ken.

Anamika Dey she is a dancer
To her grace there is no answer.
All the good girls are so well-bred
Alas that they should all be wed.

BAUDDHAYAN MUKHERJI

Liffle Girl

Translated by Sampurna Chattarji from the Bengali original 'Chhotto Meye'

The nonsensical baby-speak that adults lapse into when addressing infants is the starting point for this verse.

Honky elephant wonky owl my snub-nosed sweetie-pie
Lemme lift you by your little ears, you slopy-headed peachy-eye
Sniffly-snuffle gap-toothed wuffle, girl born after beforenoon,
If you cry now I won't give you the sugar-scented smiley moon.

Why?

Translated by Sampurna Chattarji from the Bengali original 'Keno?'

Why is the beat here without the drum?
Why is the drummer trying to hum?
Why are drum-rolls with onion so yummy?
Why are they drumming on my fat little tummy?

Dead Can Dance

Translated by Sampurna Chattarji from the Bengali original 'Teering Biring'

No reason for rhyme to make the dead dance in time
Tararumpumpum to the beat of a drum
We dance old and young our song is being sung
Feathers outspread on the riverbunk bed
A grasshopper skip-hoppity hop
Dances for joy non-stoppity stop.

Suncle[25]

Translated by Sampurna Chattarji from the Bengali original 'Shujji Mama'

Tell me, why all this slurping-burping
Look instead at the Suncle chirping

[25] Title: In traditional Indian storytelling and lullabies for infants, the sun and the moon are made intimate by conferring on them the status of affectionate relatives—*chand-mama* (Moon Uncle), *surjo-mama* (Sun Uncle). Through the coined portmanteau word 'Suncle' (sun+uncle) the attempt is to create a term as close to the original Bengali as possible.

The red earth smells nice and slick,
Suncle's bathed in turmeric,
Flowers, why don't you bloom at noon,
Such colours you'll see by the gloom of the moon!

King for a Day

Translated by Sampurna Chattarji from the Bengali original 'Aami besh aaj rajar chheley'

Listen!
Today I'm a king's son
And you are my subjects.
I'll eat sweetmeats
And you'll eat insects.

Weirdo

Translated by Sampurna Chattarji from the Bengali original 'Aajgubi'

I bow to the sun on my own threshold
I stay in on the mornings I go out
My prayer room is under my bed
My house is strange, no doubt.

NAVAKANTA BARUA

This poem is an obvious imitation of 'Article Twenty-One' by Sukumar Ray, down to some fairly specific details, like the penalties for poets. Barua has also done a derivative adaptation of Ray's 'Mish-Mash'.

NINEPUR[26]

Translated by Dileep Chandan from the Assamese original 'Naugao'

The new town of Ninepur
Has nine hundred folk.
If you don't know town law
You'll some trouble provoke.

If you weep in the town
Then nine paise you'll pay;
When your smile comes again
They're returned right away.

If you wake after nine
Then your ears get a twist
By the Number Nine cops
So don't try to resist.

For composing a verse
The town locks you up tight
In a bamboo-bar cage
Where you're left overnight.

Sons of grocers[27] write just
The nine tables, it's true;

---

[26] Title: 'Ninepur' does not capture the wordplay in the real title 'Naugao', which means 'nine villages' when the words are separate, but 'new village' when they are joined as one word.

[27] grocers: The original word is '*kayahs*', for Rajasthani grocers who typically catered to the poor.

They have ninety long sheets
Of the figures to do.

If they finish their work
Then they're told it's for sure
That by thirty it can
Be divided once more.

If you simply can't solve
This math problem at all,
You will have to go kick
At an old wooden ball.

In the town, a bald man
Who is spied fast asleep
Soon will find that he has
Obligations to keep:

Nine chapters in full
Of *Ramayan* to write
On his forehead in ink,
To be done before night.

If a student just reads
When he's sitting in school,
And he won't climb a tree
To break even one rule,

Then his punishment is
Ninety push-ups performed
And nine glasses of milk
That he has to drink warmed.

For the third penalty
Given out for these crimes
His strict teacher will pull
On his earlobes nine times.

If your grandfather beats
Your bent back with his stick,
And from your favourite playground
He snatches you quick,

If he prods you to list
All the hard words you know,
And you write them down neatly
For him, row by row,

And if later he marks
All your math with red lines,
Still for all of these things
You won't pay any fines.

You now know of the laws
For the new town Ninepur.
Come in if you please—
I will not reveal more.

ANUSHKA RAVISHANKAR

Lost and Found

I lost it
I lost it
my mantra
on a contra
rily judged
word
it fell
with a plop

like a mighty
wallop
and bounced
in a handsome
heavily flounced
and ruffled-with-laces
under painted-up-faces
shapely, bosomy bosom.

I found it
I found it
my magical
comical
quite anatomical
mantra I found
in the entra
ncing mole
of an eskimo
under an
electric pole
it wobbled and fell
with a ringing
like that of a tolling
a warning
a bringing
of morning
a dinging a donging
of some earthly bell.

I found it
I found it
my magical potion
that drank as it sang
and constantly rang
an electric beep

like the bleating of sheep
And nobody
nobody does
realize
how awfully nice
it is to find
a lost, given up
and cast-out-of-mind
a forgotten
beloved
and hopelessly shovéd
a magical, tropical
topical, tragical
infernal
eternal
and final
as ending
unbending
severe
deliverer,
that singing
that chanting
enchanting
that
free-as-a-bird
that silent, unspoken
that gleeful
that wicked
that suddenly heard
and carelessly pickéd
that wholly incomparable
word.

If

i

If you see
An empty tin
With a stupid toothy grin
Let it be
It's me.

If you spy
A funny fly
Going with a hum
And an attitude
That's glum
Pass it by
It's I.

ii

If you see
A wollop
Going at
A great gallop
Don't ever let it go.
Take it by it's tiny tail
Put it in your bathing pail
And use the shower
For evermore.

iii

If you see
A letter-writer
Writing in the sun
Fix him to a banyan tree
With a bit of gum
Then give him all the letters
That you never wrote

And tell him he can read them, but
Needs permission to quote.

iv

If you see a mountain lion
Looking ill and forlorn
Tell it plainly
Where it's at
Teach it how
To spell a cat
Then stick its toe
(the littlest one)
into its ear and show
it how
to go
the way it's come.

If you see
A mountain lion
Looking starved
And forlorn
Run.

v

If you see
An old Momentum
Trudging in the heat
Tell it about Newton's laws
And let it rest its feet
Or greet it with a howdy chum
And ask it sadly
Ain't life rum
Then tell it
That it's lost its way
That poor ageing Momentum.

Discovery of India

My cousin Nibboo—Boo for short
Once traversed India
South to North

At Parur he was very pleased
He said, 'I am—'
And then he sneezed

Srirangapatnam turned him soft
He sighed 'I do—'
And then he coughed

At Wardha he was feeling well
He claimed 'I can—'
And then he fell

In Meerut he was rather mild
He said 'I will—'
And then he smiled

Ferozepur filled him with fear
He cried 'I think!'
Then disappeared

Boo got famous overnight—
He proved Descartes
Wasn't right.

from Excuse Me Is This India?

A cow stood on the sunny beach
Eating paper from a bin
I went to her and asked her, 'Ma'am,
Which country am I in?'

'It's East of this and North of that
And Southwest of the other'
At this four crows that stood around
Began to caw together.
'It's East!' 'It's South!'
'It's North!' 'It's West!'
They circled round my head.

I put a seashell to my ear
To hear the sea instead.

I saw a girl outside her house
I thought we could be friends
'Where am I?' I asked her
She replied, 'That depends.'

She drew a map without a place
And said, 'Let me explain the case:
If you were standing on your head
I'd say you're on your hair
But since you're standing on your feet
You could be anywhere.'

I left her with a silent sigh
She waved her broom to say goodbye.

FROM WISH YOU WERE HERE

UNCLE TETTRA HEDRAN IN A PYRAMID, EGYPT

Uncle Tettra had four points to make
He made them clear and slow

The first was
One

The second
Two
The third was
Eighty-four

'The fourth'
He said and then he stopped
And never spoke a word
He now lives in a pyramid
In Egypt, so we heard

Cousin Collum at the Tower Bridge, London

Cousin Collum likes to measure
Everything in sight
He measures them from up to down
And from left to right
He measures them from inside out
And by day and night
He measures them in colour and
Also in black-and-white

He once measured the Tower Bridge
And secretly confessed
It was longer from the West to East
Than it was from East to West

Brother Marbel at the Taj Mahal, India

My brother Marbel's rather slow
He likes to think things through
He ponders for an hour if you
Should ask him 'How are you?'

He sat before the Taj Mahal
For thirteen days and nights
And at the end he quietly said,
'This building's very white.'

FROM <u>OGD</u>

Once upon a time in the Kingdom of Ogd there was a nuclear holocaust. The explosion blasted the kingdom out of shape and it became a strange-looking thing that had no inside or outside. This was an evolutionary necessity because the only way not to have a nuclear holocaust inside Ogd was by not having an inside of Ogd.

The geographical transformation of Ogd led to many developments. It was, for instance, the origin of the famous saying: ALL ROADS LEAD TO OGD, since any road that led outside Ogd also led inside Ogd.

There were, of course, dissidents who by the same logic claimed that: ALL ROADS LEAD OUT OF OGD.

But those who listened to both the assertions got extremely confused. If they believed that all roads led to Ogd and that all roads led out of Ogd then they had to conclude that all roads led everywhere and that all roads led nowhere, which was not possible unless everywhere was the same as nowhere.

These were the people who inhabited the insane asylums of Ogd.

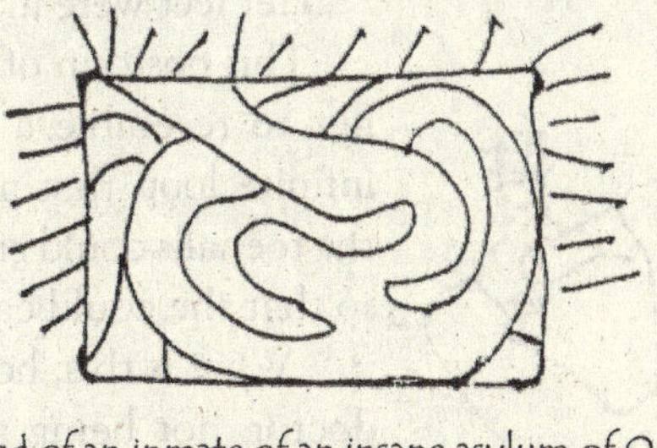

The mind of an inmate of an insane asylum of Ogd

However, what was of Ogd was also of not-Ogd. Xenophobia was eradicated because all Ogdians were non-Ogdians. And so forth.

But when the cartographers came to draw maps of the New World, they were shocked. Never in the history of cartography has there been such a thing as an unbounded kingdom, they declared, delicately drawing a line between infiniteness and unboundedness. So they drew an imaginary line and said this side is Ogd and that side is not Ogd. Be as infinite as you please, they said, but you have to be bounded.

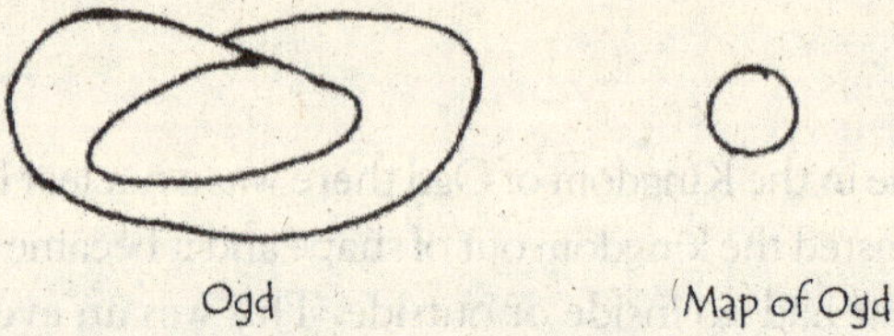

The Kingdom of Ogd was thus placed on the map and people were let out of the insane asylums.

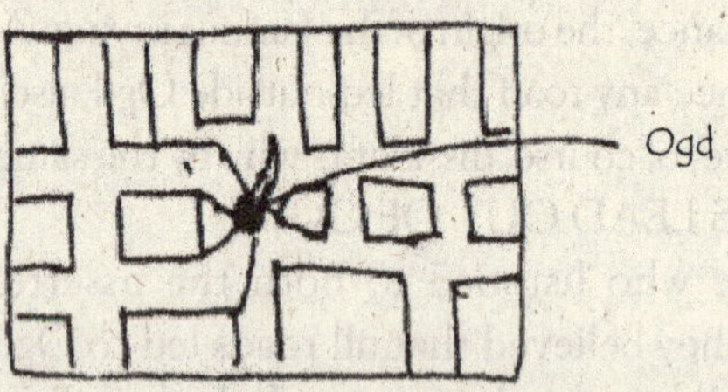

Mind of an outmate of an insane asylum of Ogd

Once upon a time, the same time as the last time upon which once was, a Messiah was born in the Kingdom of Ogd.

The paisa-worm Messiah

Her feet were in her mouth.

This position of foetal gaffe caused her to resemble a paisa-worm or an infinite loop that ate toenails so that the toenails could grow long and strong so that she could eat them.

What is this, her mother asked the doctor, not being able to distinguish between a paisa-worm and a newborn Messiah.

This is an outcome, the doctor replied.

Subsequently the Messiah grew up and began to hop on one foot, having judiciously removed it from her mouth in the interests of locomotion. [. . .]

Under the circumstances it was fortunate that the Messiah went to school. They insisted there that she remove her foot from her mouth. *Oopf*, she said, shaking her head and spurting saliva like a fountain in Caesar's courtyard, thus signifying her dissent in the matter.

They pointed out to her the practical difficulties of the situation. The bench, for one, and more so for two, was too narrow, and whatever the other advantages (though they, they declared, failed to observe any) of putting one's foot in one's mouth, it had to be conceded that she would not be able to write. But the Messiah stuck to her (metaphorical, for she was an ardent pacifist) guns. Messiahs, she explained, need not be scholars, merely literate. Besides she could not compromise on her lofty foot-in-the-mouth principles merely on account of inconvenient ergonomics. [. . .]

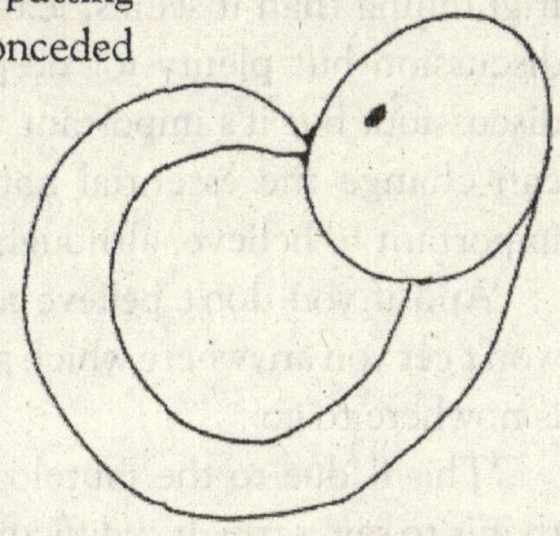
The Messiah grows up

The school authorities deplored the influence of the Messiah but since they couldn't beat it they decided to join it and soon all the furniture in the school had to be replaced to allow for the newly acquired propensity of the staff to put their feet in their mouths.

The school placard which bore the legend 'TRUTH ALWAYS PREVAILS' was taken down and another one put up in its place:

'EVERYTHING THAT IS NOT TRUE IS NOT FALSE'.

This posed a problem during the exams. When the True-or-False questions were asked, the children wrote 'not true' and the teachers did not know whether to mark them right or wrong. If it was true then since they had written 'not true' it was not false hence true. If it was false it was not true. They pondered and reasoned but whichever way they looked at it, it seemed right.

So they went to the Messiah.

It does not matter, said the Messiah, whether it is right or wrong. The true seeker transcends opposites, definitions, truth and falsehood.

The profundity awed the teachers but in the next exams they had only Fill-in-the-Blanks. [. . .]

[Here follows the unpublished manuscript of the Critic, a once-time foe of our Messiah, but soon her speech-writer. *Ed.*]

It was all about the meaning of the Universe:

'The Universe, I'm afraid, is made up of tautologies. This is more frightening than it seems, leaving as it does no room for doubt and discussion but plenty for despair. Again, there can be doubt and discussion, but it's important to know that no amount of verbosity can change the essential nature of the Universe. It is therefore important to believe, although it is not important what you believe.

'And if you don't believe anything it is perfectly all right but it won't get you anywhere which again is perfectly all right because there is nowhere to go.

'This is due to the tautology that every destination is a journey, that is to say, a trip. It is difficult, however, to distinguish between the travelling and the reaching. So it is better not to try reaching because that way you reach faster.

'Another tautology that the Universe is made of is that there is no truth in words. This cannot be proved because it is neither true nor false. Besides, it cannot be disproved because it is both true and false. This is all because of language and thought. Therefore, to understand the Universe one must forsake both language and thought. But the greatest mistake is to think that you understand. If you think, then you are. But if you think that you are not, which is the only way to think of the Universe, then you are and are not and you neither are nor are not. This is difficult to understand so if you think then it is difficult to understand the Universe. If you don't think you may still not understand the Universe but that does not matter because even if you do understand the Universe there is nothing you can do about it. You cannot even say you understand the Universe because no one will believe you. Unless they have belief in you, in which case you will become a Messiah and then it does not matter whether you understand the Universe or not, because they won't believe it if you tell them you don't, and if you tell them you do they still won't believe it because they will think you *are* the Universe. Then they will try to understand you.'

When the Messiah read this she found it strangely familiar, so she went to the Critic and asked him, where have I heard this before?

The Critic looked contrite and admitted that it was mostly paraphrased from the Messiah's discourses. [. . .]

Since the PRO[28] and the Critic were now there to look after things, the Messiah went on an astral tour and when she returned she had many things to talk of.

She decided that she would speak to the people of Ogd on VOO[29] about her astral experiences.

Just to expand their vision, you know, she explained to her faithful followers. So the PRO organized the event and the Critic wrote her a speech.

People of Ogd, the Messiah said over the VOO, I am here to tell you about my interdimensional travels.

Among other things, she added. The Critic was offended for he had not written that.

Travel broadens the mind, the Critic had written.

So, travel broadens the soul, the Messiah said, for she always drew a fine distinction between the mind and the soul. (For one is of time and the other is not, she wrote in her book *Time and Again*.)

In the nineteenth dimension, for instance, she continued, I met a tribe called the Bellingtons who said that the Earth is not round. Now, it is commonly believed, not only in Ogd but also in other kingdoms and dimensions, that the Earth is a global kind of lump.

---

[28] PRO: Public Relations Officer.

[29] VOO: Video of Ogd [*author's note*].

But this tribe had submitted a referendum stating that the Earth is shaped like a bell.

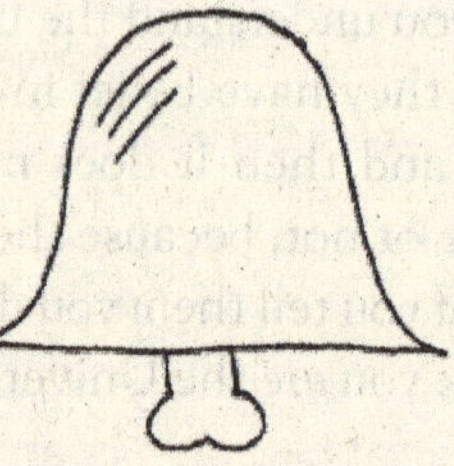

The shape of the earth according to the Bellingtons

The Bellingtons, the Messiah went on, are a taciturn people and the only answer they gave to all my questions was

'Ding dong.'

The meaning of the statement depended upon the pitch and tone of the 'ding dong'.[30] Finally, using the local properties of a sphere, I proved to them that the Earth is round.

Besides, I told them for good measure, if the Earth were a bell, it would toll.

The argument convinced them. So they renamed themselves the Ballingtons and revised their vocabulary. Then the only answer that they gave to all my questions was

'Ping pong'

since they now believed that the Earth was shaped like a pingpong ball not a ding-dong bell.

Then, proceeded the Messiah, there is a kingdom called Ugh which is so full of mirrors that one cannot take a step without walking through a looking glass. (Here she paused, because the phrase sounded extremely familiar.) These mirrors, she continued by and by, do not laterally invert. (Here she paused, for effect.)

The advantage of this, she went on after the pause had become sufficiently pregnant, is that you can shake hands with yourself. These

[30] Here the Messiah gave examples which are unprintable due to the phonetic limitations of printed words [*author's note*].

mirrors do not vertically invert either, so that if you stand under a mirror and look up, you will see the soles of your feet. This is not at all a nice sight, which is how the kingdom got its name: the people are always looking up and saying 'Ugh.' The people of Ugh never wash their feet.

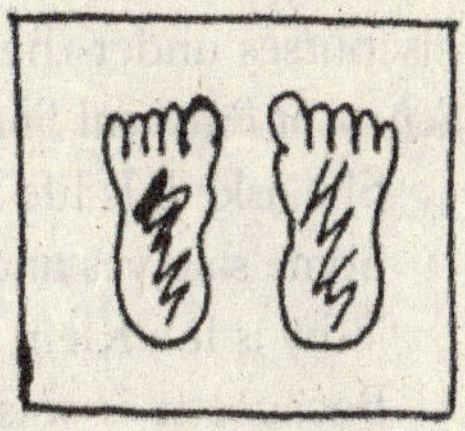

Ugh

Ding dong. (Commercial break.)

But my favourite dimension is the one in which the doughnuts are shaped like Möbius strips and they drink water in Klein bottles.[31]

Stars in the Messiah's eyes

Here the Messiah went into a deep trance from which she did not awaken until her hour was up.

The people of Ogd were enthralled by the Messiah's talk and also by her silence and they asked for more.

But the King of Ogd forbade it because he felt that her hairdo might influence the youngsters of Ogd who might try to imitate it. Do tell her not to take it personally, he said anxiously, it's just a matter of aesthetics. [. . .]

The day nooned and in the evening thousands of people gathered to hear the Messiah speak, between sucks and clips, of Life and Death.

Life is a Möbius strip, she declared.

Her disciples took down notes furiously, in shorthand. Wait, O Revered One, we're catching up, they said.

The thing, the Messiah said, is not to catch up but to catch on.

Oh yes, of course, they said, writing it down for posterity.

But the Messiah was not satisfied. She had been through all this before, and indeed there was a completely compiled book of her

[31] Möbius strip: A band that has a single boundary curve, or, in other words, only one side. Formed by taking a strip of paper, giving one end a half-twist and attaching the ends. Klein bottles: Named after Felix Klein, this is a 'bottle' that can only exist in four dimensions, as it must pass through itself without a hole. It can be created by joining two Möbius strips along their boundaries. It has only one side and thus no inside or outside.

discourses under the title *The Foot-in-the-Mouth or The Klein-Möbius School of Practical Philosophy*. But still no one Knew.

She asked, Is life a Klein bottle?

Some said yes and some said no.

Why is it a Klein bottle, she asked those who had said yes.

Because it is washed with soap and water, they replied, for the Ogdians were a literal people.

The Messiah sucked her toes sadly. You don't Know, she sighed.

Then how, O Enlightened One, shall we Know?

The Messiah paused meaningfully. This was, as her PRO would have told her (had she asked him), a psychological moment and she must not, she knew, blotch it up.

So she drew a deep breath and said, PUT YOUR FEET IN YOUR RESPECTIVE MOUTHS.

(She added the 'respective' because she did not want any mix-ups at this crucial time.)

A murmur of puzzlement ensued from the crowd. The people of Ogd and not-Ogd thought that they had heard wrong, which was quite possible because the Messiah's voice was often thick with toes, saliva and profundity.

But the Messiah swallowed the saliva and repeated,

PUT THOU THY FEET IN THY RESPECTIVE MOUTHS.

So they did and suddenly they Knew.

The Messiah saw their faces light up with Knowledge as they sucked their toes and she said, Now you will hop across the line that separates the Mortal from the Immortal, the Known from the Unknown, the Finite from the Infinite, etcetera.

Etcetera, the congregation intoned, their voices muffled by their toes. They had given up writing notes now.

There is no difference, the Messiah shouted, between Life and Death. The inside is the same as the outside.

Death is also a Möbius strip, her disciples chanted, catching on fast.

And a Klein bottle, said the Messiah.

And a Klein bottle, agreed the disciples.

And everything that has a beginning has an ending. But nothing begins, so nothing ends.

But now the Messiah found that no one was listening to her. They were too busy eating their toenails in newfound omniscience.

So she coiffured her hair and went to live in the Palace of Ogd as the consort of the King.

Etcetera.

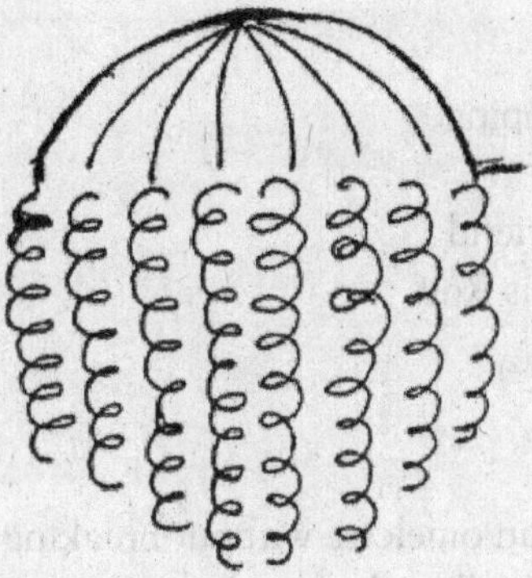

The Messiah's new hairdo, from behind

SAMPURNA CHATTARJI

FROM The Food Finagle: A Culinary Caper

Idli-Pom

Idli lost its fiddli
Dosa lost its crown
Wada lost its wiolin
And let the whole band down.

Very Fishy

There was a fish who called himself
THANKYOUBHERYMAACH.[32]
Till the fishermen caught and salted him
And ate him with boiled starch.

Explained[33]

Idiyappam keeps yapping
Puttu plays golf
Utthapam's my girlfriend
Mutthu's real name is Rolf.

Easy

How can you make an omelette without breaking any eggs?
Easy, fry tomatoes in yellow flour and eat it standing on your legs![34]

Frankie[35]

i

Frankie oozes meaty juices
But he's not a boy

---

[32] bherymaach: Since the Bengali alphabet does not have a 'v', v-sounds in English and other languages get softened into a 'bh'. Hence 'very' becomes 'bhery'. In addition, Bengalis have a habit of prolonging vowel sounds which turns English words like 'much' into '*maach*'. Significant to the wordplay here, '*maach*' in Bengali means 'fish'.

[33] Menus in South Indian restaurants detail their selections in roman script, and the lurking presence of English words within those essentially South Indian words was really the starting point of this verse.

[34] omelette: For vegans, eateries in Bombay offer an inventive option—the tomato omelette made of chick-pea flour, fried into a round thick pancake.

[35] Title: One of Bombay's favourite fast food options, a 'Frankie' is a fried roti roll with meat, egg or vegetarian fillings. It was started by Amarjit Tibbs in the late sixties, who also coined the advertising slogan 'Tibbs, I love Frankie, so will you'. The name 'Frankie'

You can get him anywhere
So stop being so coy.

ii
I love Frankie you love Frankie
Obviously there's some hanky-panky.

iii
Frankie's not a little boy
who lives down the lane.
He's a fat and juicy roll
with a kebab for a brain!

FROM The Boy Who Had Never Seen a Town

There once was a boy who had never seen a town. A clown a frown he had seen. But not a town. Now that may seem strange to *you* but to *him* it was perfectly normal. That is, until he saw one and then . . .

This is what happened.

(Of course it may have been a city but to a boy who has never seen a town but who has seen a frown and a clown, it really doesn't matter which is what, and so . . .)

This is what happened.

Our boy burst out laughing.
His eyes laughed.
His toes laughed.
His ears laughed.
His nose laughed.
His legs hands shins laughed.
His hips elbows chins laughed.

---

is said to have been inspired by the then West Indies cricket captain, Frank Worrell, whose team was apparently pulverizing the Indian team in an ongoing series. While Tibbs continues to be the 'authorized' version, me-too 'frankie' stalls are found at every other street corner.

In other words, a town to him was better than a sad joke, or a clown falling up, better than funny faces and better than being tickled with an enormous tickly leather-feather in funny places. It made you laugh and that too simply by sitting there.

Where?

Anywhere? Somewhere? Somewhere else? Or nowhere?

(For a boy who had never been anywhere in his life, somewhere was better than somewhere else and nowhere was funnier than the town. And so . . .)

He laughed till he cried.
Till his laughing tears dried.

And then he blinked his eyes and said:

Ha! If only I had brought my book!

Then of this town I could've pictures took!

(That's how it was in the boy's country or village or planet or cowshed or galaxy or wherever it was that he came from. You took pictures with a book. It was perfectly normal so there's *really* no need to laugh. You held up a blank and empty book full of blank and empty pages and aimed it at what you wanted taken, then you shut the book with a snap and, believe it or not, next time you opened the book at *that* page—there was the picture sitting pretty, like it had been there all the time! Nobody *read* books in the boy's country or village or planet or cowshed or galaxy, no, when they wanted to read they just shut their eyes and did it without any help. Everything, you see, was already written down inside their eyelids, and all they had to do was look at it with their eyes closed. Simple. Which is why . . .)

Our boy now wished he had brought his book. How else would anyone believe he had actually seen something this funny? No one, not even Gullible Go-Away, would believe it. Unless he showed them. So now what? He would have to write it all down, loud and clear, and save it inside his eyelids so when he went back he could ask for a telepathic conference and everyone could read what he had written. And so . . .

He began.

(You see where he came from they didn't need pen and paper to write. They wrote by speaking. Don't ask me how it works because *I don't know*. If I did, would I be writing this down the old-fashioned way for you to read out of an old-fashioned book? No, this book would be blank and then, since it's looking at *you*—you would be inside this book the moment you snapped it shut and the next thing you know . . .)

But then that's not *this* story is it? No. And so . . .

He began.

SHREEKUMAR VARMA

Grandmother's Tales

This is the story of truth,
Our childhood and family roots;
And our grandmother's stories that drew
Her entire brood to sample and savour her brew—
From a cauldron her ladled-out memories and scary old tunes

From mountains and seas, and the shivery silence
of inky-black dunes.
Today we remember her face like a bird, and the glow
of her nose in the dark,
Her swingy arms and chirp, and those feathers she scattered
about in the park.
And today, of course, we know for a fact that nothing she said was a lie
Even the promise she made that never in this life would she die;
For how could we guess that the day would soon come,
When she'd pack all her tales with a hum,
And climb atop our tallest old tree
And fly away, forever free?

Ghost Office

Last night I went out to post a letter I'd written to my dear classmate who is now head of the boiler room in the North Pole's ice-making factory because it was Christmas and I had baked him a nice little Indian corn cake with date seeds I had chewed myself and corns from my father's feet and our favourite cat's ear-wax, though unfortunately my sister ate it up by mistake, and I wanted him to know that it was okay and that I'd bake him another one soon enough and I wrote that it would have much more interesting ingredients in it and I took this letter to post at our local village post-office which is situated in the middle of a stream in a small compound surrounded by trees bursting with grey mangoes and pink jackfruit and vines of jasmine oozing out of the earth like night-worms, and all this basking happily in the milky moonlight, but I heard strange sounds coming from inside the locked building and remember being rather scared because I'd heard that thieves and rascally men had come from the city and made a den of the building and spent their time doing things that we decent villagers would never do like walking on their hands and swinging from the rafters by their ears, so I decided to post that letter and get the hell out of the place as fast as I could, but as I was putting my letter into the grinning slot in the red pillar-box, I heard a distinct sigh and felt a hot breath on my hand from within the pillar-box slot and a whispery tired old voice addressed me and told me to come back tomorrow 'for I feel a little too full tonight'.

VINDA KARANDIKAR

THE SMART ALECK

Translated by Anita Vachharajani from the Marathi original 'Untavarcha Shahana'

A smart aleck I know of old,
Has shoes of solid gold.
He goes begging from gate to gate
Crying, 'People are such cheapskates!'

I know a smart aleck, *alack*!
Gives advice from a camel's back;[36]
His brother he calls 'mister'
His aunt he now calls 'sister'.[37]

Says a smart aleck I know,
'I'll build myself a bungalow:
No dogs will enter in though
Horses pop in through the window!'

---

[36] advice from a camel's back: This is the literal, and colourful, translation. To give advice 'sitting on a camel's back' is to advise from a distance, with no sense of reality.
[37] His aunt he now calls 'sister': Here is a typically complex, and untranslatable, web of Indian relationships. The original is more like, 'His *aatya* he calls *mami* /And his *mami* he calls *kaki*.' '*Aatya*' is the term for one's father's sister, '*mami*' refers to one's mother's brother's wife, and '*kaki*' refers to one's father's brother's wife.

Hospitality

Translated by Anita Vachharajani from the Marathi original 'Mejwani'

Hoonka Choo
Choonka Hoo
—They are brothers two.

Chenka Foo
Foonka Che
—Nephews two are they.

Four Chinese guys came one day,
Had some dinner and went away.

Four full plates of rice, I served
Four feet long the chopsticks were![38]

They burped four times without a word
So loudly some in China heard!

Ever since they've left our shore,
We haven't had roaches any more!

Aatpaat Town[39]

Translated by Anita Vachharajani from the Marathi original 'Aatpaat Nagaramadhye'

In Aatpaat Town no crimes are there,
The dark kids are smart, the crazies are fair.

[38] chopsticks: The Marathi word used is '*kaadi*', which means a 'twig', but, at the risk of making too much sense, 'chopsticks' seems more appropriate.
[39] Title: Aatpaatnagar is a common mythical town in Marathi folk stories. Literally, it means 'a certain city/town'. Aatpaat is also a children's game.

In Aatpaat Town the fun always reigns,
The ministers fetch water, the king sweeps the lanes.

In Aatpaat Town all the money is gone,
You get kilos of jaggery for singing a song.

In Aatpaat Town, child, holidays aren't missed;
'Coz in Aatpaat Town schools don't exist!

Pishi Mavshi's[40] Backyard

Translated by Anita Vachharajani from the Marathi original
'Pishi Mavshiche Parasu'

The cat digs up the backyard soil;
Pishi Mavshi sows the seeds.
They will grow as tall as her
By morning-time when darkness flees.

If the plants are taller than Pishi
Or seem shorter by a fraction,
Pishi Mavshi'll wring their necks and
Dance deliriously to distraction.

On the jackfruit tree of Pishi
Mangoes grow in season and out
On the mangoes, guavas grow and
Banana trees on them soon sprout.

When banana bunches appear
Pishi kicks the troubled tree;
The tree starts trembling terribly and
Out pop saplings one, two, three!

---

[40] Title: A '*pishach*' is a devil, a witch or a fiend, while '*mavshi*' is the term for one's mother's sister. 'Pishi Mavshi' could be loosely translated as 'Auntie Witch'.

The cat digs up the backyard soil,
And people say that they have seen
At high noon Pishi from a skull
Pour water on her garden green.

Pishi Mavshi's Journey

Translated by Anita Vachharajani from the Marathi original
'Pishi Mavshiche Yatra'

At the time of the solar eclipse,
Pishi starts on one of her trips.
'Where are you going? Are you going to Kashi?'
She'll turn if these words leave your lips.

Seven steps back she will tread
And then carry on straight ahead.
When Pishi Mavshi begins once again,[41]
A bear cries out loudly in dread.

The villagers hear the bear's cries
And they all get the runs in surprise
The temple begins to burn in the fire
And the well, in a fever, dries.

Where Pishi on her journey steers
None know—'Is it there or here?'
Although she travels towards the East
From the West she suddenly appears.

At the lunar eclipse, the old crone
Comes back from her trip, to her home.

---

[41] She'll turn . . . again: This refers to the common superstition that asking one's destination as he or she is about to leave the house is bad luck. The only way to avoid this is to walk back a few steps and begin again.

A snake begins to whistle a tune,
And the door opens out on its own!

The Zoo

Translated by Anita Vachharajani from the Marathi original
'Ranichi Baag'

One day I dreamt of the zoo:
On the elephant's back, a snake or two.

And playing cards with the deer
Two wily cheetahs sat quite near.

The monkey read the Puraan
While the camel read the Koran.

The lion lectured so long
The donkey wrote it all down wrong.

The giraffe sang ever so well:
High as his neck his tune would swell.

The jackal managed the shop;
He thinned the milk to watery slop.

The animals of the zoo
Saw me and said, 'Give him a cage too!'

That's when I woke up—*phew*!
One day I dreamt of the zoo.

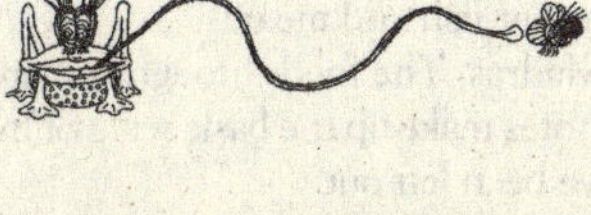

MANGESH PADGAVKAR

THE FISHING LINE

Translated by Anita Vachharajani from the Marathi original 'Gull'

Chintu Bhatt[42] tossed in a line
And tied his tuft up tightly,
When he pulled upon the line,
Up came a pea boiled lightly!

The Saraswat tossed in a line[43]
And cleared his throat—*ahem*,
When he pulled upon the line,
Up came a fish to him!

The Madrasi[44] tossed in a line
And sang, sa re ga pa dha sa,[45]
When he pulled upon the line,
Up came an idli and a dosa!

POOR LITTLE SPARROW

Translated by Anita Vachharajani from the Marathi original 'Bichari Chimnni'

There was a cow
She told the sparrow
'Give me a bath, now.'

---

[42] Chintu Bhatt: 'Bhatt' is a term for the Brahmin who officiates as a priest at ceremonies and in temples. Brahmins and other members of higher castes were required to sport a tuft of hair at the top of the head as a caste mark. The rest of the head was usually shaved bald.
[43] Saraswat: Saraswat Brahmins come from the coastal parts of Maharashtra, and are said to trace their origin from the eastern and northern parts of India. Unlike most other Indian Brahmins, they eat fish and meat.
[44] Madrasi: a person from Madras. The foods brought up are typical southern fare.
[45] sa re ga pa dha sa: Seven notes make up the basic scale of Indian classical music. Here, two notes—*ma* and *ni*—have been left out.

There was a rat
He told the sparrow
'You give me a pat.'

There was a fly
She told the sparrow
'You wipe me dry.'

There was a crane
She asked the sparrow
'What is your name?'

There was a bumblebee
He told the sparrow
'Put on my knickers for me!'

FROM *VAATRATIKA*

These verses are in a form invented by Padgavkar which he calls *vaatratika*, a self-coined portmanteau word. To explain, he writes in his Preface to the book with the same title: 'Between 1960 and 1962 I wrote some *vaatratika*. I combined the word "*vaatrat*" (mischievous) and the word "*tika*" (comment) and created the word *vaatratika*. I wanted to indicate that this was a form that contained very few lines . . .' This form resembles the limerick, not in the particulars of structure, but in its being a concise, tightly structured nonsense expression, the kind of form that seems particularly suited to the controlled yet chaotic vagaries of nonsense.

INTRODUCTION

Translated by Anushka Ravishankar from the Marathi original 'Prastavna'

Lala lala lalala
Aala aala salala
Haha haha heengheengheeng
None of these mean anything

A Little More Introduction

Translated by Anushka Ravishankar from the Marathi original 'Annkhi Thodi Prastavna'

Old Professor Solemnface
Makes very studious comments:
A few of these mischievous drops
I sprinkled onto his garments

Uncle's Wife

Translated by Anushka Ravishankar from the Marathi original 'Kaaku'

She accidentally cut her finger,
Chopping onions with her knife.
Ever since, she chops her onions
With her nose, my uncle's wife.

Pious

Translated by Anushka Ravishankar from the Marathi original 'Dhaarmik'

In the town of Piouspur
Lived such a pious sage
When he caught a cold he read
The Gita, page by page!

Is it true?

Translated by Anita Vachharajani from the Marathi original 'Khara Ki Kaay?'

On Saturdays people who eat figs
Will soon turn into portly pigs.

On Sundays rising early in the morn
Will make you grow two curly horns.

On Monday chewing betel leaf
Will make you grow a long pair of teeth.

On Tuesdays studying's not nice
You get a headful of itchy lice.

On Wednesday one who flowers plucks
Will grow a pair of big buttocks.

On Thursdays those who eat dal might[46]
Be beaten in a pestle fight.[47]

On Fridays those who dare to bathe,
Policemen come and take away.

THE NEST

Translated by Anita Vachharajani from the Marathi original 'Gharta'

Did-dill, bid-dill
Flour that's in the mill.
The flour flew into the black crow's eye.

Treasure-pot freasure-fot
The tom-cat, a cunning sort,
Stole away all the salt on the sly!

Timpant-a-tampant
There's a dancing elephant!
She sprayed the water up so high!

---

[46] dal: A rather dull translation of '*usal*', a popular, spicy, gravy-based snack made of sprouted and boiled green gram.

[47] beaten in a pestle fight: The original uses the word '*musal*', which means both a 'punch' and 'pestle'. This fairly violent image is common in folklore. Cruel stepmothers, stern fathers or brutal in-laws are said to resort to this rather horrific instrument.

Birrow-o-barrow
The poor little sparrow,
Her nest's so wet, it might never dry!

No

Translated by Anushka Ravishankar from the Marathi original 'Nasail'

A ripple has no rip
If there's no bottom in a ship

An eater has no mouth
If there's an elephant with no snout

A needle has no eye
If jackals do not howl or cry

A sandwich has no bread
Without any needle, if there's thread

A tambura has no string
If there's a fire without kindling

With no wheels a car goes
If there is breath without a nose

A tiger eats no mutton
If there are pants without a button!

Mr Big Nose

Translated by Anushka Ravishankar from the Marathi original 'Naakoba'

A double-sized nose
No one should grow
On that nose
Should sit no crow

If a crow
Should sit on top
When it leaves
It might just plop!

On the nose
No filth should show,
A double-sized nose
No one should grow

THERE ONCE WAS A MAN

Translated by Anita Vachharajani from the Marathi original 'Asaa ek manoos'

There once was a man with a beard
How long do you think it could be?
It was so long, so very long,
That his feet he never did see!

There once was a man with two hands
How big do you think they could be?
He could just reach out and pick
Some coconuts off the tree!

There once was a man with two legs
How long do you think they could be?
With just a single stride he could
Step over the moon easily.

There once was a man with a head
How large do you think it could be?
Even the toughest sum would take
One look at him and flee!

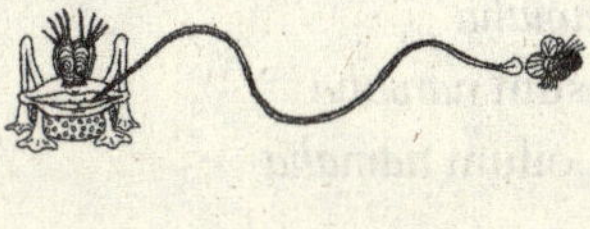

SARITA PADKI

SIXED-UP MONG

Translated by Anushka Ravishankar from the Marathi original 'Gulte Aanne'

Bold bold kreeze blows
Po the tark let's go
Let's fave hun, come, let's fave hun

Let's on the ring swock
Let's on the ree-raw sock
Let's fave hun, come, let's fave hun

Let's sneat acks come
Let's jink druice come
Let's fave hun, come, let's fave hun

Plide-n-seek let's hay
Platch-platch let's cay
Let's fave hun, come, let's fave hun

Plots and plots let's lay
Let's holl in the lay
And then, brailing in the seeze,
Let's ho gome
Let's fave hun, come, let's fave hun

THE BATHING HYMN

Translated by Anushka Ravishankar from the Marathi original 'Aanghol Stotra'

Om havum bathum *namaha*
Om take offum clothesum *namaha*
On the body applyum oilum *namaha*

Scrubscrubum *namaha* rubrubum *namaha*
Scrubscrubum *namaha.*

Om on the body pourum waterum *namaha*
Glugglugum *namaha* blugblugum *namaha*
Glugglugum *namaha.*

Om applyum soapum *namaha*
Scrubscrubum *namaha* rubrubum *namaha*
Work upum latherum *namaha.*

Om pourum more waterum *namaha*
Glugglugum *namaha* blugblugum *namaha*
Wash offum soapum *namaha.*
Om wipeum bodyum *namaha*
Wearum clothesum *namaha*
Om niceum cleanum *namaha*
Bring outum snacksum *namaha!*[48]

USHA KHADILKAR

THE MANGO JUMPED RIGHT OFF THE TREE . . .

Translated by Anita Vachharajani from the Marathi original
'Jhadavarun amba padla'

The mango jumped right off the tree,
And hopped into a basket
Uncle Jackfruit chuckled in glee,
Held his belly, and sat in a casket.
The jackfruit casket and the mango basket
Skid slowly to the boat,
Bho, bho, bho, went the boat's siren,

[48] The description of taking a bath is written with many words having suffixes that make the whole sound like a droning Sanskrit strotra or hymn.

As they reached Mumbai afloat.[49]
They hopped on to a horse cart
Clip-clop-clip the horse did run
But *blam!* It hit a motor car!
Uncle Jackfruit's head, it spun!
Jackfruit tumbled *thump, thump, thump,*
The mango went down *bump, bump, bump!*
The mango paled to a fearful yellow
The jackfruit was squished and shattered.
'To Mumbai we will no more go!
Our Konkan is much better!'

ANANT BHAVE

Bananas, Bananas

Translated by Anita Vachharajani from the Marathi original
'Kele, Kele'

Bananas, so many bananas,
Been munching them for weeks!

Banana peels, banana peels,
Ate so many, it hurt my cheeks!

On gobbling bananas of every sort,
The lion went and climbed a fort!

[49] Mumbai: Known as Bombay earlier, the city is said to have a faster pace than the slow, sylvan villages of the Konkan belt. Mangoes and jackfruits are among the seasonal fruits that grow in the coastal parts of Maharashtra, also known as the Konkan region. That probably explains the fruits' rather provincial phobia for the big city!

After eating banana fries,
Granny, asleep in a cradle, lies

When, Then

Translated by Anita Vachharajani from the Marathi original 'Jehva-tehva'

When the clock tocks suddenly
And strikes the thirteenth time,
Then
To tie the elephant
The mice, with sand, make twine.

When the days within a week
Move on from seven to eight,
Then
The rabbit tells the tiger,
'Beware! We have date!'

When the month of February
Thirty days assumes,
Then
Upon the crow's head bloom
Two purple peacock plumes.

When there are an extra couple
Months within the year,
Then
The bullfrog teaches the lark
To sing tuneful and clear.

USHA MEHTA

A Blast

Translated by Anita Vachharajani from the Marathi original 'Dunga'[50]

Donga Dunga Donga, and Dunga Donga Dunga
Donga Dunga Donga, and Dunga Donga Dunga

Mister Magan and Mister Chhagan,
Start your blubbering, there's the onion!

Dabbu Rao and Gabbu Rao all fall into some slush—
If it gets too much, go fly off in a rush!

O Meenakshi, O Kamakshi, O what's what, I say!
There goes your chunni on the wind—flying away!

The salt tastes sour; the bitter gourd's sweet,
The sun's gone nuts and the moon steals treats.

A raucous ruckus, a chaos insane
Inside the forest the cockroaches reign.

Madly, sillily, madly-ho!
Sillily, madly, sillily-ho!

Donga Dunga Donga, and Dunga Donga Dunga
Come on, have a blast—hey, cowabunga!

[50] Dunga: The word refers to a riot or, by extension, to riotous fun.

LEELAVATI BHAGWAT

THE SNAIL

Translated by Anita Vachharajani from the Marathi original 'Gogalgaay'

Snail, old chum, has feet in his tum
Its shoes are black and darkly shining
A hundred kids go out a-running

A hundred kids with a hundred chins
When they popped red berries in
Red and crimson turned their faces
They roamed around the woodland places

Ohmigosh! So much blood!
Mom's caught out
The kids laughed out
Gurr-gurr, gurr-gurr, they tumbled about

SHANTA SHELKE

ONCE ...

Translated by Anita Vachharajani from the Marathi original 'Ekda'

Once, flowers became children
And children became flowers!
The children sat in the garden,
And the flowers went to class!

Busy bees began to buzz
Around the children's heads

Meanwhile the flowers went to school
To study in their stead

The bees couldn't get
The children's smell
The flowers couldn't learn
Their lessons well

The kids in the garden
Wilted, poor mites!
The flowers couldn't get
A single sum right

There in the garden
The children grew sour
While in the school
Boo-hoo bawled the flowers!

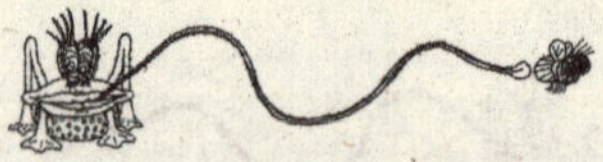

GULZAR

The One-Eyed Town

Translated by Sampurna Chattarji from the Hindi original 'Kaano ki ek nagri dekhi'

I came upon a one-eyed town
Jam-packed with just One-Eyes,
On one hand they were crazy
On the other shrewd and wise.

In that one-eyed town I found
The rituals were so strange,

Sickness flourished in strange places
Strange cures remained unchanged.

Their rivers flowed on bridges
And trains ran on water not land,
On bushy tails of apes there grew
Thick grapes in bunches grand.

Umbrella in hand, on moonlit nights,
They'd go out and say 'Oh my!
The dew is falling down it seems
And breaking our heads from high.'

When the mice would bell themselves
And go chasing after the cat
On empty bellies they'd drum their hands
And sing qawallis just like that.

'In the land of the blind the one-eyed man
Is king,' they say, but it's untrue,
Go see for yourself—in the one-eyed town
Reigns a blind king—I swear to you.

SARVESHWAR DAYAL SAXENA

Mr Footloose

Translated by Sumanyu Satpathy from the Hindi original 'Batuta ka Joota'

Mister Footloose laced his shoes
And stepped into a typhoon

The wind whipped up inside his nose
And into his ears, too.

As he tweaked his ears and squeezed his nose
Off flew his shoes from below his hose.

They flew and flew and flew
and flew to distant Japan—
Mister Footloose, now sans his shoes,
Was stranded at the cobbler of Hindoostan.

The Copycat Raja

Translated by Sumanyu Satpathy from the Hindi original 'Nakalchi Raja'

Building a fort of green chillies,
a gateway of coriander
and cannon balls of brinjals, quickly,
fought this copycat of a Raja.

One, Two, Three, Four

Translated by Sumanyu Satpathy from the Hindi original 'Ek, Do, Teen, Char'

One, two, three, four,
Let's go to Qutb Minar.
Five, six, seven, eight
Let's go to India Gate.
Nine, ten, eleven, twelve,
Into Humayun's tomb we'll delve

Thirteen, fourteen, fifteen, sixteen
At Connaught Place the cock said[51]

SRI PRASAD

THE JAMUN

Translated by Sumanyu Satpathy from the Hindi original 'Jamoon'

It was a jamun tree for sure
Yet mango fruit is what it bore.
I picked out one to eat and savour,
But found it had a cashew flavour.
I sowed the cashew, it is true,
From which two pomegranates grew.
They ripened into oranges sweet
Of which four baskets I did eat.

K. AYYAPPA PANIKER

MURDER

Translated by J. Devika from the Malayalam original 'Kula Patakam'

This piece has a certain rhythm that resembles that of a thief trying to steal a bunch of plantains from a tree at night. This translation does not capture the play with language, however. In Malayalam it starts *'Kam, takam, patakam,*

[51] cock said: The last line is intentionally incomplete.

Kulapatakam . . .' '*Kulapatakam*' means murder, but '*kula*' also means plantain-bunch, so, '*kula-patakam*' is twistedly made to mean 'plantain-bunch murder'. The following line is '*Netravazhakulapatakam*' which distorts the word '*nentravazha*', a particular sort of plantain and so on.

Er
D-er
Mur-der
Plantain-bunch murder
Eye plantain-bunch murder
Inner-eye plantain-bunch murder
Universal eye plantain-bunch murder
Auspicious universal eye plantain-bunch murder
Universal eye plantain-bunch murder
Inner-eye plantain-bunch murder
Eye plantain-bunch murder
Plantain-bunch murder
Mur-der
D-er
Er

MUTHALAPPURAM MOHANDAS

Two Sad Souls

Translated by Anushka Ravishankar from the Malayalam original

The coconut said 'My Mango!
I fell off the coconut tree.'
'My Coconut!' said the mango
'My fall's made squash of me.'

The two of them then continued
This back-and-forth bemoaning
The coconut sat and cried, whereas
The mango kept on moaning.

VAIKOM MUHAMMAD BASHEER

Me Grandad 'ad an Elephant! (1951) is one of Basheer's most popular works. It is the tale of the Muslim girl Kunjupattumma, whose rich grandfather is reputed to have owned an elephant. The song at the end of the extract is pure gibberish, which is not literary nonsense but obviously related to it. The sheer play in the sound illustrates an important aspect of nonsense and here the transliteration allows us to hear the music of the original Malayalam. It is also interesting to note the spiritual connotations given nonsense here, including the 'amen' and the mock spiritual tone used to introduce the piece.

FROM ME GRANDAD 'AD AN ELEPHANT!

Translated by R.E. Asher and Achamma Coilparampil Chandersekaran from the Malayalam original

'What were you singing?' Kunjupattumma asked.

'Don't ask me,' said Aisha. 'I'm a complete ignoramus. When that great guy comes, ask him. He's the one who wrote it. Nobody knows in what language. He composed it for the girls in our college to sing in a procession. And we sang it for the procession.'

'When you were singing, I was saying "amen"!'

'I noticed!'

'Is it bad to say "amen"?'

'Silly booby, it can never be bad.'

'Then sing it again. It's beautiful.'

'Sit there in an attitude of meditation. Put everything else out of your mind, and pay careful attention. Imagine this: There is a big procession of college girls. They—I should say we—are moving forward, carrying flags and singing!'

'All right.'

'Then listen!' And she sang:

'La . . . la . . . la!
Huttini halitta littapo
Sanjini balikka luttapi
Halitha manikka linjalo
Sankara bahana tulipi
Hanjini hilatta huttalo
Fanatta lakkidi jimbalo
Da . . . da . . . da!
La . . . la . . . la!'

KUNJUNNI

A TONGUE-TWISTER

Translated by Saroj Sundar and Anushka Ravishankar from the Malayalam original 'Padippum Theettayum'

A sesame ball in the middle of the sea
A sheep on the sesame ball
On top of the sheep is an elephant
Going for a little stroll

To catch the elephant, chase it, dimwit

In the southern part of the garden
At the root of the flowering tree
You will find a strand of hair
As fine as it can be

With this hair, tie the elephant, dimwit

Tie it, dimwit
Tie it, dimwit
Tie it, tie it,
Tie it, dimwit

Because

Translated by Saroj Sundar and Anushka Ravishankar from the Malayalam original 'Kondaavaam'

Because the poppadum is round
So the cow's milk is white
Because the cow's milk is white
So the milk-pot's made of clay
Because the milk-pot's made of clay
So Pappu's pipe goes *papparappay!*

Tell Me a Story

Translated by Saroj Sundar and Anushka Ravishankar from the Malayalam original 'Katha Parayu'

Tell me a tale, little grandma
If I tell a tale, you'll sprain your foot, child
What if I sprain it, little grandma?
If you sprain your foot, a crow will come, child
What if a crow comes, little grandma?
If a crow comes, it will tell a tale, child

Caw caw caw caw
Here comes the crow

Caw caw caw caw
The crow tells a tale

NANDA KISHORE BALA

Raven, O Raven

Translated by Sumanyu Satpathy from the Oriya original 'Damaru Kau'

Raven, o Raven
You caw from the murk
Of the shifting high hills
Where the Threeseedy[52] lurks.

It's eight times twenty
And twenty times three
Ask brother to count
The cowries for me.

The nighttime descends
With coins counted out,
The kajal pot's stolen,
A thief is about.

The six-rupee ox
Lays his head down to die.

---

[52] Threeseedy: The Oriya word '*tinimanjika*' is a nonsense portmanteau used to rhyme with '*ghunchi-ghunchika*' (shift-shifting) of the previous line. '*Tini*' means 'three' and '*manjika*' means 'whore' and is a variant of the word '*manji*', meaning 'seed'. *Tinimanjika*, along with the suggestion of sitting on top of the mountain, conveys a vague sense of foreboding.

Only the black cow
Today will survive.

MANOJ DAS

The Yellow Bear

Translated by Sumanyu Satpathy from the Oriya original 'Haladia Bhalu'

A yellow bear on Iceland's shore
Would sweetly speak and never roar.
None might believe, I guarantee,
Except Abanie Mahantie.

Poor Abanie, his soul has passed
At four-score-one he breathed his last
He never quite could understand
That trains existed in this land.
It's one like you, dear Abanie,
Our planet does so rarely see.

I know my Abanie would laugh
To hear this told on his behalf:
Last week atop the old dam's brink
I told the moon just what I think
About a crone that I had found
Nine cubits tall and five around,
Quite ungainly, I must tell,
In Indonesia did she dwell.

The old maid moon, not once in doubt,
Believed my tale, then hopped about

From cloud to cloud so daintily
Delighting in her levity

O Abanie Mahantie, dear,
If I could hear your voice draw near,
If I could see you sometime soon,
Around your neck I'd tie that moon.

J.P. DAS

These Oriya verses by J.P. Das are meant to imitate limericks, though they do not follow the form strictly. While they have the requisite number of stresses, they do not attempt to have an exact number of syllables.

Vain Cock

Translated by Sumanyu Satpathy from the Oriya original 'Poda Kapala'

Taught to say *ku-ku-du-koo, ku-ku-du-koo*[53]
He only said, 'cock-a-doodle-doo'
    Such a vain cock—
    You're in for a shock:
Not tandoori, you'll only be stew.

Bhagrathi Bhaina

Translated by Sumanyu Satpathy from the Oriya original 'Bhagrathi Bhaina'

From Bhimkhol, one Bhagrathi Bhaina[54]
Desired a voyage to China,

---

[53] *ku-ku-du-koo, ku-ku-du-koo*: The Oriya equivalent of 'cock-a-doodle-doo'.
[54] Bhimkhol: A village in Orissa. People from this region are often ridiculed. 'Bhagrathi' is a first name and 'Bhaina' is an honorific term, literally meaning 'elder brother'.

But couldn't quite find
A visa, so dined
At the zoo, staring straight at the myna.

Professor Kar

Translated by Sumanyu Satpathy from the Oriya original 'Professor Kara'

Short of temper was Professor Kar
Blood rushed to his head, oft, therefar
When mad with despair
He pulled at his hair
Till his head went as bald as the Thar.

Sadanand Satpathy

Translated by Sumanyu Satpathy from the Oriya original 'Sadananda Satpathy'

He, of Sarankul,[55] Sadanand Satpathy,
Went off riding his brand new phat-phati[56]
The red traffic light
He crossed with delight
And thus did the babu attain sadgati.[57]

Fear

Translated by Sumanyu Satpathy from the Oriya original 'Dara'

The goat is terrified of the tiger
The tiger is frightened of the figer

55 Sarankul: A village in Orissa.
56 phat-phati: An onomatopoeic coinage, imitating the putt-putting of a car.
57 sadgati: The rites of passage to death.

The figer is fearful of the goat—
They are all in the very same boat.

Flying Rumours

Translated by Sumanyu Satpathy from the Oriya original 'Uda Khabar'[58]

The cormorant soared, shaking dust from his wings[59]
The duck en route from Bhadruk on to Srikakulum sings
The raven was appointed referee in the park

---

[58] Title: The translation tries to express the literal Oriya, in which, '*khabar*' means 'news', and '*uda*' means 'that which has flown'; '*Uda khabar*' is 'rumour'.
[59] This first line is commonly found in romantic Oriya folk songs.

The kingfisher jumped into the jaws of a shark
The lark always flings a distant sound in the air[60]
The water-crow has drowned in knee-deep water over there
The white kite died when he accidentally dove
The woodpecker's banned from ever landing in the grove
The yellow finch's money has all vanished down the drain
The bone-swallow writhes in wretched stomach pain.
The hummingbird decides to sell her flowers in the sun
The swan looks on in hunger at the Lotus Award she's won.

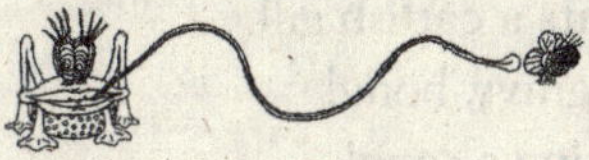

DASH BENHUR

Sing a Song, Brother, Sing!

Translated by Sumanyu Satpathy from the Oriya original 'Geeta Bol, Bhai, Geeta Bol'

Sing a song, brother, sing a song!
If not a song, maybe a fong![61]
Tap, tap, tappity tap
On the wooden clatter-clap[62]

[60] Sound in the air: Literally translated. This is also the name of All India Radio.

[61] fong: In Oriya, a reduplicative phrase can be created that expresses dismissiveness or a casual attitude to any given noun, by giving the word, then repeating it, but with an initial sound of 'f' replacing the original, as in '*gita-fita*', or, translated, song-fong. In this case, '*fita*' only makes sense with its companion word '*gita*'. Alone, at the end of the line, it is nonsense—one can't sing a 'fong'—yet there is sense implication because of the association with the implied 'song-fong' phrase.

[62] wooden clatter-clap: A musical instrument called '*das-katiya*', literally two sticks, made of two flat, narrow, rectangular pieces of wood, clapped together. It is usually

Brimming pots with trickling molasses.
Teeming red ants attack them in masses.
Chomp, chomp them in a queue.
Gnaw and gnaw, the marauding crew.
One night and all the molasses is grong.[63]
Sing a song, brother, sing a song!

Crink, clackle, clinkling coals
Fiery, fire-bright crackling coals.
Fried lentils, fried on a fiery grill.
Deep in the gravy floats a catfish gill.
Slurp, slurp, the thin gravy, bong!
Sing a song, brother, sing a song!

Tom, tom, the tom-tom, beat!
The younger woman is a betel-leaf neat!
Scorching is the August steam.
The calf toddles off with a left-side lean.
It moos; must open the gate before long—
Sing a song, brother, sing a song!

Ickity-Sickity

Translated by Sumanyu Satpathy from the Oriya original 'Uluru Uluru Bai'

Ickity-sickity gas:
Piles and piles of fire—

accompanied by the player singing stories from traditional texts. The entire performance is also called *das-katiya.*

[63] grong: In the original, this word sounds like the word for 'gone', but is altered slightly to rhyme with 'song'.

On water, shadows are cast—
The blustery blowing winds gasp.

Squishily splashy mud seeps;
The grass is standing standing;
The wild creepers creep
The Boguli bird's beak peeps.

Munching and crunching the hole,
Its face is fidgety fidgety:
A tiny hungry mole—
The snake looks away at the pole.

Drip-drop drip-drop drip,
Sliding slowly slowly
Down a muddy strip,
The snail and the worm on a trip.

Whoo-whoo screams the owl in flight
Whose eyes are glowing glowing
Darkness covers the night
Sleeping, the kite hides from sight.

Flickering flickering flame
Must study and study some more:
Exams are coming again
He's scared not enough's in his brain.

Clippity-cloppity tread
With sandalwood paste on his head
And wooden-sandalled feet,
The priest will walk here next week.

The Shadow-Catching Baiya

Translated by Sumanyu Satpathy from the Oriya original 'Chhaidhara Baiya'

The shadow-catching Baiya [64] came
Sunshine filled the midday sky
Kaiya[65] was his given name

Who can tell what trick he played
Back behind the clouds that day
Skies of brightest sapphire splayed

The rain-cloud-catching fiend appeared,
Blackest Night, his kinsman, too
They approached as evening neared

Seated, he guffawed like thunder
Clouds soon hid or went astray
Moonlight shone in all its wonder

The moon-catching fisherman stayed awake
High inside the Tungle Tree[66]
Holding his net above the lake

The full moon cast its image bright
Upon the lake, to fake a swim
And fool the fisherman that night

The liar-catching cop barked out
Coming quick that early eve
'Bring me Hilsa!' was his shout

---

[64] Baiya: The Oriya word for boogey-man, also meaning 'shadow'.
[65] Kaiya: An imaginary proper noun to rhyme with '*baiya*'.
[66]Tungle Tree: A nonsense tree, '*jeuta*' in the original.

'Where's the hilsa?' liars asked
Not in total innocence—
        Jumping in the river fast

The river-catching engineer
Came with minister in tow
        Bringing words for all to hear

Both of them did rant and shout
For a dam they must construct
        A raucous rally came about

Explanation's hard to hear
Rallies turn to bitter lies
Sounds of truth resist the ear

NIRANJAN BEHERA

MADHIA HUNDAY OF KANDIA KUNDAY

Translated by Sumanyu Satpathy from the Oriya original 'Gaan'tire Nama'

In the village of Kandia Kunday
There lived one old Madhia Hunday
When his pen full of goats
Was fed buckets of oats
They laid dozens of eggs every Sunday.

Ant-King's Grandson

Translated by Sumanyu Satpathy from the Oriya original 'Tankatiya Dhan'

The Ant-King's grandson, a rupee in his pocket
And a rope in his hand, set out to the market.
They asked him, 'What would you buy there, Ant?'
He replied, 'Why—only an eleph-ant.'

The King and the Ant

Translated by Sumanyu Satpathy from the Oriya original 'Raja Jaithile Uttara'

Long ago the King went north and saw to his relief
The tiger took to taking naps while chewing betel leaf
Just then a red and angry ant reared up its jaws and bit him
Before his servants saw the ant and had a chance to hit him.
Hearing this sad tale the Queen then swooned in utter grief
She called the court snake charmer who could any snake enchant
And asked him quietly to draw the venom of the ant.

SRI SRI

Clerihew

Translated by Dr E.M. Rao from the Telugu original 'Quin Eight'

Clerihew the bard said:
King Edward the Third
Ought never to have occurred.

The unappreciative poor bird
Would merit not even a word.

M.D. MUTHUKUMARASWAMY ('SYLVIA')

This is an example of modern Tamil stream-of-consciousness writing; a form that is not technically in the genre of literary nonsense, but borrows from it in significant ways. In the original Tamil version, the story appears as you see it here, as a wall of text with diamond-shaped blank spaces in the middle of each page.

A Detective Novel

Translated by Latha Ramakrishnan from the Tamil original 'Marma Naaval'

Mu. Who went in search of the frontiers of knowledge, became mad and disappeared and so worried . . .

With the umbilical chord dangling on the floor, with the small white beard that kept growing at great speed touching the floor, a baby boy who came into being just then, in a toddler's soft, unsteady walk as against the current of a chill wind cloud in Tirunelveli at dawn, when the time was 3 a.m. and thirty minutes + three seconds. With walls whitewashed, fixed like dark glasses on whichever direction one turned, with the stench of excretion in the gutters revealing raw nudity, that child became a vulgar image with sunken eyes, swollen belly and protruding teeth. In the struggle of the hands which stretched towards the image before the blood in the umbilical chord could dry, in the manner of a villager seeing halwa.[67] The word

[67] Halwa: A sweet typical of Tirunelveli. Halwa can be found in various forms in India and differs greatly from some forms of halwa found in the Middle East or in Europe.

'Mu'. Mu filling up the media space I came to be. When I the Mu filled up my mother who had but dry, milkless breasts, in the semen bag of he called father, from the moment I came and located myself inside to the moment I reached at the womb of she called mother, the more or less one crore, nine lakhs and sixty thousand seconds, calculated approximately by me passed safely with no hurdles for my being visible and invisible and safeguarding the atom particle of a great grand atom that was myself, with love and concern from all sorts of evils within and without—for which to convey my thanks I stood wondering, bewildered. The very fact that I am not one of the twenty million children who die without breast milk in this Indian subcontinent is but more than enough reason for me to thank. But whom I had to thank I didn't know and also for what. This confusion turned me into a corrupt child. And my corruption became cruel, thanks to my fellow urchins. Let's first begin with the frog, and dog—what great ecstasy it was tearing apart the legs and other parts of the frog and tying a string to them, each one of us carrying one such string and running along the streets and lanes of Sindupoondurai,[68] rolling in a frenzy unleashed. In the end, they would be aimed at an old widow or an insane boy and thrown with a shocking suddenness. And would hear their bitchy curses like 'go to hell, you devils', revelling in them, with ears relishing them. Then come the dogs. It was still better if the weapon was a sharp, rough-edged stone. And we would aim it with such expertise that it would slam into the soft, white belly or bottom of the creature. More than the dogs, if girls of my age were caught, the pleasure then proved unparalleled . . . Ah, ah. Can there be a bliss more than this? Here they would keep the filth and dirt in a heap street after street. Picking a handful, we would throw it at a girl who came by—words such as, 'you scoundrel, son-of-a-bitch', the fetid scraps would fill the air with their fragrance. This is prestigious land where sweet, honey-oozing Tamil words nourished Shaiva Siddhantha, you know. Let's overpower shit with more shit. Let's linger in the gutter itself hours on end, enjoying the smell and the feel. For attaining a philosophical look so early in life is

[68] Sindupoondurai: Sindupoondurai is an area in the town of Tirunelveli.

there a better place than this, tell me. Sir, please excuse me, Sir, I was coming in search of you only. My father was seriously ill, Sir. That is why I couldn't come. Please, forgive me, Sir. I promise that I will never do such a thing again. I will definitely give back the stolen object, Sir—Doesn't that suffice? When at the age of six after stealing a golden chain weighing solid five sovereign I kept wandering, away from the police station, it seems like, the practised words would come to one's aid throughout life. Enough if we become enraged. We can use these terms and phrases any time, anywhere and so save our skin. And, it is these very words which have made the writers' world look at me wonderstruck, praising me as someone great indeed. 'Mu is indeed a very wise person, or rather, a very shrewd one', they would remark. Yes these very same words. Deceit, Cruelty, Rage—three excretions. Husband, Cow, Affection—three excretions. We will win over these three filths. While I am penning all these things you may get the doubt that I am but writing about my own self, my dear reader. No, no, not at all. Because right from my seventh year to my twenty-seventh year, all I had done or seen, I remember not. As I came to be born of the assertion of images I was but a mixture of many an image, they say. MGR, Karunanidhi, Indira Gandhi, Shobana Ravi, Malavika Kapadia, Rajiv Gandhi, Kapil Dev, Pataudi Nawab, Gold Cafe Rani teacher Manohar Rameshkumar Baby Loose Mohan, Bama Booma Ragunathan Fathima Sujatha Swarnalatha Jayalalithaa Panrutti Prabhakaran[69]—so many a name and image shaped my I and me. I became that I, became 'He', She, They. During this period, in all that he had written, Mu had invariably lamented not being able to know for certain whether he was

[69]Karunanidhi is the former chief minister of Tamil Nadu. Shobana Ravi is a Tamil television newscaster. Kapadia is the last name of a famous Hindi actress. Malavika is just a first name. Kapil Dev and Pataudi Nawab are famous Indian cricket players. Gold Cafe Rani teacher is an advertisement character. Mohan is the name of a Tamil cinema comedian. Fathima is a Tamil television newscaster. Sujatha is a famous and popular male Tamil writer who writes under the pseudonym of a woman. Swarnalatha is another male Tamil writer who writes under a female pseudonym, but in this case, very much an unknown writer. Jayalalithaa is the present chief minister of Tamil Nadu—an actress turned politician. Panrutti is a small town in the northern part of Tamil Nadu. Prabhakaran is the leader of LTTE (Liberation Tigers of Tamil Elam) in Sri Lanka.

a man or a woman, a point which has been thoroughly overlooked by the critics at large. 'Can't fuck the images,' so shouting, as if he had discovered some great grand truth of life, he ran along the streets in an ecstatic state, was viewed on the television and devoured by millions of thrilled Tamils. But, 'Mu's claim that all those incidents are beyond the grasp of his memory is but a strategy adopted to shield his criminal days,' says a policeman, and a doctor views it as but an illusory disease sexually transmitted. Maybe we are not talking about Mu. God, what's this, some kind of a mysterious riddle sort of thing? But whose history in this blessed land of Tamil Nadu reads different from this? Aa ha. That's what the history of words is, discovered Mu. And he realized history was the language of the human worms' struggle. Their pains and irregularities, their uneasiness, their struggle for grabbing power exactly as fourteen different things or objects. During those days when he was wandering in the streets, in the manner of someone gone out of his mind, suddenly, on one fine day he gave his name in full as 'Muniyandi' and claimed that everything should be renamed and so wrote on all the streets with the help of a piece of charcoal, they say when he came to his senses in his twenty-seventh year saying that writing the novel was the damned thing he was destined to do, he shrunk into his own self. He had realized the real enemies of the novel as the theme, the characters, setting, background, backdrop and plot. He began his novel with the words, 'Nothing but the fullness of vision or its structure alone could remain unravaged in the twentieth century. Damned lonely ones along with demons, ghosts, criminals reveal nothing else except melodrama and frailty. The one dangerous and menacing aspect in them is that they dread loneliness, coming across the feeling even in their dreams. But, desert or the facades of the textile shops which are created artificially, three-dimensional posters, the television that keeps vomiting images, those skeleton-people who dance in tune to the swing and sway of those images, their ass of a culture, legal rules and regulations, lifelessness, the vacuum that is all-pervading both within and without—this is the deadly horror that the twentieth century has brought over Tamil Nadu. And, the body of the man who is caught in this morbid trap will have not even the dignity of a shadow—a miserable state of mind that stands in stark contrast to our onward march to the twenty-first century. Oh, my fellow-men of the city! Please listen! Let all of us research how we are to continue being alive in this world. We don't want children with beards. We should free ourselves from images. Where is the mentality of revolt against what is called "History". For all those signal rules and symbolic boundaries, for coordination and history—how are we to show our protest jointly? How to fill up that gap that could never be reduced, and also the burning emptiness? Dance, Snake, Dance. "Being alive" is only in the nonstop surging of the snake and nothing else.' These words spoken by the shadow of one of the characters in Mu's novel are but his own speech, several critics commented. Realizing that Physics alone would be of use in getting out of the clutches of history Mu got involved in research in the faculty of Physics till he turned thirty-three years old. That this entire universe is ruled by a fourteen-dimensional force, and that, because we see only four of them (Length, Breadth, Volume, Time), we don't feel and comprehend the other ten, and that the movement of these fourteen dimensions is History—Mu had found out and explained at length. The fundamental forces of Nature that even those men like Albert Einstein, Niels Bohr couldn't apprehend and the coordination of all of them, Mu was able to unravel without much difficulty, the scientists who have recommended Mu's name for the prestigious Nobel Prize wrote in their correspondence. Mu's 'Law of Physics' is called 'Garland Theory'. For instance, imagine a chain made of those fourteen rings entwined in the shape of a ring with another big chain. And, in that, another, and another—so you bring fourteen chains into your heart, visualize it. That is the Universe. It is their continuous harmonious and joint movement that moves and rotates the Universe. History moves on. And Mu after substantiating his theory with the help of mathematics, named those fourteen forces as follows: 1. The force of gravity 2. The strong force and weak force referred to in quantum mechanics[70] 3. The two-tier bridge over Tirunelveli 4. Time 5. van Gogh's torn-off ear 6. Electromagnetic power 7. Ernesto 'Che' Guevara's severed

[70] quantum mechanics: In English in the original.

hands 8. The heat and humidity of Tirunelveli 9. The female organ 10. Images 11. Such others or etc. 12. Meanings 13. The intellectuals of Tirunelveli and also Kovilpatti 14. Cypher or vacuum or Tamil. 'The very universe keeps going, thanks to those "so-called" intellectuals of Tirunelveli and Kovilpatti—there is no doubt about it. But, our Tamils can never understand either cipher or vacuum or poverty'—so writing, Mu in his work has drawn many circles one on each and every page denoting vacuum or poverty. In order to stress the fact that we are in a third-world country Mu has made constant use of the digit '3', it is said. In the chapter 'Some Dialogues with Cypher' it is written, 'We should only write essays, theses, biographies. We are neck deep in filthy mud. God knows when we may become fortunate enough to enjoy the cool weather and the soothing environment of the East European countries, but we should free ourselves from this literary suffocation.' The fake intellectual on reading it commented 'all rubbish', implying that Mu had lifted it straight from Sundara Ramasamy's '*J.J. Some Notes*'. And they all raised a great cry, uttering such terms as parody, forgery,[71] rewriting *J.J.* and all that. Mu argued that he didn't spit red, with the delicious munch of the betel leaves, on any buffalo. Whether he was writing seriously, whether it was a satire, mockery or the pranks of some mischievous monkey—none could arrive at a veritable guess about Mu's detective novel until the end, starting from Nabokov, Borges, Barthelme, Parth, Kooler, Pynchon, right up to Hawkes, such queries never came to be in the case of any other—this we should remember. The signifiers that have discarded meaning, he had opened them all up like the sea unleashed and the unleashed sea and pea and nut and yet wet as a great deluge. So huge a stooge, in quick succession, one by one, calling them daydream, cream, beam so seemingly, leaving the eyes open and closing and firing. Tadadak tadadak tadadak dak . . . So shot and ate Mu. I didn't know how you were able to produce 'meaning'. Even if I buy soap, I also buy a Bofors gun too, I am told. How is this at all possible? How at all possible . . . possible, promise,

[71] forgery: In English in the original.

middle octave, fiddle octave, riddle octave—mud, thud, blood, drink blood, eat, lick, suck, unsettle annihilate, Revolution on an individual level, J. Krishnamoorthy, Jittu Krishnamoorthy, Van Gogh's torn ear, Che Guevara's severed hands—give answers for all these things Mr Krishnamoorthy . . . Goddamned soul, how have you belittled Tamil—J.J. Joseph Keller, John the Killer . . . Twenty million children dying without milk. The individual revolution to reach the zero-level, pure experience is a must. Shun the institutions, O Cypher . . . humble to your good self. You are the source of all the images and reflections, we will pray to thee, the veritable god. You are the master of Virtue. You are the ocean of Kindness. You are the ever-glowing divine light, you are the lord of female organs . . . What a great boon it is to live in this same age in which you too are existing. Aren't you the one who had allowed me to record on this Tirunelveli bridge the reflection of the reflection of my shadow, my one and only master. From that bridge seated like the eye of a monster the thin stream of river Thamirabarani flowing as the tears of urine of a small boy the heat of the soil of which is but Time unaware of the Sky. Cast off the comprehension. What is taking place without taking Sri Lanka into confidence. No No No No No No No No No No No No No No No No No No No No No No No No Krishna's manoeuvring, Buddha's silence. *Mahabharatham* has commenced on the TV Frooti advertisement. Malavika Kapadia Karthik married the one who did not kill animals, but was kind to them—when the flesh and blood of the body burn and burn in hunger what kills what, that becomes the love for fellow-beings. Breakfast the green leaves 'Musumusuk-Keerai', Thoodhovalaik Keerai,[72] milk boiled to the maximum, everyday discipline, shouldn't sleep during daytime, shouldn't waste semen. Can waste away the very life, can make some other sacrifice, his or her life. Ten crores worth of drugs, seized. Though we lead a very usual everyday life, that is, living mechanically and meaninglessly, eating whatever is cooked

[72] The names of green leaves. The reference is to a text written by the Tamil poet and saint Ramalinga Vallalar. The text is called *Nithya Jeeva Olukkam* (Everyday Discipline).

and breathing our last when the time comes and even living so our economy enables the imperialist countries to amass profit, it seems . . . you, the lord, the source of all reflections . . . what is this? You can do it, brother. This is our man. Close your eyes and be blessed. Hey, you Barthelme, come here, you speak of something called cheerful nihilism, they say. What is that, you fella—initiate me into it, won't you, yeah, you, do you know . . . These fellas have no roots, do you know . . . Do they know how to climb the palm tree? Drinking liquor do they know 'cotton-wood'—the type of soil called 'karisal'. Do they know at least sisters-in-law. What bloody story they build, my brother—There are those four to hear all that—Sir, please, excuse me. Without fail I will come and meet you tomorrow. Folklore, what is that, my boy. These fellas have no roots, my girls . . . Do they know rowdyism. Who have written these to these no-gooders. Weren't we listening to the story of Mu? Garland Theory has gone away, missing since, my dear lady, he has gone mad, that fella, how many days have gone since we lost trace of him, you know how many. And, it is for him that I have told the other to come sing a 'Gaanaa'[73] song and so brought him here. That fella, not being able to comprehend what is what and how the how is, blabbers all nonsense. Looks like he had come, having a belly full of liquor. In that morning time when the cool breeze was blowing Sharmila got up and went out adjusting her jeans. How long to wait for this Ramesh. Poor she, such an innocent girl she is, not knowing the havoc that her voluptuous breasts and bum would create in any man, pulling at his innermost heart, oh how she walks with that bouncing gait. While the entire nation was raging with internal war a political leader sitting with the Chakra is like Lord Krishna reciting the Bhagavad Gita right in the middle of Kurukshetra. How soon new phrases turn highly attractive. With the help of a slightly altered structure and syntax the fundamental issues of philosophical processes could never be done away with—never—Ostwald's Law of Energy is a fine example

[73] Gaanaa: A genre of Tamil folk song sung in slums and among the fishermen of Chennai.

of this. Suffice it if the story is not told, somehow. All we want is fragments. Let's say all that we have already said again, again, and again. What is this then? This is no book. This is sheer abuse. Throwing a handful of sand at you, an act accompanied with filthy curses. Character assassination. This is not a book in the usual sense of the term. Lying in wait for a long time and calculate the worst possible attack at the appropriate moment, saliva spat at what is called 'Art'. A kick in the dhoti of god, an incorrigible indifference thrown at man, Destiny, Time, Beauty, Love, Everything. Outrage, Atrocity. The Circles with their central points you when turned voiceless I go on singing. Standing on your reeking corpse I would sing. You would never understand it. I would pose challenge after challenge against your power of comprehension. Do cry desperately. The impeccable Maruti cars, the young women who go round and round in them. Five-star hotels. Fashion shows, virgins in black paying homage to Nelson Mandela. Women and the Treasuries. How have one and all of them become pregnant? Quantity would transform into Quality. That, the quantum weight of an atom alone determines. Their characteristics or quality—we now know these things very well, Koodankulam[74] and the possible mass destruction therein are the real qualitative changes. Let us bring the emptiness outside too. Again, physics, again 'Garland Theory'. Generally, as examples though we use human–social concepts such as law, purpose, objective, rules and regulations, etcetera in association with things pertaining to these, and if by reason of the basic necessity the characteristics of our language in such usage have become sharp, Nature alone is a being incapable of handling any human–social scales. Everything has become quite calm. Doesn't emptiness feel loneliness? Doesn't it feel fatigue and boredom? If emptiness copulates with emptiness, emptiness alone would remain. Can't a shadow being bear human pregnancy? The intense sun would cool. Madness would lose its intensity. The earth would continue to

[74] Koodankulam: A village in Tirunelveli district where the Indian government had set up a nuclear power plant, displacing thousands of villagers.

hold us in its tight grip. Come, rise up and play like a Greek Olympic champion and seize the space. Become a signifier in the media and with the meaning losing its meaning every now and then turn meaninglessness unto yourself and live a meaningless existence. Vacuum would shroud you on all sides, brimming and blooming. Everyone would see for themselves all the fourteen dimensions. Total disintegration. Total formlessness. And the tragedy of having to record all these etcetera etcetera o, ye, Donald Barthelme. Are you the villain, my dear sir? The Detective novel would go on with the period intact. But, someone would turn into an antagonist of history and tearing off the last pages we would prevent or destroy meaning. The etcetera would become 'They are.' But etceteras would become 'They are.' But etcetera etcetera etcetera be born.

S. RAMAKRISHNAN

THE HISTORY OF THE RAMASAMY LINEAGE: THE HIDDEN TRUTHS

Translated by Latha Ramakrishnan from the Tamil original 'Ramasamigalin Vamsa Saritram:Sila Maraikkapatta Unnmaigal'

It was a completely unexpected morning that had to be confronted. The crowd, thick and dense, moved in rows. It was not clear where they were coming from. Sitting on the Gemini Flyover, legs dangling, many were conversing. Two people were atop the stallion warrior statue, taking photographs. News kept coming that the crowd was larger and thicker along the beach road.

Whose brainchild this was, none could tell. Indeed, it is highly doubtful that a similar event had ever taken place before. 'An assemblage of everyone endowed with the name Ramasamy—the first of its kind in the whole stretch of human history'—so the news flashed across the pages of all leading dailies. Ramasamys from every nook and corner of the world kept coming to attend the Grand Convention. You can't dismiss it with the old line, 'What's in a name?' How can any other name stand on par with Ramasamy?

'Ramasamys of the world, come together. Your world is coming into being at Seerani Arangam'[75]—the clarion calls went out all over Tamil Nadu. There were posters and banners everywhere in the city. Literary, agricultural, medical, linguistic, political, philosophical, postmodernist, social, religious, realist, irrealist, surrealist, structuralist, intellectual and the tri-Tamilist Ramasamys were taking part in large numbers in the three-day convention. As the news spread everywhere, those who were not Ramasamys listened intently and agitatedly.

The special guests of the convention were Umberto Ramasamy of the country of Kango, Edwarti Ramasamy of the nation called Nuva, the popular superstar who was also the renowned linguist of Hollywood, Arnold Ramasamy Wasnekkar, and also Ramasamysky, Su en Ramasamy (UN Special Emissary). Thus, more than a handful of special Ramasamys were expected to attend.

And, I would like to place before you, objectively and impartially, led by my inner vision and thirst for truth alone, historical truths of those grand days when lakhs and lakhs of Ramasamys gathered under one roofless roof. As information and data are brimming and overflowing within my senses, let me cast aside some of them and tell you about some others with the help of my imaginative power.

The Ramasamys, arriving in lorries and buses, had begun to assemble there the day before. We had been informed that some eight thousand Ramasamys were apprehended in Tambaram Railway Station for travelling without tickets. For the purpose of the Ramasamy Convention all fourteen floors of the massive LIC building were vacated, and all fourteen floors were filled with Ramasamys. All the windows of all the

[75] Seerani Arangam: An open-air stage on Marina beach, built in the seventies and used by political parties, evangelical groups and others. It was demolished in 2003.

floors were clogged with Ramasamy faces and fluttering, freshly washed dhotis hung out to dry. Many a Ramasamy stood there, right from the one-year-old to the too-old-to-remember-how-many-years-old. They were wandering, their faces changing colour and contour with time. When someone clapped his hands and called 'Ramasamy!', innumerable faces of varying ages turned, swelling like a huge wave. The BBC made an official announcement that four crore Ramasamys had gathered. To maintain that revolving bed, two hundred Ramasamys toiled day and night.

Outside the convention tent, martyr Ramasamy portraits were kept. Ramasamys themselves saw those portraits of Ramasamys, where all faces looked alike. Beneath every portrait was kept a packet of salt. The Ramasamys tasted the salt and remembered the salty days when they extracted the salt filling their minds, and they shed tears for the martyrs.

Bringing the torch for the convention from the Andamans was the duty handed over to Aaravayal Ramasamy. A thousand Ramasamys joined hands and set out in a ship from the Andamans. Many Ramasamys had assembled in the port to give them a warm send off. They waved and waved to the voyaging Ramasamys.

Inside the ship, Ramasamys' faces were everywhere. Sitting atop the roof of the ship the great freedom fighter, Aaravayal Ramasamy, delivered a spirited speech on independence. Some thought-provoking excerpts of it are as follows:

> My dear Ramasamys, we had proven to the British in those bygone days that Ramasamy was a name distinct from other names, that it was unparalleled. Ramasamy is the symbol of Tamil identity. Even if he is at the other end of the world, a Ramasamy would never lose his exclusive, special identity. Ramasamys alone have preserved Tamil life, politics, philosophy, and literature for centuries. The very first man who set foot on the moon was a Ramasamy. History has concealed this veritable truth. But who can ever refute the fact that the pages of history are so full of Ramasamys? (Applause) As our dear genius of philosophy, Hegel Ramasamy, claims, Ramasamy is a name that remains the same. And, this great convention will determine the future of Ramasamys, my dear Ramasamys . . .

Before this speech could conclude, the sea's rage had worsened and the waves began to lash higher than the ship. Caught in the sea's grip, the ship lost its sense of direction. The Ramasamys who had to sleep listening to the roaming waves throughout the night were afflicted with yellow fever, with the result that by the next afternoon 999 Ramasamys had breathed their last. With those bodies lying spread on the deck like wood blocks floating on the salty water, Aaravayal Ramasamy, standing on the deck of the ship, sang *'Behold, the precious flag of Mother'*, in an effort to get rid of his gripping fear. The ship loaded with the bodies of 999 Ramasamys wandered aimlessly. Aaravayal, all alone with the corpses, stood staring at the sea. Wild birds hovered in circles above the ship.

Unaware of this great tragedy in the history of the Ramasamys, crowds and crowds kept on alighting at Central Station, causing great tidal waves everywhere. The world-famous poet Theppa Kulam Ramasamy, neo-critic Little Finger Ramasamy, Waterfall Ramasamy (who cares to pen global novels alone), and also Uproar Ramasamy, Realism Ramasamy, Romantic Ramasamy, Extravaganza Ramasamy, Ever-Your Ramasamy and their near-and-dear ones, readers, fans, well-wishers, ardent lovers, suicide squads. Joining these Ramasamys, an abundance of Ramasamys kept on crowding the special Literary Locomotives.

In each and every station non-writer Ramasamys thronged to catch a glimpse of writer Ramasamys. There were placards bearing the name 'Ramasamy' everywhere along the entire stretch of the platform. The train came to a halt at the platform.

'Hot-pot novel, sir, steaming short story, sir, poems, sir . . . novel, sir, story, sir . . .'—so shouting, the blue employees went along, selling the books. Waterfall Ramasamy, who was sitting in his AC coach, spoke to his dear disciples: 'The novels of this place read too well . . . the idiosyncrasies of the place are such . . .'

No sooner had he spoken these words than his dear disciples leaped out to buy a novel each, and they began to read these novels the very next moment, breathlessly. When the train arrived at Kokkalanchery Station, spotting senior writer Pavalakodi Ramasamy who was sitting there all alone, Little Finger Ramasamy clapped his hands and called out, 'Ask him to come in. He is the senior writer who used to write in Pavalakodi, long ago . . . call him inside.'

Eighty-year-old Pavalakodi Ramasamy boarded the train with his eighteen unsold books. Little Finger Ramasamy gave him a place to sit. As the senior writer was in the habit of chewing Thangapaspam tobacco, he sat near the window. As soon as the train began moving he began pulling out tales and anecdotes from the pages of his old 'Pavalakodi' days. The Ramasamys went to sleep.

In the next coach, Uproar Ramasamy was narrating his uproarious memories to his followers. His recent rebellion took place in front of Thaluk office. Along with a hundred odd Ramasamys, Uproar Ramasamy staged a protest outside the office rejecting the recent growing literary '-isms' in Tamil: magical realism, postmodernism and others. A petition to the effect was handed over to the tehsildar. This uproarious protest took place in all the district capitals. The complaint made by Uproar Ramasamy was inscribed on a tin plate and given to the tehsildar which the latter promptly returned marked with a zero and so the rebellion was declared a resounding victory.

Proclaiming Seerani Arangam to be 'Ramasamy Arangam', participants continued their preparations, including honouring Ramasamy, the first fountain pen writer. Prior to him everything was written by dipping a peacock quill into ink. In those days, only Ramasamy had the guts to start using the pen, an innovation for which he should get all the credit. At the convention a huge painting of him with one hand on his cheek and the other holding a pen was put up. A gigantic ink bottle was spilled in front of his house as a mark of respect to his memory.

Sitting at the rear side of the Ramasamy Arangam, Realism Ramasamy was penning his new realist novel *17:17:17*. The Agro-farming Association had come forward to publish it. While writing the novel, which deals with the ways and means of harvesting cotton in summer, he sobbed and sobbed, unable to control his emotions and consequently breaking three pen nibs.

Meanwhile, the ship, gone astray with its direction lost, dashed against the shores of TeluguLand[76] and came to a halt. Ramasamy, who had slept with the torch, set out on foot to visit the rural areas of Andhra. The dogs eventually began to chase him and so, changing his walk to a run, he came towards Chennai.

At Egmore Station innumerable Ramasamys were waiting to welcome the Literary Locomotive. The other popular Ramasamys who were to be honoured at the convention were escorted to various lodges. Under the leadership of Pon. Ramasamy, 108 or so had gathered and were busy preparing a memorandum.

Meanwhile Levistro Ramasamy of the Department of Anthropology, inside the caves of Mainalla Draw, was writing by candlelight a historical document entitled, 'The History of the Ramasamy Lineage: The Hidden Truths', An excerpt follows:

[76] TeluguLand: He has hit the coast of mainland India a little too far north, in the state of Andhra Pradesh, just above Tamil Nadu.

> In the beginning, all the Tamil letters started with the first letter 'Ra'. From that the Tamils came to be named 'Ramasamy'. Ramasamys from time immemorial have cultivated a civilized style of make-up and couture, and this truth has been amply substantiated by significant archaeological evidence gathered in Rappa, located on a small strip of land near Mohenjo-daro. The clay-pots excavated in this region bore the letter 'Ra' which could be seen distinctly. (See photograph, courtesy Rappa Archaeological Research.) Veteran archaeological scholar Na. Altan Singalo Ramasamy himself confirmed this claim. Therefore it is beyond doubt that the first name of the world was none other than 'Ramasamy' (Ra.Va.Sa PR 24).

The very sight of Pavalakodi Ramasamy, who spoke ill of modern stories with his mouth full of tobacco which he chewed incessantly, was disgusting to Theppakulam Ramasamy. With the literary quarrel between the two reaching an ugly peak, Theppakulam pulled out the tobacco wad and threw it away. The senior writer then pulled the alarm chain, bringing the train to a halt. There erupted a bitter fight between the Ramasamys regarding the humiliating treatment meted out to the veteran Ramasamy. At that point the train was standing half a mile away from Virudhachalam Station.

At the Ramasamys Convention, they turned Gemini Flyover into a dais for the purpose of conducting literary debates. Arrangements were made for the crowd to stand on the roads beneath and listen to the speeches. When the lists of the literary speeches were announced, the Ramasamys vied with each other to read the titles.

Horror Ramasamy gave a talk titled, 'The History of the Universe and the Art Form Called Devarattam',[77] Little Finger Ramasamy spoke on 'My Little Finger and Tamil Literature', and Realism Ramasamy delivered the speech 'Go Hang the Storytellers'. Thus, unheard-of varieties of international titles had found a place. Only Pavalakodi Ramasamy was given the exclusive freedom of selecting his own title.

[77] Devarattam: A folk dance of Tamil Nadu.

As soon as the train stopped at Egmore Railway Station, Ramasamys ran to receive the new load of Ramasamys. Giving each a fountain pen and a badge bearing the picture of Ramagirisami, they escorted them along with the dance of a Karagattam team. The Ramasamys of the 'Tamil Readers' clan who had travelled on the roof of the train wandered all over the city in search of water to bathe. Seeing the waterless corporation taps making strange moaning and hissing sounds, they sat beside them and wrote complaining odes on the woeful state of affairs. Some Ramasamys were fast asleep in the Burma Bazaar Road. The religious Ramasamys multiplied their religiosity by having a mouthful of neyyappam in the corridors of the Mylai Kapaleeswarar temple.

Apart from these, one Ramasamy from Erichanatham, a remote area situated at the southern end of Tamil Nadu, sent a translation of his, along with a milk can, in city bus number thirteen. The Ottanchathram Ramasamy, after completing his long-term dream of writing a 4000-page novel, divided it into two segments and hung the two on either side of a *kavadi*.[78] He bore his Kavadi Novel from Palani to Chennai and some eighty budding poets accompanied him carrying his Kavadi Poem. In each and every village en route, throngs of women gathered to watch the 'novel pilgrimage' of the Ramasamys and welcome them with great pomp. They even arranged for a 'Feeding of the Poor' to mark the occasion, but all these events form part of a separate story.

Before Aaravayal Ramasamy could arrive with the torch, the convention had commenced. The welcome speech was given by Nunna konda Pettai Kadhavu Ramasamy, a Gandhian and the former governor of Andhra Pradesh: 'Ikkadalu, Ramasamygalu, Maanaadulu, Nassalu, Nadakkalu, Akkadalu, Kavidhailu, Sirukadhaiyilu, Vimarsanamilu, Raasilu, Nobalu Parisulu, Pettraarulu, Ramasamygalu, Edhir Kadamulu, Nammalu, Desathalu, Mukyamalu, UlagaRamasamygalu, Uttrumaigalu, Vallargalu.'[79]

[78] kavadi: An upside-down, U-shaped canopy, supported at the lower ends by a wooden rod. The rod rests on the shoulders of the bearer, someone who has gone through strict abstinence to earn the right to bear the *kavadi* in a southern Hindu religious festival.
[79] These are nonsense Tamil words, a parody of speaking Tamil in a Telugu accent. Telugu is a language that often uses the 'ulu' ending.

Before the speech was completed, Aaravayal Ramasamy came on the dais with the ever-glowing torch which his men helped light. As the torch was lit a bit belatedly, it was then that Ramasamy told the Ramasamys of the deaths of the Ramasamys. With tears welling up, those at the convention postponed it for half a day, in memory of the 999 Ramasamys. Also, Ramasamy placed before the Ramasamys an appeal to the Central Government that a stamp with Aaravayal Ramasamy floating in the ship along with the dead bodies of 999 Ramasamys be released.

As the convention was postponed, the writers dispersed hurriedly and went with their groups. Small-Magazine Ramasamy went round amidst those Ramasamys present, selling small booklets with captions like 'You have made me into a Ramasamy' and 'From Ramasamy to Ramasamy'.

If I were to narrate all that which took place between the Ramasamys, it would prove another 'Angaputhran Tale' of counting sand grains. I think it would be better just to give the self-introduction of the writers and leave it at that.

Among the senior writers was Pazhath Thottam Ramasamy, who had so far waved aside all awards; he, the great warrior, is alone the Godfather of the world of Tamil stories. Beyond all doubt, no one can excel him in writing. This unparalleled writer was for a while the disciple of Piggymount Swami (Pandrimalai Swami). Then he was deep in philosophical ponderings concerning Nietzsche, Schopenhauer and others, and then he got involved in the arts and put his heart and soul into it. His inward silence had a distinct artistic clarity, said many critics. In an anthology compiled by them there is an article called 'On Some Times in the Life of Pazhath Thottam Ramasamy'; here is an excerpt for your edification:

> There are different varieties of fruit trees all around the abode of Pazhath Thottam Ramasamy. His friends always call him 'Sultan'. He never writes when there is no fruit smell surrounding him. Every morning, after completing a story, he shows his excitement in his success in arriving at a real artistic peak by plucking and eating the fruits. In that overjoyed state he would be a treat to watch. He also owns a publishing house called 'Mukkani' (the three primal fruits)—(*On Some Times in the Life*, 18)

Of the lot of neo-critics of Tamil literature who branched out from Pazhath Thottam Ramasamy, Little Finger Ramasamy is quite important. The postal department had reserved all eight employees who toiled day and night to deliver the loads of books that came to his address every day to be reviewed by him, running a kind of relay race from the post office to his house and back.

Little Finger Ramasamy never handled those books with his hands. He would turn the pages using only his little finger. If his little finger signalled that it was a good book then he would start reading it. The rest he would press hard with his little finger and force them deep beneath the floor where they would remain buried for ever. With so many books being buried, the house swelled in size. The books which had the good fortune of earning a mention from Little Finger are but half a handful. As the little finger is crowned with the status of Class A critic, it started viewing the other fingers with scorn and disdain, feeling so proud of its stature. The other fingers, taking note of the elevated position enjoyed by the little finger, became afraid of it. Still, every now and then there erupted literary quarrels, fights and wars between the little finger and the other fingers.

The other fingers: You, Little Finger critic—who is crowned with literary reviews, who tells tales to the scarecrows![80]

Little finger: You goddamned straw-heads,[81] don't you dare blabber about such things as story, tale . . . the beautiful blend of the inside and the outside is what is called 'story'.

The other fingers: Then, what do you have to say about the jackal's story of betrayal called 'Abandhaga'?[82]

Little finger: Whatever the others say, I am the unparalleled emperor of criticism!

---

[80] tell tales to the scarecrows: To 'tell tales to scarecrows' is to tell stories that are lies or rubbish.

[81] straw-heads: The original Tamil is '*vaikoel moodhigalae*', or 'straw-scoundrel', meaning a dull-headed clod.

[82] The jackal is traditionally a cunning, dishonest figure.

In this way the discussions and debates continued. From all the rural and urban regions of India, people came in large numbers and vied with each other to get a glimpse of the little finger of Little Finger Ramasamy. He would always walk concealing his little finger with his dhoti. How he became the one and only one, unique 'little finger' in the entire gamut of the field of literature, is a separate episode.

Among the novelists, the skills and expertise of Waterfall Ramasamy defy all description. With only the words that remained after not having been washed away by the waterfall, he would bring out a book. His most popular novel *The Counterfeiters and the Hundred Little Lambs* was an existential novel nominated for the Nobel Prize thrice but rejected due to errors in proofreading. In this, he constructed the central theme around a lamb that goes to an empty house every day and looks at itself in a mirror, thus dealing with the essence of life on a philosophical plane. His novel, *A Big 'No' to Conversing with Cats*, was going to be released at the convention.

Realism Ramasamy would prepare blank white sheets at home with his own hands, and, on principle, would only pen his creations on these handmade white sheets. He was a man capable of writing about anything and everything he encountered. His stories are being used in UN pamphlets. He has the habit of taking snuff, and every cough comes out '*realism*', '*realism*'.

Some hundred more Ramasamys were honoured at the convention. Kalladaikurichi Ramasamy, Boli Ambur Ramasamy, Nellivalai Ramasamy, Thisayanvalai Ramasamy, So.Pa. Ramasamy, Ko. Ramasamy (ex), Ramayya Pillai Pulimootai Ramasamy, Ettu Veettu Ramasamy, Moopan Ramasamy, Thamizh Ramasamy, Esthapan Ramasamy, Britto Ramasamy, Ramasamy Kumar, Kavik Kizhaar Ramasamy, Nadai Vandi Ramasamy, and so the potential of many Ramasamys gained special attention at the convention.

The next day at the convention, thousands of Ramasamys kept wandering down to the beach in bikinis to bathe. Some Ramasamys lay on the lawns and sang poems. Other Ramasamys read and applauded themselves on their own reading. On one side, a christening went on for those who were not Ramasamys. The name 'Ramasamy' was suffixed to their names and thus Britto Ramasamy, Farook Ramasamy,

Alexander Ramasamy, Mubaraq Ramasamy entered directly into the convention.

As the cry went on, soaring higher and higher, Alleluyah Ramasamy, who lived in Gemini Complex, was afflicted with verbiage fever. Standing around him, the Ramasamys who went along with his 'word-blabbering' sang 'Alleluyah' day and night. On the walls of his house, the saying 'Ramasamy never leaves you' could be seen. When the convention reached its dizzy heights the torso of 'Alleluyah' Ramasamy twisted and jerked and jumped and leaped in frenetic frenzy.

Though a Ramasamy, a man in black was not allowed inside. Leaning against a signal post outside, he lamented: 'What good things our reverent Ramasamy made and made possible this day . . . But for him, could we talk like this today? And, Mandhrasamis have become more powerful.'

Outside the decorated roof of the convention some Spanish speeches could be heard, so some went in that direction. The special convener of the Ramasamy Convention was giving a speech on how his fountain pen leaked and drenched his shirt. The crowd outside the tent turned delirious. In its midst, Counter-Culture Ramasamy stood, while men circled all around him. Raising his hands to the heavens, he said: 'I am a fan of Umberto Ramasamy. I have come here to listen to his speech. After he finishes I will leave at once. Please go away from here.'

When Umberto Ramasamy was said to have come with his Name-of-the-Rose-Tamil, Counter-Culture Ramasamy beat a hasty retreat. Outside, a person was selling non-linear lollipops.

The memorandum of the convention was read out. Resolutions were passed to the effect that Ramasamys, in order to stress their uniqueness, should wear dresses of a particular shade, that free bus passes should be provided to Ramasamys, that Ramasamys should shun non-linear writings, that the residential areas where Ramasamys dwell should be renamed 'Ramasamisthan', and much more.

The Ramasamys who disagreed with the memorandum discussed it near the Gandhi statue. Pavalakodi Ramasamy spoke for more than four hours about his first-ever poem 'Murugesan in the World of Fools'. The crowd wandered and dispersed. The moment the discussion on the memorandum began, uproar ensued. With many staging a walk-out the convention was again postponed by half a day. That day, many Ramasamys left for Tirupati and returned with tonsured heads. In the evening it was officially announced that the convention of the Ramasamys was split into two owing to ideological differences.

There came to be two groups—the moderates and the radicals. Writers, political personalities, traders, poets, publishers, doctors, historical researchers, copy-writers, health officers and others, everywhere, established themselves within the newly enshrined divisions.

'This ideological split, both vertical and horizontal, is a historical event!' cried both Ramasamy groups. A statue along the beach road stood stretching its finger, asking 'Are you a Ramasamy?' 'Yes, yes,' swayed the heads as they walked past. That day, when this great historical phenomenon of Tamil Nadu took place, the city of Madras suffered nature's fury in the form of a storm. Convention tents became deconstructed and papers flew away. The next morning those who were not Ramasamys came, saw thousands of books and photographs of Ramasamys lying scattered all over the beach, and then dispersed.

Nonsense in Hindi Film

FROM AASHIRWAD

This song, sung by Ashok Kumar in the film *Aashirwad* (1969), has acquired folklore status among Hindi speakers. It is considered to be one of the earliest rap songs in Hindi. It is also perhaps one of the earliest Hindi nonsense songs in Hindi movies.

THERE GOES GRAN

Lyrics: Harindranath Chattopadhyay
Translated by Sampurna Chattarji from the Hindi original 'Nani ki Nao'

There goes Gran
There goes Gran
There goes Gran in her catamaran
The catamaran of Geeta's Gran

On a long jaunt a-ho
All set from home they go
Out from Gran's home they go
And into the catamaran they go
But what goes in a-ho
A rifle a trifle
A timer a primer
A casket a basket
A pajama a llama

A horse's boot
A drum and a flute
A horse's saddle
A fisherman's paddle
A potato a parrot
A bear and a carrot
A rope and a rack
A knap and a sack

A fly and a swat
An egg and a pot
A banana a mango
One ripe and one raw
And in the basket
One kitten not four

Then a croc chased old Gran
Chased old Gran and her catamaran
Chased the catamaran of Geeta's Gran

And then oh my gosh
From behind and in front
With a growl and a grunt
It pulled out stuff with a slosh

One kitten not four
A banana a mango
One ripe and one raw

An egg and a pot
A sack and a swat
A bear and a parrot
A potato a carrot
A fisherman's paddle
A horse's saddle

A drum and a flute
A horse's boot
A pajama a llama
A casket a basket
A timer a primer
A rifle a trifle

But what was she doing Gran dear
Poor old Gran she couldn't hear

Geeta's Gran she couldn't hear
Her sleep was deep and without fear

How deep was her sleep
As deep as a river
Afternoon shiver
The moon's daughter
Ice cold water
Spicy hot
Belly in a knot
Sixteen and a jot
Fifteen times two
Is thirty to you
Triplet forty-five
Quartet sixty
Quintet seventy-five
Sextet ninety

FROM <u>NAMAK HALAAL</u>

I CAN TALK ENGLISH

In this scene from *Namak Halaal* (1982), Bhairon has brought our hero, Arjun Singh (Amitabh Bachchan), into the manager's office of a four-star hotel for a job interview. The manager asks Arjun if he can speak English. This is his enthusiastic reply, all in English except for the very beginning.

'*Sir, I know such English* [in Hindi] that I can leave Angrej behind. You see, Sir, I can talk English, I can walk English, I can laugh English because English is a very funny language.

Bhairon becomes Baron
and Baron becomes Bhairon[83]
because their minds are very narrow.

'In the year nineteen hundred and twenty-nine, Sir, when India was playing against Australia in Melbourne City, Vijay Merchant and Vijay Hazare, they were at the crease, and Vijay Merchant told Vijay Hazare, "Look Vijay Hazare, this is a very prestigious match, and you must consider this match very carefully."

'So considering the consideration that Vijay Hazare gave Vijay Merchant, Vijay Merchant told Vijay Hazare that ultimately we must take a run. And when they were striking the ball on the leg side, Sir, the consideration came into an ultimatum, and ultimately Vijay Hazare went to Vijay Merchant . . .'

The hotel manager screams: 'Oh, shut up!'

Arjun continues, to the chagrin of the manager: 'Similarly, Sir, in the year nineteen hundred and seventy-nine, when India was playing against Pakistan in Wankhede Stadium, Bombay, Wasim Raja and Wasim Bari, they were at the crease. And Wasim Bari gave the *same* consideration to Wasim Raja.

'And Wasim Raja told Wasim Bari, "Look, sir, this ultimately has to end in a consideration which I cannot consider. Therefore, the consideration that you are giving me must be considered very ultimately."

'Therefore, the run that they were taking . . . Wasim Raja told Wasim Bari, "Wasim Bari, you take the run." And ultimately both of them ran and, considerately, they got out!'

[83] Bhairon: The ending of this name is pronounced nasally, in a countrified manner, and rhymes with the word 'narrow'. Part of the joke is also that Bhairon, the character, is a powerless and somewhat pathetic man, quite the opposite of a 'baron'. One aspect of 'sense' in this line might also lie in the inability of most English speakers to pronounce or even hear certain aspirated consonants in Hindi, like the letter representing the sound 'bh' (say the two words 'bob harrow' together quickly, to get the sound of 'Bhairon'). Hence, to an English speaker, 'Bhairon' really does become the simplified and perhaps not coincidentally English title, 'baron'.

FROM AMAR AKBAR ANTHONY

MY NAME IS ANTHONY GONSALVES

Lyrics: Anand Bakshi

The scene in the film (1977) is an Easter celebration dance. A giant Easter egg is wheeled out on to the dance floor. The top half of the egg revolves to reveal our hero, Anthony Gonsalves (Amitabh Bachchan), seated inside, wearing a black tuxedo complete with top hat, monocle and an umbrella, apparently every inch the English gentleman. He sits in a mock dignified, stiff manner, quelling the enthusiasm of the gathering crowd by imploring them, 'Wait! Wait! Wait!' He then rattles off the following line in English, meant to mystify and impress the crowd with his borrowed English 'erudition':

> You see the whole country of the system is juxtapositioned by the haemoglobin in the atmosphere because you are a sophisticated rhetorician intoxicated by the exuberance of your own verbosity.

The song itself, otherwise all in Hindi, is about Anthony's ideal woman and general state of availability. As he woos his present love interest on the disco floor with song and his wiry dance moves, he also idealizes his own poverty by claiming that only the love of the poor is real. Later in the song, Anthony presents other English-language crowd-stoppers, continuing to spoof on the English and perhaps the kind of overblown English language that English-influenced, and probably wealthy, Indians supposedly speak:

> You see, such extenuating circumstances coerce me to preclude you from such extravagance!

And once more he professes to the kneeling, mesmerized crowd:

> You see the coefficient of the linear is juxtapositioned by the haemoglobin of the atmospheric pressure in the country!

Folk Nonsense

NURSERY AND FOLK RHYMES

CUSTARD-APPLE MUSTARD-PARROTS

Translated by Sampurna Chattarji from the Bengali[84] original 'Aata gaachhey tota-paakhi'

Custard-apple mustard-parrots[85]
Pomegranate-bees[86]
Won't you speak, my wife, oh please?
Why should I?
On what pretence?
Speaking makes me sick and tense!

SKITTER-CHITTER FRUIT BATS

Translated by Sampurna Chattarji from the Bengali original 'Aadur baadur chatla baadur'

Skitter-chitter fruit bats
The banana bat's going to wed
So ring the bellflowers red.
The titmice are playing drums
With broomsticks on their head.

---

[84] These nursery rhymes are in variations of the East Bengal (now Bangladesh) dialect in which the inflections differ from standard Bengali. These inflections are not reflected in the translations.

[85] Custard-apple mustard-parrots: For the sake of the metre, what is really 'parrots in custard-apple trees' (in Bengali the word for 'parrot' rhymes with the word for 'custard-apple') has been condensed into two rhyming compound words.

[86] Pomegranate-bees: Similarly in this case, where the original literally reads 'Bees in pomegranate trees'.

The bears are eating tamarind

Translated by Sampurna Chattarji from the Bengali original 'Aaye re aaye, bhalukey tetul khaaye'

The bears are eating tamarind; hurry, come and see
Six old women are rolling under the lichen tree.
The spade hits the grinding stone
The mustard creaks to the bone
Mr Pumpkin as his witness, Spinach starts to moan.
Why do you cry, dear Spinach, rolling in the dust?
My little boy will eat his rice
With only fried fish, I trust.

Sleepy eyes peepy eyes

Translated by Sampurna Chattarji from the Bengali original 'Aaye rey ghoom jaaye re ghoom'

Sleepy eyes peepy eyes
Sandman's looking for you
Sleepwalking through the door
Are catfish one and two.

Scrawly-molly skin-crawly

Translated by Sampurna Chattarji from the Bengali original 'Ikid mikid chaam chikid'

Scrawly-molly skin-crawly
Box his ears Majumdar[87]
Down swoops Damodar.

87 Majumdar: A Bengali surname.

Damodar's pots and pans are nice
Within four walls there's heaps of rice.
Cleaning the rice took all morning
In-laws dropped in without warning.
Fly fell into the rice that's made
Scraped it off with a sharp spade
The spade has gone blunt and dead
Now go eat the smithy's head.

NITTER-NATTER

Translated by Sampurna Chattarji from the Bengali original 'Iching biching'

Nitter-natter
Son-in-law's chatter
A spider fell down splitter-splatter.
The spider fought all arms and legs
Seven pumpkins laid seven eggs.

THE BLACKEST CAT THAT PURLED

Translated by Sampurna Chattarji from the Bengali original 'Ekey bedaal kaalo'

The blackest cat that purled
Down the Ganga hurled
On the bolsters curled
His beauty lit up the world!

SHILLY-SHALLY ASKED FOR RICE

Translated by Sampurna Chattarji from the Bengali original 'Ech-chi mech-chi dhaan chailo'

Shilly-shally asked for rice
Inside the grain he found some mice
The king of birds fished in a pail
The captured serpent wagged its tail
Tasty-hasty rice we sing
Cut off the thief's hand says the king.

SRI GANESHJI

Translated by Sumanyu Satpathy from the Bhojpuri-Hindi original 'Sri Ganeshji'

This rhyme uses the strategy of rapid and successive decontextualization in order to generate the sense of nonsense. Some words are corruptions of well-known words. The nonsense here is also the result of extreme colloquialism and the technique of using words from the previous lines but by changing the context. The rhythm is fast, imitative of a horse on a gallop: ta-dak-ta-dak-ta-dak-ta-dak.

On his horse Ganeshji hurls.
Resplendent in nine hundred pearls,
Of which just one was green.
Our guru taught a spelling scheme.[88]
Panditji did blessings give
May you for six lakh seasons live.
Many lakhs of lotions bought.
Twenty Delhi gajmots[89] sought.
Delhi's Minni is a one-eyed thief,

[88] spelling scheme: In the original, the term used is '*pandit mala*', which is a mnemonic table, similar to the multiplication tables, containing formulae to guide the pre-primary learner to spell words.
[89] gajmot: A large pearl.

The peacock-master is Thief-in-Chief
The Thief-in-Chief's arrow headed straight
The arrow struck the lover's fate.
The lover seeks a pretty lass
Putting out two chairs in the grass.
Sahib, he can hurl the javelin
That flies to eighty-kosh[90] Multan
Travelling at eighty like a bullet
One bullet after you fire to kill't
Go! Set the jungle on fire, go.
In the forest elder brother Kesho
Kesho has daughters-in-law four
Who play with gold nuggets in the wood.
The woodpecker pecks at the wood
In the wood the parakeet goes on
On the riverbank the crane goes on
What Ram wills will surely be.

While playing I found a cowry shell

Translated by Sumanyu Satpathy from the Bhojpuri-Hindi original 'Khelte Khulte'

While playing I found a cowry shell
I gently let it flow with the Ganga's swell.
Mother Ganga gave me sand
To the goudnia[91] I gave the sand
The goudnia gave me bhuja
I gave the bhuja to the grass-cutter
The grass-cutter gave me grass
I gave the grass to a cow
The cow gave me milk
I gave the milk to the cat

[90] eighty-kosh: 'Kosh' is a unit of measure, roughly two kilometres.
[91] goudnia: A woman of a lower caste who milk cows and sell dairy products.

The cat gave me a rat
I gave the rat to the kite
The kite gave me a feather light
I gave the king the feather
The king gave me a mare
On the mare I rode away
Clap, for I am happy today!

THE BUFFALO CLIMBED A PEEPAL TREE

Translated by Anushka Ravishankar from the Gujarati original 'Paado chadyo peepale'

The buffalo climbed a peepal tree
And sucked a lemon whole;
When he flew into the yard
The horse jumped in a hole.

Bluffer

Translated by Anita Vachharajani from the Gujarati original 'Gappi'

A bluffer came to a bluffer's house
Come in, Bluffer-ji,
There's a melon that's twelve feet long
With a seed that's thirteen feet!

Wormtooth[92]

Translated by Anushka Ravishankar from the Malayalam original 'Puzhupallan'

When Wormtooth bathed in the tank
In the south the rains began.
He shot a lemon in the air
And everybody got a scare.

Word for word[93]

Translated by Sumanyu Satpathy from the Hindi original 'Baat ki baat'

Word for word, *kur-a-fat kur-a-furd*,
On a berry bush leaf
All the groomsmen stirred.
A wee mosquito gave a kick
And Gujarat—it flew right off!
(I tell you what I've seen myself
Not only what I've heard.)

Emperor Rashul, made by God.
Human emperor, made by Rashul.

---

[92] The rhyme is about the monsoon and represents the rain and thunder.

[93] Source for 'Word for Word', 'Fat Cat', 'A, B, C, D', 'Barber's Brother', 'The Match' and 'Gadbadjhala', *Gadbadjhala, Khel Kavya: Ek Parichay*, eds. Ashish Ghosh and Manish Manoja, Delhi: Maulana Azad Centre for Primary and Social Education, Delhi University, 2001.

(Oh—what was I saying just now?)
There was an emperor, long ago,
Whose pocket held another emperor
(Then, after that?)
Another emperor in *his* pocket.

Fat cat

Translated by Sumanyu Satpathy from the Hindi original 'Niche chai ki dukaan'

Fat Cat has a bungalow
Above an old tea stall
Fat Cat caught a terrible cold
And hid in a football.
On giving the football two hard kicks
It flew so very high
It went and got itself transfixt
For ever in the sky.

A, B, C, D

Translated by Sumanyu Satpathy from the Hindi original 'A, B, C, D'

ABCDEFG
Out came old man Panditji.
Panditji, he dug a hole
An old man popped up like a mole.

Barber's brother

Translated by Sumanyu Satpathy from the Hindi original 'Nayee ke bhai nayeeke'

Barber's brother
Barber's brother

Tabla-playing barber's brother
Parrot in the barber's tabla
Barber calls me old grandfather.

THE MATCH

Translated by Sumanyu Satpathy from the Hindi original 'Ram ke darbar mein'

In the regal court of Ram
There was a cricket match
Kumbhakaran hit a six
Hanuman caught the catch
Ram then shouted, 'Out'
Sita said, 'Get out!'

GADBADJHALA[94]

Translated by Sumanyu Satpathy from the Hindi original 'Gadbadjhala'

Child 1: Turn the sky green,
The earth blue, and tree violet.
Let the car drive Mr Lala—
Then what?

Chorus: Gadbadjhala!

Child 2: If the frog sang sweetly like the cuckoo,
And the barn owl always hooted at noon
If brine were sweet,
And the moon turned black in colour—
Then what?

[94] Title: The word '*gadbadjhala*' is somewhat unusual in Hindi. It is not in everyday usage and does not appear in some dictionaries, yet it appears in print occasionally, connoting a state of general chaos and confusion.

Chorus: Gadbadjhala!

Child 3: If Grandpa were to borrow our teeth,
And ice cream tasted tart, not sweet,
If the keys were in,
And the lock were out, O Allah—
Then what?

Chorus: Gadbadjhala!

Child 4: If milk rained down from the sky in streams,
And all the ponds skimmed over with cream,
If chocolates were full of masala—
Then what?

Chorus: Gadbadjhala!

Mister Rat

Translated by V. Geetha from the Tamil original

Mister Rat, Mister Rat
Where are you going?
I'm going off to London
To see Elizabeth Queen.

You've got to cross the seven seas
Pray, what's your solution?
I'll buy a ticket for a plane
And fly across the ocean.

You will get hungry on the way
Pray, what will you eat?
I'll buy bajjis and vadas, hot,
And give myself a treat.

Grandpa's Beard

Translated by V. Geetha from the Tamil original

When Grandpa stuck his finger
Deep into his beard
He found many strange things there
The strangest things you've heard:

Out came a turtle dove
Not just one, but two.
In flew a sunbird
Not just one, but two
A yellow bird has got inside
And a blackbird too.

They'll make their cosy nests in there
And lay their eggs inside them
And dear old Grandpa's long, white beard
Will quite completely hide them.

DON'T STICK OUT YOUR TONGUE

Translated by V. Geetha from the Tamil original

Don't stick out your tongue
Marry, you should not
And do not have your babies
In a big, bald pot.

SINGAPORE DANDY[95]

Translated by V. Geetha from the Tamil original

Ai ai ai ai ai ai ai
Half a pint of butter
Make a pot of porridge
And lay the silver platter
Here comes Singapore Dandy
In his silken sweater.

FOOD FIGHT

Translated by V. Geetha from the Tamil original

Downstairs is a clothes shop
Selling clothing bright
No, no, it's an idli shop
You're wrong, and I'm right
Idlis and chutney get into a fight
The ten-paise banana
Slips down in fright.

[95] *Singapore Dandy*: This verse seems to deride the Indian emigrants who come back from Singapore, perceived as wealthy and somewhat spoiled.

Urdu Nursery Rhymes

Translated by Sumanyu Satpathy from the Urdu originals

i

Half past twelve it happened to be
When he got ready, good Mullahji
By one he called out for namaz
By two they say quite dead he was
By three the awful news they gave
By four he rested in his grave

ii

Come you boys, and let us play
We will break the lump of clay
Then we'll break the hard molasses
Till the wolf comes to harass us
When we thrash it right away
It will fly to far Bombay

iii

Oh Allah, syrup fills the plate
Young boys in sacks go meet their fate
A bunch of flowers sits in place
And Allah's touch lights Munna's face

FOLK DRAMA

When an epic play is staged through the night in villages, a fool figure invents the following kinds of 'fool's verses' to be recited during scene changes or at particular moments in the action, often immediately before a sad moment, to amuse the audience, provide catharsis and, possibly, to keep them awake. These interludes are not related to the plot of the play and can include comic songs, rhymes, parody or religious text, usually accompanied by music and dance. Such verses are not restricted to drama; an artist might create such a verse for any gathering in the village.

FOOL'S SONG[96]

Translated by Nabin Chandra Sarma from the Assamese original 'Endur aatai mekuritook khale'

The rat has eaten the cat
The kid ate the elephant, just like that.
The catfish drinks hot tea.
The prawn now plays the *khunjuri*.[97]

THE CAMEL PERCHED UPON A BRICK[98]

Translated by B.S. Talwadi from the Kannada original

The camel perched upon a brick
Was selling fried cake rather quick
With bag in hand the roguish rat
Rode to the fair, upon a cat

An ant sold at the market stall
An elephant two storeys tall

[96] This song comes from a folk drama form called Khulia Bhauriya, popular in the Darang district of Assam.
[97] khunjuri: A drum with jangles, usually used in prayers.
[98] Source: T. Govindaraju. This is a 'fool's' oral chain verse, to which there is little order and no conclusion. Many of the creatures here have some significance in devotional or traditional literature, yet here such meanings only tease, for these verses mean not to mean; it is a game of nonsensical banter.

A wolf sat on the elephant's head
The passers-by played golf instead

A sheep sat happily astride
The wolf, and went off for a ride
The hen sat on the fox's back
Serving it a tasty snack

The seed was lying in the bin
Forecasting futures to the hen
The blind bird sitting on the fence
Uttered words that made no sense

Beneath a tree, upon the coast
A bird perused its morning post
The snake and mongoose had a fight
They went to court to set it right

Interludes from Oriya Operas

Translated by Sumanyu Satpathy

i

An '*opera*' is a form of folk theatre (with the English term misapplied). Up to a certain time, operas were in the oral tradition, but from the late nineteenth century they have been authored. This example is from an *opera* by K.C. Pattnaik.[99] This is in a form coincidentally like a limerick.

The porter, young Dunder,[100] set out Astride a bullock-cart's snout
The pundit, his brother Lovelorn for another
Eats snails now instead of fresh trout.[101]

[99] Source: *Oriya Loko Sahitya o Loko Sanskriti*, ed. K.C. Pradhan, Cuttack: Vidyapuri, 1995.

[100] *Dunder*: The original name is Dunda, a country name denoting a foolish person. '*Snout*' has been used loosely to describe the poles that the bullocks are tied to.

[101] Snails were typically eaten by the poor, so those who eat snails are generally looked down upon.

ii

If the ploughman now has already gone
And yet the ploughshare trundles on
And if the son's cremated in the meadow
And yet the daughter-in-law is not a widow
And if farmers farm in the sky,
Then, Son, this stunning news will fly!

If the broom and the winnowing fan
Both went on a trip to greet their gran
And the rice-thrasher fell into a fever fit
The frog a bamboo lath did knit
And the sieve will be a man in demand,
Then all this news will be so grand!

FOLK TALE

Man and Spirit

Translated by Dileep Chandan from the Thado-Kuki original

In the beginning of the world, people and spirits were the same. Later, when humanity constantly was physically abusing the spirits, the spirits went to God and complained: 'If man keeps beating us like this, he will soon kill us.' God then told the spirits, 'If you make some yeast cakes with black centres and drop them in the men's wells, the centres of their eyes will become black and they will not be able to see you or beat you any more.' From that time, men have not been able to see spirits.

Shedding Skin

Translated by Dileep Chandan from the Thado-Kuki original

Once upon a time animals and men used to shed their skins. As this did not seem fair, the toad and the lizard drew up a contract stating that only two kinds of beings would be allowed to shed their skins, and these kinds would be determined by whomever could name them quickest. The lizard said, 'Snake change, lizard change' followed by the toad who said, 'Man change, toad change.' The toad was slower and thus lost, so snakes and lizards can now shed their skins while man cannot. If man could, he would never become old, for when he aged, he would just shed his skin and become young again like a snake or a lizard.

Dao Sharpening

Translated by Dileep Chandan from the Thado-Kuki original

The Dao-sharpener was sharpening his dao when the crayfish scuttled along and pinched his posterior. At this, the Dao-sharpener accidentally sliced off the tip of the bamboo. The tip of the bamboo cut the cheek of a jungle bird. The jungle bird flapped itself away and scratched a red ant, who ran up and bit Mr Wild Boar's testicles. The wild boar running in circles knocked down the wild plantain tree which was the bat's home. The bat flew out and fluttered in Mr Elephant's ear. The elephant stampeded off and flattened the widow's house.

'Mr Elephant,' said she, 'why have you flattened my house?'

Said the elephant, 'The bat flew into my ear.'

'Bat, why did you fly into Mr Elephant's ear?'

'Mr Wild Boar knocked down the wild plantain tree I live in.'

'Mr Boar, why did you do that?'

'The red ant bit my testicles.'

'Red Ant, why did you do that?'

'The jungle fowl scratched me.'

'Jungle Fowl, why did you scratch the ant?'

'The bamboo tip cut my cheek.'

'Bamboo Tip, why did you cut the jungle fowl's cheek?'

'The Dao-sharpener sliced me off.'

'Dao-sharpener, why did you slice off the bamboo tip?'

'The crayfish pinched my posterior.'

'Crayfish, why did you pinch the Dao-sharpener?'

The crayfish did not know what to answer. He said, 'Putting me in the fire will do nothing. If you put me in a deep pool, I shall turn very red and the Dao-sharpener will be charmed to see it.' He then jumped into the pool.

'The pool I live in is very deep,' said he, and in the pool he stayed.

Four Friends

Translated by Sumanyu Satpathy from the Haryanvi original 'Chaar Log'

There were four friends: one was blind, another was lame, the third one was naked, and the fourth one was deaf. Suddenly, the deaf one said, 'I can hear the sound of horse hooves. Are the robbers coming? What shall we do?' The blind man said, 'Yes, indeed, I can see the robbers riding towards us. We must do something about it.' The naked one started to panic and said, 'Oh, what am I going to do? I shall be robbed of all my clothes!' The lame one said, 'What is the problem? Let us run!'

NEVER-ENDING TALES AND CHAIN VERSES

Mother of the Woods

Translated by J. Devika from the Malayalam original 'Katha, katha ammay, kaananathammay'

A tale, a tale, Mother, Mother of the woods
A measure of rice in a nutshell is cooked
The Menon[102] ate, the Menoness ate

[102] Menon: The word is derived from the Tamil word for 'overseer' and originally denoted a person who oversaw the agricultural activities of the feudal Nair community, which used to be the predominant matrilineal Hindu community in Kerala. But gradually it has come to denote a subcommunity of the Nairs. Now both Nair and Menon, to

The children of the Menon house ate
A hundred and one elephants, crosslegged, ate
The parakeet too, in great style, ate.

Never-Ending Tale

Translated by Sumanyu Satpathy from the Oriya original 'Asaranti Katha'

This kind of poem is used to put children to sleep. The child asks, 'What happens next?' and the parent answers with the last line until the child sleeps. This type of tale is also found in Hindi and Telugu.

Once there was a granary full of grains. All the sparrows in the world came for the grains. One sparrow came, took one grain and flew off. Another sparrow came, took one grain and flew off. Another sparrow came, took one grain and flew off.
Another sparrow came, took one grain and flew off.
Another sparrow came, took one grain and flew off.
Another sparrow came, took one grain and flew off.
Another sparrow came, took one grain and flew off.
Another sparrow came, took one grain and flew off.
Another sparrow came, took one grain and flew off.
Another sparrow came, took one grain and flew off . . .

My tale has ended

Translated by Sumanyu Satpathy from the Oriya original 'Kathani'

This is a doggerel told at the end of every tale. As it finishes, the mother pinches the child's bum. This kind of verse also exists in the Bengali and Assamese traditions.

---

conform with the requirements of a patriarchal society, have become surnames. Originally, a Malayalee was identified by the ancestral house he or she belonged to; that is, paternity was irrelevant. Menon is thus a title, a name and a sub-sect. In the Kerala context, a Menon is almost an Everyman.

My tale has ended
The flower has died
Oh flower, why did you die?
The gardener did not water me.
Oh gardener, why did you not water?
The baby cried.
Oh baby, why did you cry?
The red ant bit me.
Oh red ant, why did you bite?
Beneath the ground I live,
When I find some tender flesh, a little nibble I give.

LET'S TELL A TALE I

Translated by Sumanyu Satpathy from the Oriya original 'Kathatiye kahun'

Let's tell a tale,
Let's tell a tale.
What tale?
The ice cream tale.
Who stole the ice cream?
Pussycat.
How far did you chase the cat?
To the partial pond.
What did you fetch from the partial pond?
A shoulder-load of soil.
To whom did you give the load of soil?
To the potter.
What did the potter give?
A shoulder-load of pots.
To whom did you give the load of pots?
To the oil man.
What did the oil man give?
A shoulder-load of oil.
To whom did you give the load of oil?

To the sweet seller.
What did the sweet seller give?
A shoulder-load of sweets.
To whom did you give the load of sweets?
To the Brahmin.
What did the Brahmin give?
Betel nut, sacred thread and sandalwood paste.
To whom did you give the betel nut, sacred thread and sandalwood?
To the Raja.
What did the Raja give?
Elephants, horses and more.
What happened to the elephants and horses?
One drowned while drinking water.
One sunk in a hoof hole.
One was buried in an ant hole.

What's up?

Translated by Sampurna Chattarji from the Bengali original 'Ki kotha? Banger maatha'

In this verse, the rhyme and rhythm depend on two things—a word being carried over from the previous line into the next, and the answer in the first line becoming the question in the second, and so on till the end. This kind of wordplay is common in other regions as well.

What's up? Frog in a cup.
What sorta frog? A musical frog.
What sorta music? Brahmin music.
What sorta Brahmin? Eulogic Brahmin.
What's eulogic? A horse's kick.
What sorta horse? A good, mild horse.
What's good and mild? A monkey's child.
What sorta monkey? A head monkey.
What sorta head? Leaf-wrapped and red.
What sorta leaf? Me liar, you thief.

Jaggery Square

Translated by Prathibha Nandakumar from the Kannada original 'Achchachchu'

This song is sung while clapping hands. It is in the form of questions and answers, with each question and answer picking the clue from the previous ones. There is no end to this game.

Square square square
Jaggery square
See there
See here
See the crowd in the margosa tree
What crowd?
Crow crowd.
What crow?
Black crow.
What black?
Charcoal black.
What charcoal?
Firewood charcoal.
What firewood?
Forest firewood.
What forest?
Burning forest[103] . . .

And Then, Bhurrah!

Retold by A.K. Ramanujan in Folktales from India, from Rev. A. Manwaring's Marathi proverbs

A storyteller was tired of telling stories, but the children and the grown people who were around him were not yet tired of listening to them. They asked for more.

[103] Burning forest: In Kannada, this phrase also implies 'cremation ground'.

So he began to describe how a vast number of birds were sitting on a tree. People asked as usual at a pause, 'And then?'

He said, 'One bird flew from the tree with a sound like bhurrah!'

'And then?'

'Bhurrah went another bird, flying from the tree.'

'And then?'

'Another bird went bhurrah!'

'And then?'

'Bhurrah!'

This went on until nothing was heard but 'And then?' and 'Bhurrah!' Finally someone asked, 'How long is this going to go on?'

The storyteller answered, 'Till all the birds are gone.'

GAME RHYMES

Where Is That Mango?

Translated by Praphulladutta Goswami from the Assamese original[104]

This is a game rhyme, recited while children hide their hands.

O crane, who has taken away your hand?
—The mango, when I tried to pick it.
Where is that mango?—It fell into the wood.
What became of the wood?—The fire consumed it.
Where are the ashes?—The washerman carried them away.
What did the washerman do?—Washed the king's clothes.
What became of the king?—He is out on a deer hunt.

[104] Source: *Folk-Literature of Assam: An Introductory Survey*, Praphulladatta Goswami, Guwahati: Department of Historical and Antiquarian Studies in Assam, 1954, 42–43.

Where is that deer?—It crossed the river.
Where are the fish?—The crane ate them up.
Where is that crane?—It's perching on a bough.
See, out come our hands!

Curds Gurdew[105]

Translated by Anita Vachharajani from the Gujarati original
'Adko daduko, dahi daduko'

This poem accompanies a game where the players spread their fingers on the floor. One player touches the space between their fingers with her finger and 'hops' between them as the poem is recited by all.

Durdew-burdew curds gurdew,
Drank some curd and a creeper grew
Tars-towers, datura's white flowers,
Sugar cane, dates and jaggery,
A Brahmin wandered home with me
The Brahmin, he was very hungry
He stood, poor soul, with his dinner bowl
The bowl held many coconut pieces
He gave them all to my hungry nieces!

Close your eyes

Translated by Prathibha Nandakumar from the Kannada original
'Kanna muchche kade goode'

This song is sung in a game of hide-and-seek. The child who is 'it' sings this, with eyes closed, while the other children hide. When the song is over, the child then begins to look for the others.

[105] Source: Chani Shah, age eleven.

Close your eyes
Wreck the nest[106]
Black gram sack fell down
Our bird flies—let it out, let it out—
Your bird you should hide.

Frog, frog

Translated by Prathibha Nandakumar from the Kannada original 'Kappe kappe haalkodtheen'

Another short poem children sing when they are making frogs' houses in sand. They pat wet sand into a heap on their feet to make a mould and slowly take out their feet to make a 'house'. It is also believed that playing this game brings rain.

Frog, frog, I will give you milk
Will you give me water?
Frog, frog, I will give you milk
Will you give me water?

The Circle Game Song

Translated by J. Devika from the Malayalam original 'Aruppotti tiruppotti'

Aruppotti tiruppotti
In Aruppan's tent
There sat in a circle
Twelve elephants.
Can't find the comb,

[106] Wreck the nest: In Kannada, this phrase also means 'the forest itself is the nest'.

Can't find the cloth.
Who has got it?
The dame has got it.
From the dame's hands
It's been snatched
The dame's been spun
Upon the roof-thatch.
You girl, who three cups of oil has drunk
You girl, who's bitten the drumstick trunk
Stretch out the legs of the old lady
Sitting in faraway Pandy.

Dumdee Dandy

Translated by Anita Vachharajani from the Marathi original 'Aapdi thapdi'[107]

The first five lines of this rhyme work as an accompaniment to clapping. The child's hands are placed on the floor, palms down. The adult taps on them repeatedly. When the sixth line is said, the players reach out and grab each other's ears. The rest of the poem is recited in a sing-song fashion, with the ear-holding partners rocking back and forth.

Dumdee Dandy,
Sweet sugar candy!

A sugary smack[108]
Oil in the sack!

The telangi has just one leaf, I fear,
Raise your hands, and grab your ears!

---

[107] Source: *Navneet Baalgite*, Mumbai: Navneet Publications (India) Ltd, 2003.

[108] sugary smack: This refers to the original '*dhammak laddoo*'. *Dhammak* is a thump given with the fist on the back, while a *laddoo* is a traditional sweet. The common collocation is meant to be humorous.

Munch-monch and sip-sup
There's some water in the cup
Gulp—it's gone!

LET'S TELL A TALE II

Translated by Sumanyu Satpathy from the Oriya original
'Kathatiye kahun'

Let's tell a tale,
Let's tell a tale.
What tale?
The head of a snail.
What head?
The urchin's bread.
What urchin?
The oil man's tin.
What oil man?
The musk-oil can.
What musk-oil?
Quilt foil.
What quilt?
Musk-root quilt.
What musk?
Nose tusk.
What nose?
Goat goes.
What goat?
King's moat.
What king? . . .

Hopscotch Rhyme

Translated by Nirupama Dutt from the Punjabi original 'Eereeye pambhiriye ni kehrha'

Spinning Top, O Spinning Top[109]
In the game of scotch and hop
Where lies your home?

In a cellar full of mangoes
A courtyard of pomegranates[110]
Where is Baba Nanak's place?[111]

Jump and do a hop
Spinning Top, O Spinning Top
In the game of scotch and hop
Where lies your home?

Kikali kalir di

Translated by Nirupama Dutt from the Punjabi original 'Kikali kalir di'[112]

This is a whirling dance for adolescent girls performed at festive occasions and during normal play. It is performed by two girls crossing their arms, holding hands and spinning around fast, chanting this rhyme. This version is being chanted at a wedding, for the brother and his newly wedded wife. The phrase '*kikali kalir di*' is rhythmic nonsense to build the tempo and speed of spinning.

Kikali kalir di!
Hold hands and whirl around
My brother's turban is brown
His wife's veil is red
Which she just won't shed

---

[109] spinning top: '*Pambhiri*' in Punjabi, refers to a girl who is agile and quick.

[110] mangoes, pomegranates: Both mangoes and pomegranates are much-loved fruits and reference to them is sensuous.

[111] Where is Baba Nanak's place?: This is the equivalent of asking where God lives.

[112] Source: *Punjabi Lok Geet*, compiled by Devendra Satyarthi and Mohinder Singh Randhawa, New Delhi: Sahitya Akademi.

Heer comes from Kashmir[113]
Ranjha is of Hindustan
Fair as a swan
Just look at his wife
She's sharp as a knife
Fast I whirl around
Feet leave the ground
I sit by their side
And say with pride
The lord has blessed
Those who love have met!

FESTIVAL AND CEREMONY VERSE

Naming Rhyme

Translated by Anita Vachharajani from the Gujarati original 'Oli jholi'[114]

This poem is meant to be recited at a child's naming ceremony, performed on the twelfth day after the child's birth. The aunt referred to in the original is specifically the father's sister. In Gujarat it is customary to have the father's sister name the child. The ritual involves swinging the baby on a sheet held at the four corners by family members who are each holding a peepal leaf.

Ting-ping, swing-ing,
The peepal leaf game,
Auntie's given me
This nice name:
[*The child's name is said here.*]

[113] Heer, Ranjha: The legendary lovers of Punjab who met a tragic end because of social taboos. Any pair of lovers can be called Heer and Ranjha.
[114] Source: Amit Vachharajani.

Onam Song

Translated by J. Devika from the Malayalam original

This is a song sung during the festival of Onam, a harvest festival peculiar to Kerala. According to the myth, there was a king who was growing so powerful that the gods dethroned and banished him. He was granted a boon though, and he chose to come and visit his people every year during Onam. The festival goes on for ten days, with all kinds of festivities, including dances and boat races, culminating in the final day, called Thiruvonam. The last two lines of the song are the usual refrain of Onam songs.

A thumba-flower blooms, come and see
In the yard of the Trikkakara deity
From the flower came boats fifty
From the boat's bow grew a banyan tree
On the banyan's bough was born a boy
For the baby boy, here are some toys:
A grain barrel and a stick to flay with
A drum and a drumstick to play with
And Jester and his children, so
Let the flowers bloom and grow,
Let the flowers bloom and grow.

The duck chased off the civet

Translated by Navakanta Barua from the Assamese original[115]

This is actually a song of a mystic cult, though it is often used as a nursery rhyme because of its amusing absurdity.

The duck chased off the civet,
The owl observed the scene.
The roast fish from the trivet
Gobbled the cat down clean.

115 Adapted from *Cradle Songs and Playtime Verses of Assam*, trans. Navakanta Barua, Guwahati: Anundoram Borooah Institute of Language, Art & Culture, 1999.

A Mocking Wedding Song

Translated by Dr B.S. Talwadi from the Kannada original[116]

In rural weddings, singers among the bride's relatives target the bridegroom's people and vice versa by singing, in the name of humour, these mocking songs, which can be harsh, silly or profane. This kind of song is common in many areas of India, including Assam.

Ye! You who attempts to slay
A wandering mongrel in the hay
Have exposed your loin flesh
And lo! The vultures on you rush!

Wedding Songs from Punjab

Translated by Nirupama Dutt from the Punjabi originals

An evening of music and dance is a must before the actual wedding ceremony in Punjab. The following songs are sung in traditional women-only gatherings of passionate dance and song, still exclusively for women in rural areas. Among urban Punjabis now, both men and women participate in them.

Pumpkin Song

This is a wedding song of the 'ladies' sangeet' (as it was known in colonial times) taken from the oral tradition. Here the daughter-in-law has a dig at her mother-in-law at the risk of getting a thrashing from her husband.

The pumpkin sale is on, my love
Come, let's sing a song, my love

116 As told to T. Govindaraju in Kannada by Muni Akkayamma (age sixty, untutored housewife) of the Dalit community in Channadevi Agrahara, Bangalore Rural District.

One pumpkin to a rupee, my love
I want to give your mom a shove.
La! My love will bash me up
The turbaned one will bash me up.

Two pumpkins to a rupee, my love
Your mom has lost her glove, my love.
La! My love will bash me up
The turbaned one will bash me up.

Three pumpkins to a rupee, my love
Your mom's chasing a dove, my love.
La! My love will bash me up
The turbaned one will bash me up.

She Will Come

This bawdy wedding song, in the form called *sithni*, is sung by the female relatives of the bride to tease the bridegroom and his party. The same women ask the questions and give the answers. All insinuations are a part of the social bonhomie on such occasions. Such songs are rarely published because they are, understandably, not considered 'proper'. These songs often rhyme with little regard for reason.

So you have come
Yes you have come
But where have you
left your mum?

She will come
She will come
She's just busy
Shaking her bum.

What's the matter, dear mister?
What's the matter, dear mister?

Where have you left
your little sister?

She'll be here soon
So don't you titter!
She's just fucking
the barrister.

My Husband's Woman

Another piece performed at a ladies' sangeet, this is a brutal dialogue between two women claiming the same husband. Bigamy was common in old Punjab, and even now many men take a second wife in spite of the law against bigamy. The play is on repetition and the refrain of 'you die'. The grand finale is an enactment of the two women pulling at each other's hair and grappling.

My husband's woman,
O my husband's woman,
Take a saucerful of water
Drown yourself and die!

May you die!
May you die!

Who was the man
Calling on you yesterday?

He was my brother!

So he was your brother!
My husband's woman
Take a saucerful of water
Drown yourself and die!

He is mine!
No he is mine!

The suited one!
Yes, the suited one!

The booted one!
Yes, the booted one!

I will take him!
I won't give him!

My husband's woman,
O my husband's woman,

Take a saucerful of water
Drown yourself and die!

May you die!

LULLABY AND FOLK SONG

O FLOWER: A LULLABY

Translated by Navakanta Barua from the Assamese (Upper Assam) original[117]

O Flower, O Flower,
Why don't you bloom?
The cow eats my buds
So why should I bloom?

O Cow, O Cow,
Why eat the buds?

---

117 'O Flower: A Lullaby' and 'Lullaby' adapted from *Cradle Songs and Playtime Verses of Assam*, trans. Navakanta Barua, Guwahati: Anundoram Borooah Institute of Language, Art & Culture, 1999.

The cowherd doesn't tend me,
So why not eat the buds?

O Cowherd, O Cowherd,
Why don't you tend?
The cook does not cook,
So why should I tend?

O Cook, O Cook,
Why don't you cook?
The woodcutter doesn't fetch wood,
So why should I cook?

O Woodcutter, O Woodcutter
Why don't you fetch wood?
I felled the big tree
So why doesn't it dry?

O Tree, O Tree,
Why don't you dry?
The clouds go on raining
So why should I dry?

O Cloud, O Cloud,
Why do you rain?
The frogs go on croaking
So why shouldn't I rain?

O Frog, O Frog,[118]
Why do you croak?
Why should I give up
My forefather's ways?

[118] The frog is traditionally associated with rain. Children celebrate the 'frog marriage' (*bhekuli-biya*) when there is a drought.

Lullaby

Translated by Navakanta Barua from the Assamese (Boro-Kachari) original

Come down O Moon,
        O Moon come down,
If you do not come
        then give us a banana;
If you do not give one,
        You must give us two
O Moon, come, come!

Hoote-maate Lullaby

Translated by Nirupama Dutt from the Punjabi original 'Hoote-maate'[119]

Hoote-maate[120]
Eat sugar and candy
My lad is a dandy.

A carriage of gold is drawn
For my little one to sit on
Spun silver for a seat
My child will have a treat.

Mothers! Sisters!
Rain and storm have come[121]
Run and put away all your stuff
My lad has grown whiskers rough.

[119] Source: *Punjabi Lok Geet*, compiled by Devendra Satyarthi and Mohinder Singh Randhawa, New Delhi: Sahitya Akademi.
[120] Title: 'Hoote-maate' is rhythmic nonsense, akin to 'rock-a-bye', indicating a mother rocking her child in her lap. Punjabi folk literature has lullabies only for the male child, as a female child was and is still not so welcome.
[121] rain and storm: While comforting the child the mother also often introduces an element of fear, which in this case is from the rain and storm.

Parrot Lullaby

Translated by Nirupama Dutt from the Punjabi original 'To ve totarheya'[122]

P for Parrot
Parrot's come all the way
From Sikandar town[123]
Wearing a jewelled crown
He works all day
Without taking any pay
Old man's sheet is white
Spread out for the night
Thus I lull my child to sleep
Let the moon and stars peep

Folk Songs from Mizoram

Translated by Laltungliana Khiangte from the Mizo original[124]

These two texts are very early examples of Mizo folk songs. They are repetitive mnemonic rhymes that are nonsense mainly in their lack of referents. With 'Folk Song I' we include the transliteration of the original, to demonstrate the music of the language.

Folk Song I

Heta tangin kha kha a lang
Khata tangin hei hi a lang.

That is visible from here
This is visible from there

122 Source: *Punjabi Lok Geet*, compiled by Devendra Satyarthi and Mohinder Singh Randhawa. New Delhi: Sahitya Akademi.
123 Sikandar town: A reference to the Greek conqueror Alexander. In Punjab, names of various foreign conquerors are often used to scare children so that they may sleep. The 'old man' is another figure meant to cause fear.
124 Source: *Mizo Songs and Folk Tales*, edited and translated by Laltungliana Khiangte, New Delhi: Sahitya Akademi, 2002.

Folk Song II

Up up above, up up above
Down it rolls on, it rolls on
And so on.

Nursery Song

Translated by Anushka Ravishankar from the Kannada original

Underwear-gunderwear you can wear
And ride away upon a mare
Hoi hoi hoi.

Petticoat-getticoat you can wear
And ride away upon a mare
Hoi hoi hoi.

Children's Songs

Translated by Dr B.S. Talwadi from the Kannada originals

These compositions,[125] spoken and sung by children, appear in form to be normal songs, but they are quite nonsensical. They are often just jugglery of rhyme and alliteration. The meaning is less important, even absent. The aim of telling these is in *not* communicating any 'message' at all.

Frogs twitter

Frogs twitter, ghee glitters
Mango's pulp, tree's help
The hawk a message carried,
The crow, meanwhile, is married
On Monday Saumi's wed
On Saturday for lunch we're fed.

In a government bus

In a government bus
Upon a numbered seat
Are sitting Bulge and Bulgy
Bulge's stomach bursts,
Bulgy shouts a curse.

Oh! Caw!

Oh! Caw! Caw! Crow,
Come! Hanumant Rao!
Let the kids get wed!
Make Granny some bread!

---

125 'Frogs Twitter', 'In a Government Bus' and 'Oh! Caw!' told to T. Govindaraju in Kannada by Shyamala, age seven, of Channadevi Agrahara, Bangalore Rural District; 'Look Up At the Sky' told to T. Govindaraju by T. Manjula, Channadevi Agrahara.

Let Grandpa tie the thali! Come!
Dum! Dum! Dum! Dum!

Look up at the sky!

Look up at the sky!
See the plane fly!
A nanny's in the plane
She plays a baby game
The baby holds a plate
Of sweets the baby ate
In comes a housefly
All the children beat it dry.

Fib Song I

Translated by J. Devika from the Malayalam original

In this fib song, a common folk form, the singer is making up fanciful things to tell a *kunhatthol*, a young Brahmin wife in a Nampoothiri family. (Nampoothiri is a Malayalee Brahmin caste specific to Kerala and entirely different from Brahmins in the rest of South India.) The young Brahmin woman becomes the gullible target of such fibbing because the mobility of such women, as well as their exposure to the world outside the *illam* (the homestead of the Nampoothiri joint family), is limited.

This-dee that-dee, Little Lady,
I went to town to see a play
No farce, no fibbing, Little Lady,
Pebbles have sprouted roots, they say
The storehouse, it seems, has shrunken in size
It's so narrow, it squashed two flies
No farce, no fibbing, Little Lady,
In Palakkad, I went to see
A jackfruit grow on a banyan tree
In Kochi, the mouth of a river was aflame

An ant has pierced its ears, they claim.
A coconut tree was chopped right down
To sweep a speck of dust from the ground
In Calicut, an elephant flew on the roads
Hundred and one elephants in a hundred bowls
No farce, no fibbing, Little Lady,
I went to see a play, truly.

Fib Song II

Translated by J. Devika from the Malayalam original

A bedbug bit the elephant
And the elephant died
The rats in the forest all together
Ploughed the ocean tide
At dawn a tender seed was sown
By noon the areca nuts had grown
When they were dug up and cut
The winnow was full of mangoes, but
When the mango skins were stripped
Out came five hundred Portuguese ships
When they tugged the ships away
They tied the waves above their heads
In Kayamkulam town, they say,
A tiger and a leopard have bred![126]

Farmer's Song

Translated by J. Devika from the Malayalam original

When I planted cucumbers in the ground
What sprouted and flowered were okra, I found,

[126] Kayamkulam is a coastal town and these creatures can certainly be nowhere near.

When I plucked the okra and put it in my bin
What I found was a breadfruit lying within
When I deep-fried the breadfruit to make some fries
What got served was gruel of rice
When I drank rice gruel with great relish
What landed in my stomach was a chicken dish
The chick when little goes 'pyoo-pyoo'
When I was small I went 'coo-coo'

Rain Song

Translated by Anushka Ravishankar from the Marathi original

Come, come, rain
Money you will gain
The money's fake, so
The rain began to pour!

Come, come, shower,
Come and fill my jar
The shower came running,
The jar went spinning!

Rice Song

Translated by V. Geetha and Anushka Ravishankar from the Tamil original

This song is probably sung while pounding rice.

In the flowing river
Two eggs are floating by
While the god of Aalangudi
Looks down from the skies

Two wooden dolls
Are pounding at the rice—

Your mother is a teacher
And my mother too
Your father is a policeman
And my father too
My brother is a dancing drum
And your brother too
Your sister is a drumstick
And my sister too
And both our little sisters
Are coconut shells, two.

A Mango Tree

Translated by V. Geetha and Anushka Ravishankar from the Tamil original

A mango tree
A jasmine tree
In the Madaswamy shrine
A coconut tree

The mango tree
And the jasmine tree
Have a peacock-mirror
But the boy called Maaman
Will have two wives for ever

'THORN' TEXTS

A study in cross-cultural folk nonsense

This section contains what we have called 'thorn' texts, as many of them begin with the image of a thorn. This is a folk/literary/mystical form found in various regions throughout India, but the versions can differ dramatically. The basic format is exemplified by the first piece here, in which we have a story of accretion, using the image from one section as the starting-point for the next. The nonsense device shared in all pieces is nonsense tautology (see the Introduction for more on accretion and tautology). These techniques are common to all these texts, yet we can also see the great variations created by the folk imagination. The Oriya version, for instance, takes one of its images, an eel, and, in sheer exuberance, cannot help but go off on a tangent, pulling it away from its base form. The age of such texts is unknown, though we have two examples here from poet-saints, a sign of considerable lineage from at least the early medieval period (late fourteenth or early fifteenth century). In some ways, these texts exemplify quintessential Indian nonsense with their folk and literary heritage, their mixture of adult and child audience, topsy-turvy reversals and unquestionable 'Indian' cultural provenance. They are all presented here as literal translations. No effort has been made to 'versify' them—so that we may make a more trustworthy and accurate comparison.

THREE VILLAGES

Sant Namdev

Translated by Anita Vachharajani and Gouri Patwardhan from the Marathi original 'Teen gaav' from Sakalsantha Gaatha

On the tip of a thorn were three villages
Two were barren and one hadn't any people at all!
To the village with no people came three potters
Two were limbless and one wasn't formed at all!
The unformed potter made three pots
Two were leaky and one wouldn't hold at all!
Nama says that being without a guru
Leaves you incapable of seeing the truth at all![127]

[127] The last couplet is a traditional closing in the oral tradition that allows the speaker self-attribution. 'Nama' is a shortened form of 'Namdev'.

Shikar Nama[128]

Khwaja Banda Nawaz Gesu Daraz

Translated by Sumanyu Satpathy from the Urdu original[129]

Though the story that follows seems absurd and meaningful in itself, Khwaja Banda Nawaz has presented in it the concepts of Bhakti in the language of Islamic Sufism.[130]

We four brothers were only from the countryside. Three were without clothes and the fourth one was absolutely naked. The brother who was naked had money in his *aasteen*.[131] All four went to the market to buy bows and arrows. Death came, and all four died. But twenty-four came back to life and stood up. Just then four bows came into view. Three of them were broken and were quite useless. The fourth one had neither any end nor a bowstring. The naked brother who had money in his *aasteen* bought the bow with neither any end nor a bowstring. Now the thought of the arrow was worrying. Four arrows came into view. Three were broken, the fourth one had neither a point nor a feather. We bought the pointless and featherless arrow, and headed for the jungle looking for prey. Four deer came into view. Three were dead, and the fourth one was lifeless. The lifeless deer was shot with the pointless and featherless arrow. Now, a rope was needed to tie up the victim. Four ropes came into view. Three were in pieces, and the fourth

[128] Title: *Shikar Nama* is said to be an Urdu translation from a Persian text entitled *Majmuu'a-e Yaazdah Masaail* (A Collection of Twelve Puzzles). The title of this story in the original Persian text is *Burhaan-ul Ashiqeen, Almaaruuf bah Qissa Chahar Braadar* (Arguments/Manifestations of Lovers, known as the Story of Four Brothers). Sources: Anwar Sadeed, *Urdu Adab ki Mukhtasar Tareekh*, Lahore, 1996, 49–50; Sayyid Ehtesham Husain, *Urdu Adab ki Tanqeedi Tareekh*, New Delhi, 1983, 27–28.

[129] Source: *Qadeem Urdu Adab ki Tanqidi Tareekh* (Critical History of Early Urdu Literature), ed. Mohammad Hasan, Lucknow: Uttar Pradesh Urdu Academy, 1986.

[130] Sources: Dr Anwar Sadeed, *Urdu Adab ki Mukhtasar Tareekh* (A Short History of Urdu Literature), Lahore, 1996, 49-50; Sayyid Ehtesham Husain, *Urdu Adab ki Tanqeedi Tareekh* (A Critical History of Urdu Literature), New Delhi, 1983, 27-28. Texts compiled by Dr Abu Bakar Abbad and Dr Arjumand Ara, lecturers in the Department of Urdu, University of Delhi.

[131] aasteen: Shirtsleeves.

one had neither ends nor the middle parts. The prey was tied up with the rope whose ends and middle parts were missing. Now, a house was needed for rest and also for cooking the meat. Four houses came into view. Three were broken, and the roof and walls of the fourth one were missing. We went into the roofless and wall-less house. There in a *taak*[132] on the wall a big pot came into view. It was impossible to reach out to the high *taak* and take out the pot. A four-yard deep hole was dug into the floor beneath our feet. Only then could the pot be reached. When the meat was cooked and ready, a man came down from the roof, and said, 'Give me my share, for this is your duty.' His blood brother was also sitting somewhere nearby. He picked up a bone from the cooked meat and struck the man's head. A yellow potato-bearing tree sprang out from the elbow of the man. We climbed up that tree. We saw that melons were being cultivated and were being irrigated with the help of catapults. From the tree, we started picking brinjals and started cooking kulia, and distributed it among the masses. We ate so much that we started swelling. We thought that we had grown very fat, so fat that we could not get out through the doors, and we lay there in the dirt. We escaped through the threshold of the house quite easily, and slept at the door of the house and embarked on a journey.

A Story about a Story

Translated by Anita Vachharajani from the Gujarati original 'Ek vaat ni vaat'[133]

Here's a story about a story:
There was once a ber tree
It had an eighteen and a half foot thorn.
On its tip were three villages,

[132] taak: A crude shelf, usually very small, on the wall in traditiona constructions. It is used to keep earthen lamps.

[133] Source for 'A Story About a Story', 'The Never-Never King' and 'The False City': *Baalvartaa*, Vol. 1, 1929, compiled by Gijubhai Badheka, Ahmedabad: Sanskar Sahitya Mandir, 2001, 4–6.

Two were empty and no one lived in the third at all.
In it lived three Brahmins,
Two were fasting and one ate nothing at all.
The Brahmin had three cows at home,
Two were infertile and one could never have a baby at all.
The cow gave birth to three calves,
Two weren't there and one didn't exist at all.
The calf ploughed three fields,
Two were barren and nothing grew in one.

The Never-Never King

Translated by Anita Vachharajani from the Gujarati original 'Nako-nako raja'

There was once a Never-Never King
Who founded three villages;
Two were barren and no one lived in the other at all.
In it lived three potters,
Two couldn't make pots and one didn't know how to at all.
The potter made three little pots,
Two were broken and one wasn't mended at all.
He invited three Brahmins to lunch,
Two were fasting and one wouldn't eat at all.
He gave them three coins of copper,
Two were fakes and one wasn't real at all.
The Brahmins showed the coins to three goldsmiths,
Two were blind and one couldn't see at all.
This story was told to three little lads,
Two soon forgot that they'd heard it,
And one couldn't remember it at all.[134]

[134] remember: the original word here is 'learn', but with shades of learning it well enough to retell/remember it.

THE FALSE CITY

Translated by Anita Vachharajani from the Gujarati original 'Khotu Nagar'

There was once a city that wasn't.[135]
In it lived three princes;
Two weren't even born and the third wouldn't ever be.
All three set off on a trip,[136]
On the way, they saw three trees;
Two trees hadn't grown at all and the third would never grow.
Under the tree, the princes sat and ate three fruits;
Two fruits didn't exist and one would never exist.
The princes rode on.
On their way were three rivers;
Two rivers had no water and one was dry.
The princes drank up some water from that river.
Then the princes went to a village.
It had three houses in it,
Two weren't even built and one had no walls at all.
In it were three golden bowls;
Two were broken and one wasn't formed at all.
In it was cooking some rice;
There were ninety-nine measures of rice, of which a hundred were
being cooked.
Three Brahmins were invited to lunch;
Two had no bodies and one had no mouth at all.
The one without a mouth ate up the hundred measures of rice
And the princes ate up all the rest!

[135] city that wasn't: The city in the first line is actually described as a 'false-false' city. The reduplication sounds natural in Gujarati but odd in English, which rarely uses such forms. An echo remains in the repetition of 'was' and 'wasn't'.

[136] trip: The word used here is one that means 'they went on a trip from village to village'.

On the tip of a thorn

Translated by V. Geetha and Anushka Ravishankar from the Tamil original

On the tip of a thorn
I dug three deep wells
Two went dry, the third had no water at all

To the waterless well
Came three potters
Two were lame, the third had no legs

The handless potter
Baked three pots
Two stayed wet, the third was half-baked

Into the half-baked pot were thrown
Three grains of rice
Two remained raw, the third didn't cook

To the uncooked rice was added
The milk of three buffalos
Two were not pregnant, the third was barren

To the barren buffalo was given
Three acres of land
Two of these were deserts, the third had no grass

For the grassless land they paid
Three whole rupees
Two rupee notes were torn, the third valueless

For the valueless note stood guard
Three accountants
Two were blind, the third eyeless

The eyeless man bequeathed to the others
Three whole villages
Two were deserted, the third had no people

In the peopleless village
Lived three young women
Two were bald, the third had no hair

ON THE TIP OF A NEEDLE

Translated by J. Devika from the Malayalam original

On the tip of a needle
Three ponds were dug
Two were useless
The third had no water

In the waterless pond
Came swimming three men
Two were lame
The third had no arms

The armless potter
Made three pots
Two had holes
The third had no bottom

In the bottomless pot boiled
Three measures of rice
Two were raw
One never got cooked

To eat uncooked rice
Came three men
Two were starving
The third never ate

For the non-eater
The milk of three buffaloes
Two were barren
One never gave birth

For the non-bearing buffalo
Three fields to graze
Two were bare
One had no grass

For the grassless field
Three coins were given
Two were false
The third was phony

Three men looked after
The phony coin
Two were blind
The third had no eyes

At the tip of the needle
Three ponds were dug
Two were useless
The third had no water!

Story of a Story, Hero of a Brother

Translated by Sumanyu Satpathy from the Oriya original 'Kathara Katha, Bhai Maharatha'[137]

There once were two villages
Both were in ruins
One had no houses.

[137] Source: *Lokagulpa Sanchayana*, ed. Dash Kunjabihari, Bhubaneswar: Orissa Sahitya Akademi, 1964.

In the village without a house, there lived three potters.
Two potters were always sulking,
One potter made no pots.

The potter who made no pots had three pots.
Two were broken,
The third had no bottom.

The pot without any bottom
Cooked three handfuls of rice.
Two handfuls remained dry,
One handful was not boiled.

Three guests wait for the rice.
Two guests are sulking,
One guest refuses to eat.

This guest owns three ponds.
Two ponds are dry,
One has no water.

The pond without water has three eels.
Two eels are slippery,
One escapes capture.

The one that can't be caught
Was caught by Mr Gee
Mr Gee cut it into sixteen pieces.

Mr Gee got the tail,
But the cat snatched it away.
Mr Gee asked angrily,
'Where are the rest of the pieces?'

'The missus has eaten them all—
Listen, I know for sure!

The mongoose took two of the sixteen—then remained fourteen.
Two, the fairies took—then remained twelve.
Two went across the river—then remained ten.
Two slipped off while cleaning—then remained eight.
Two I traded for wood—then remained six.
Two the son took—then remained four.
Two went to the whole family—then remained two.
One was eaten up by the termite—one remained.
The cat ate the rest—see!'

The Rising Stars

In summer 2004, Michael Heyman gave a lecture on nonsense at the British Council in Chennai, at which there were quite a few enthusiastic audience members, but the most engaged was Kaushik Vishwanath, who composed a piece on the spot, during the lecture. One of his poems is included here. In Mumbai, at about the same time, Sampurna Chattarji held a nonsense workshop for children. She taught them some basics of nonsense and let them loose. As with adult-written nonsense, these pieces show the fun and philosophical spirit of whimsy. Featured here are a few examples from the many imaginative poems, stories and recipes some of the participants composed.

KAUSHIK VISHWANATH

Let Us Alphabetus

Do you feel queasy in easy queues,
Or clam-like on lam-like seas?
Do you think Alice with lice has the ace,
Or feel bad in an ad with bees?

ARPITA SHAH

Phony Comb

There lived a phony comb in the kingdom of fatheads. He had the face of a monstrous moon and had red ants in place of teeth. And also he had a red head which kept dozing here and there. Once he was ill and that decreased the rate of ant teeth. So he was not able to eat the kingdom of hair and this affected his health. He recovered after some time and a disaster occurred. Something fell with a plonk on his head and this changed him from a phony comb to a king comb.

POOJA JHUNJHUNWALA

The Glow-Worm and the Giraffe

The glow-worm and the giraffe are insulted
People say they can't compete
So they are going to meet in a ring
To show that they are totally complete.

The giraffe is growing less skinny, more wicked,
The glow-worms have stopped being slobs
The giraffe now uses five beds to sleep
And the glow-worms stopped sleeping in mobs.

Now the big day had finally arrived
When the giraffe and the worms would collide
But the glow-worms had a whooping cough
And coughed which made them impolite.

They went nearer and nearer and nearer still
Now they were so near they could even kill
The giraffe was advancing, ready to glow
When unfortunately the glow-worm went
        ATIIISHO!!!

VINNIE MEHTA

THE JOKING JUICE

Welcome. Welcome. I am Madso Intelligent and I am here (in the brain furnace) to teach you the most sensible recipe ever made: The Hooly Pooly Hoo Hoo. Okay so go, get set, ready. Take a footcut ball and keep it in the fire. Take some of the milk you drink during exams and put some kites in it. Kiss the ball and pray to God that your recipe turns out to be scary. Stir with eleven toothpicks. Stir and stir. Let it boil. Note that the recipe is only for those who want to lose their appetite and is eaten not during summer, nor winter, nor any other season. Okay now our recipe is ready. Let it cool, taste it, and throw it out.

SHAIVYA SONKAR

YELLO JELLO

Happy-go-lucky Yello Jello
Singing and dancing on his way,
Greeting everyone with a 'Hello'
On an island in the bay.

Skipping and stomping his huge, bare feet
When the sky becomes dark and misty,
He can only survive in the exhausting heat
And the darkness for him is risky.

He does not like tons of sidekicks,
But he digs having lots of friends.

He is usually dressed up in bricks
He's in the habit of setting trends.

He takes a bath in a basin
And cooks his food in the bathroom.
He has a particular dislike for raisins
And he dries himself off with a broom.

So forget your tensions and just say 'Hello'
Whenever you encounter the Yello Jello.

NOVNIT KASHYAP

The Mixed-Up City

In a city named Riko there lives a family of trees. There are about ten trees in the family. The trees eat pizzas with the help of cups. When a tree dies it lays an egg. After a minute the egg hatches, and a fly comes out. The moment it eats, it dies. After the fly dies it lays some eggs. The eggs hatch into a seed and the seed develops into a parrot. The parrots can do calculations. These parrots eat bananas. The monkeys are the only sensible characters in the city, because they eat bananas. The monkeys were really angry because there were only seven bananas left on the tree. So a fight took place between the parrots and the monkeys. The pigs could fly, so the pigs came and took the bananas away. The fight stopped. Then it started to rain. The monkeys quickly climbed down and ran off. The parrots were still on the tree. Then lightning struck the tree. The parrots died and the monkeys were safe.

Appendix

EDWARD LEAR'S INDIAN NONSENSE

It is perhaps fitting that the father of English nonsense wrote and published nonsense in India. These texts were written by Lear while on a trip to India in 1873–74. 'The Cummerbund' was published in *The Times of India* (Bombay) on 22 June 1874.

THE CUMMERBUND

An Indian Poem

She sate upon her Dobie,
        To watch the Evening Star,
And all the Punkahs as they passed,
        Cried, 'My! how fair you are!'
Around her bower, with quivering leaves,
        The tall Kamsamahs grew,
And Kitmutgars in wild festoons
        Hung down from Tchokis blue.

Below her home the river rolled
        With soft meloobious sound,
Where golden-finned Chuprassies swam,
        In myriads circling round.
Above, on tallest trees remote
        Green Ayahs perched alone,
And all night long the Mussak moan'd
        Its melancholy tone.

And where the purple Nullahs threw
        Their branches far and wide,—
And silvery Goreewallahs flew
        In silence, side by side,—
The little Bheesties' twittering cry

Rose on the fragrant air,
    And oft the angry Jampan howled
Deep in his hateful lair.

She sate upon her Dobie,—
    She heard the Nimmak hum,—
When all at once a cry arose,—
    'The Cummerbund is come!'
In vain she fled:—with open jaws
    The angry monster followed,
And so, (before assistance came,)
    That Lady Fair was swollowed.

They sought in vain for even a bone
Respectfully to bury,—
They said,—'Hers was a dreadful fate!'
(And Echo answered 'Very.')
They nailed her Dobie to the wall,
Where last her form was seen,

And underneath they wrote these words,
In yellow, blue, and green:–

'Beware, ye Fair! Ye Fair, beware!
Nor sit out late at night,—
Lest horrid Cummerbunds should come,
And swollow you outright.

The Akond of Swat

For the existence of this potentate, see Indian newspapers, *passim*. The proper way to read the verses is to make an immense emphasis on the monosyllabic rhymes, which indeed ought to be shouted out by a chorus.

Who, or why, or which, or *what*, Is the Akond of SWAT?

Is he tall or short, or dark or fair?
Does he sit on a stool or a sofa or a chair   or SQUAT,
The Akond of Swat?

Is he wise or foolish, young or old?
Does he drink his soup and his coffee cold   or HOT,
The Akond of Swat?

Does he sing or whistle, jabber or talk,
And when riding abroad does he gallop or walk   or TROT,
The Akond of Swat?

Does he wear a turban, a fez, or a hat?
Does he sleep on a mattress, a bed, or a mat   or a COT,
The Akond of Swat?

The Akhond of Swat

When he writes a copy in round-hand size,
Does he cross his T's and finish his I's with a DOT,
The Akond of Swat?

Can he write a letter concisely clear
Without a speck or a smudge or smear or BLOT,
The Akond of Swat?

Do his people like him extremely well?
Or do they, whenever they can, rebel or PLOT,
At the Akond of Swat?

If he catches them then, either old or young,
Does he have them chopped in pieces or hung or SHOT,
The Akond of Swat?

Do his people prig in the lanes or park?
Or even at times, when days are dark GAROTTE,
O the Akond of Swat!

Does he study the wants of his own dominion?
Or doesn't he care for public opinion a JOT,
The Akond of Swat?

To amuse his mind do his people show him
Pictures, or any one's last new poem or WHAT,
For the Akond of Swat?

At night if he suddenly screams and wakes,
Do they bring him only a few small cakes or a LOT,
For the Akond of Swat?

Does he live on turnips, tea, or tripe?
Does he like his shawl to be marked with a stripe or a DOT,
The Akond of Swat?

Does he like to lie on his back in a boat
Like the lady who lived in that isle remote SHALLOTT,
The Akond of Swat?

Is he quiet, or always making a fuss?
Is his steward a Swiss or a Swede or Russ or a SCOT,
The Akond of Swat?

Does he like to sit by the calm blue wave?
Or to sleep and snore in a dark green cave or a GROTT,
The Akond of Swat?

Does he drink small beer from a silver jug?
Or a bowl? or a glass? or a cup? or a mug? or a POT.
The Akond of Swat?

Does he beat his wife with a gold-topped pipe,
When she let the gooseberries grow too ripe or ROT,
The Akond of Swat?

Does he wear a white tie when he dines with friends,
And tie it neat in a bow with ends or a KNOT,
The Akond of Swat?

Does he like new cream, and hate mince-pies?
When he looks at the sun does he wink his eyes or NOT,
The Akond of Swat?

Does he teach his subjects to roast and bake?
Does he sail about on an inland lake in a YACHT,
The Akond of Swat?

Someone, or nobody, knows I wot
Who or which or why or what Is the Akond of Swat!

Indian Limericks

i

There was a small child at Narkunda,
Who said, 'Don't you hear! That is thunder!'
But they said, 'It's the Bonzes, a-making responses,
In a temple eight miles from Narkunda.'

ii

There was an old person of Fágoo,
Who purchased a ship and its Cargo;
When the Sails were all furled,
He sailed all round the world,
And returned all promiscuous to Fágoo.

iii

There was an old man in a Tonga,
Who said, 'If this ride lasts much longer,—
Between shaking and dust,
I shall probably bust,
And never ride more in a Tonga.'

Poona Observer, May 1875

We are able to present our readers with an inaccurate misrepresentation of the well known Author & Artist Mr Edward Lear, who has lately caused so much sensation in our city by having become a Fakeer. He may be seen any day beneath the 18th Banyan tree on the wrong hand as you descend the level road entering and leaving Poonah from Peshawar and Madras. He is constantly attended by a tame crow & a large dog of the Grumpsifactious species, & passes his days in placid conkimplation of the surrounding scenery.—

The Owl and the Pussy-cat

This poem, though written long before Lear visited India, was widely read in India before his arrival. He tells an anecdote of children raised in India with intimate knowledge of his work.

The Owl and the Pussy-cat went to sea
        In a beautiful pea-green boat,

They took some honey, and plenty of money,
        Wrapped up in a five-pound note.
The Owl looked up to the stars above,
        And sang to a small guitar,
'O lovely Pussy! O Pussy, my love,
        What a beautiful Pussy you are,
                You are,
                You are!
What a beautiful Pussy you are!'

Pussy said to the Owl, 'You elegant fowl!
        How charmingly sweet you sing!
O let us be married! too long we have tarried:
        But what shall we do for a ring?'
They sailed away, for a year and a day,
        To the land where the Bong-tree grows,
And there in a wood a Piggy-wig stood,
        With a ring at the end of his nose,
                His nose,
                His nose,
With a ring at the end of his nose.

'Dear Pig, are you willing to sell for one shilling
        Your ring?' Said the Piggy, 'I will.'
So they took it away, and were married next day
        By the Turkey who lives on the hill.
They dined on mince, and slices of quince,
        Which they ate with a runcible spoon;
And hand in hand, on the edge of the sand,
        They danced by the light of the moon,
                The moon,
                The moon,
        They danced by the light of the moon.

Notes on Contributors

TRANSLATORS

R.E. ASHER has published books on the literature of the French Renaissance, the history of linguistics, contemporary Malayalam literature, Tamil and Malayalam grammar and translations of five Malayalam novels. He is editor-in-chief of the ten-volume *Encyclopedia of Language and Linguistics* and of the *Atlas of the World's Languages*.

DILEEP CHANDAN is a writer and a journalist. He is the editor of *Asam Bani*, an English-language weekly newspaper in Assam and has written several fiction and non-fiction books, most with a focus on the North East region of India. He contributes to other regional newspapers and has received numerous journalism awards.

ACHAMMA C. CHANDERSEKARAN is a translator and political activist and has been a teacher in India. She has worked for many years in the US Department of Commerce. She has also translated the short story anthology, *Daughters of Kerala* (2004).

J. DEVIKA has a Ph.D in History and is a researcher and teacher at the Centre for Development Studies, Thiruvananthapuram. She has translated non-literary writing from English to Malayalam, and from Malayalam to English. Her work includes a collection of essays by women translated from Malayalam, titled *Her-Self: Early Writings on Gender by Malayalee Women, 1898–1938* (Kolkata: Stree, 2005).

NIRUPAMA DUTT is a poet, translator, senior journalist, and art and literary critic. She has published a book of poems called *Ik Nadi Sanwali Jehi* (1995) and edited an anthology of poetry from the SAARC countries called *Our Voices* in 2004. She has also edited two anthologies by Pakistani writers, titled *Half the Sky* and *Children of the Night* (2005).

V. GEETHA is a writer, translator, social historian, activist, and a freelance editor with a number of small research journals. She has been active in the women's empowerment movement in India since 1988. V. Geetha has written widely, both in Tamil and English, on gender, popular culture, caste and the politics of Tamil Nadu. Among the books she has authored are *An Ideal Boy* (with Gita Wolf and Sirish Rao), published by Tara Books, *Gender in the Theorizing Feminism Series* and *Towards a Non-Brahmin Millenneu: From Iyothee Thass to Periyar* (both published by Stree). Her Tamil books include *Self-respect and Samadharma: Life and Thought of Antonio Gramsci, Frankfurt Marxism* and *An Introduction to Althusser*.

PRAPHULLADUTTA GOSWAMI is the author of several books on the folk culture and literature of the North East. He is a retired professor of folklore from Guwahati University.

T. GOVINDARAJU has an MA in Kannada and a Ph.D in folklore study and has developed new concepts like candid folklore, archaic folklore, folklore through trekking and political folklore. He has authored twelve books and hundreds of articles and has won several awards for his work.

GLORIA MACHLIS HEYMAN considers her two sons her finest accomplishments. Recently she has been tending a fifteen-foot beanstalk while completing a two-volume English translation of Rebecca Machlis's Yiddish poetry and writings. Her own poetry and her book, *Fifty on Fifty*, await her attention.

RANJIT HOSKOTÉ is a poet, cultural theorist and independent curator. He is the author of ten books, which include, most recently, *Vanishing Acts: New & Selected Poems, 1985–2005* (Penguin, 2006). Hoskoté was a Fellow of the International Writing Program, University of Iowa (1995) and writer-in-residence at Villa Waldberta, Munich (2003).

LALTUNGLIANA KHIANGTE is a prolific author, essayist, folklorist, poet and scholar. He has written and co-authored more than forty-two books and has received many awards for his significant contributions to Mizo language and literature. He is a professor and head of the Mizo department at Mizoram University.

PRATHIBHA NANDAKUMAR is a poet, short-story writer, journalist, translator, and theatre and documentary-film personality in Kannada. She has been a part of the Ten Writers' Delegation to Sweden on an Indo-Swedish cultural exchange programme. She has also participated in several international conferences of writers and has won several awards.

GOURI PATWARDHAN has directed educational films for NCERT and edited several documentary films, as well as taught film editing at NID, Ahmedabad, and IDC, Mumbai. Currently she teaches at the Indus Valley School of Art and Architecture, Karachi.

LATHA RAMAKRISHNAN has published several volumes of short stories and poetry under the pseudonyms 'Anamika' and 'Rishi', as well as many Tamil/English translations. She is associated with the Welfare Foundation of the Blind and endeavours to enable the visually handicapped get easy access to modern Tamil literary works.

A.K. RAMANUJAN (1929–1993) was translator, poet, essayist, playwright and scholar. Born in Mysore, he later moved to the USA, where he was a professor at the University of Chicago for many years. His volume, *Folktales from India*, was an inspiration for this book and a standard of research from which we have inevitably fallen short.

ELCHURI MURALIDHARA RAO is a poet, scholar, translator and editor of several literary journals and medieval *kavyas*. Among his publications are *Sivamritalahari* (Telugu), *Lure of the Yore and Other Poems* (edited) in English, *Devi Saptasati* (translation) and *Subandhu's Vasavadatta* (criticism). His forthcoming work is titled *Problems in the History of Telugu Literature*.

NABIN CHANDRA SARMA is one of the top folklorists in the North East and was the head of the Department of Folklore Research at Guwahati University. He is co-author of the *Handbook of Folklore Material of Northeast India* (1994).

SAROJ SUNDAR is a retired schoolteacher who taught English and History for thirty years. She now lives in Tellicherry, Kerala.

B.S. TALWADI is an eminent folklorist in Kannada. He has an MEd. and Ph.D to his credit. He has written seventy books and published more than 200 articles on various subjects. Being a linguist, he has translated from English, Hindi, Telugu, Tamil and Konkani to Kannada and vice versa and has received several literary awards for his works.

ANITA VACHHARAJANI writes poetry and fiction for children. Her stories have appeared in *The Puffin Book of Bedtime Stories* and she has written *My Little Garden*, a book on gardening for children. She also writes educational content, book reviews and magazine articles. She lives in Mumbai with her husband, an illustrator, and their daughter.

AUTHORS

NANDA KISHORE BALA (1875–1928) was the pre-eminent and first modern Oriya writer of children's rhymes, *chhele bhulano chhoda* (which he called '*nanabaya*').

NAVAKANTA BARUA (1926–2002) was one of the best-loved modern Assamese writers, with over thirty books and anthologies, mostly of poetry, to his credit. He was also a playwright and the editor of the children's magazines *Jonbai* (1950–62) and *Pohar* (1969–70) and the literary-cultural magazine *Shiralu* (1983–85). He received many literary awards, including the Sahitya Akademi Award in 1975, the Padma Bhushan in 1976, and the title of 'national poet' in 1996 from the Madhya Pradesh government.

VAIKOM MOHAMMED BASHEER (1908–1994) was a beloved Malayalam fiction writer who won many awards for his work. Many of his thirty-four books have been translated into other languages. After much activity in the freedom movement, he settled into a writing career.

One of his stories, 'Walls', was made into the film *The Flowering of Desire* by the Malayalam film-maker Adoor Gopalakrishnan.

NIRANJAN BEHERA is a retired schoolteacher living in relative obscurity in a remote village in Orissa, called Nachhipuria, where he runs an international children's library. After trying his hand at fiction, romantic poetry and writing plays, he started writing for children in 1979. He has published several chapbooks containing nonsense rhymes and limericks in Oriya.

DASH BENHUR is the pseudonym for Jitendra Narayan Dash, a revered Orissan poet, scholar and writer for children. He was born in Khandapara in Nayagarh district, Orissa. Among many honours, he has won the Orissa Sahitya Akademi Award (1987) and the National Prize Competition for Children's Literature (1989). Presently, he teaches at S.C.S. College, Puri.

LEELAVATI BHAGWAT started her career as a Montessori teacher and went on to produce special programmes for women on All India Radio, Mumbai, for close to twenty years. She is the author of several award-winning books for children and young adults and the books she has written for the National Book Trust have been translated into fourteen Indian languages.

ANANT BHAVE has taught Marathi literature and language for many years. He is also a translator and a columnist for numerous Marathi dailies and weeklies. He has been writing poetry for children for the past thirty years and has published over twenty collections of his poetry.

SAMPURNA CHATTARJI is an award-winning poet and short-story writer. Her work has appeared in *Chandrabhaga*, *Poetry India: Millennium Voices* and *100 Poets Against the War*, among others. In 2004 she published a translation of Sukumar Ray's work, titled *Abol Tabol: The Nonsense World of Sukumar Ray*, and *The Greatest Stories Ever Told*. Her stories have appeared in *The Puffin Book of Bedtime Stories* (2005) and *The Puffin Book of Funny Stories* (2006). She won the Charles Wallace Scholarship for Creative Writing 2005 to the University of Edinburgh and her first book of poems is being published by the Sahitya Akademi.

HARINDRANATH CHATTOPADHYAYA (1898–1990) was a well-known Indian English poet who also wrote drama, composed music and painted. He was member of the Rajya Sabha for some time, and has acted in a few Hindi films and written lyrics for Hindi film songs. His romantic poems were published as early as in 1918 (*The Feast of Youth*). He was the youngest brother of Sarojini Naidu, a freedom fighter and one of India's first recognized women poets.

MANOJ DAS was born in the village of Sankhari in Balasore district of Orissa. He now lives in Pondicherry. He writes both in Oriya and English. Initially attracted to Marxist philosophy, he was later drawn to the teachings of Sri Aurobindo and Sri Maa. Primarily known for his short stories, he has also written some poetry and several novels in Oriya. He has received the Sahitya Akademi Award for his work.

JAGANNATH PRASAD (J.P.) DAS is a well-known Oriya poet, playwright, short-story writer, translator, novelist, and also writes for children. He studied in Ravenshaw College and then in Allahabad University before joining the Indian Administrative Service in 1958. In 1984 he gave up his administrative position and took to writing full-time. He lives and writes in Delhi and his works have been widely translated.

KHWAJA BANDA NAWAZ GESU DARAZ (1320?–1422?) was a Sufi saint and is considered by some to be the first prose writer in the Dakhni dialect of Urdu. He was a disciple of Hazrat Nizamuddin Aulia. He lived in Delhi and Gulbarga and had a large number of followers. He wrote several texts in Dakhni, including 'Maeraj-ul Aashiqeen' and 'Shikar Nama', though works attributed to him are not always verifiable. The theme and style of narration in 'Shikar Nama' are said to have influenced the writings of Marathi saints.

GULZAR is the pen-name of Sampooran Singh, a famous Urdu and Hindi poet, lyricist, fiction writer, script writer, film producer and director. He has also worked on many projects and albums for children. His publications include *Mera Kuchh Saman*, *Ek Boond Chand*, *Chand Pukhraj Ka* and *Dhuan*. He has won many awards, including the National Award for best lyricist (twice) and producer of the best film (*Maachis*), and the Sahitya Akademi Award.

KABIR is a celebrated poet, mystic and teacher from the fifteenth century. He was born in Varanasi to weavers who had recently converted to Islam. He is believed to have been the disciple of Ramananda, a famous Hindu guru. Such mixed history causes him to be claimed by Muslims and Hindus alike, although he viewed himself as independent (and critical) of both traditions.

VINDA KARANDIKAR is a well-known and decorated Marathi poet, essayist, lecturer, scholar, critic and translator. Karandikar was born into a farmer's family in 1918 at Dhalawal, in the Sindhudurg district of Maharashtra. He taught English Literature and became the head of the English department at SIES College, Mumbai. He has won numerous literary awards, between 1960 and 2002, and was invited on academic tenures abroad in the sixties and seventies. He is also a well-loved author of children's literature. He and his wife Suma live in Mumbai.

USHA KHADILKAR is a famous Marathi writer. She began writing in 1948 and her short stories, poems and articles have been published in magazines and broadcast on AIR, Mumbai. She has twenty-eight books, including a few novels, to her credit. Usha Khadilkar retired as head-mistress of Sharadashram English Medium School, Dadar, Mumbai and is the author of several books on spoken English.

KUNJUNNI (1920–2005), sometimes referred to as Kunjunni Master, is a renowned poet from Kerala. He wrote about a dozen books of poetry, some of which are for children. He was born in 1927 at Valappad, the son of Njayappilli Neelakantan Moosad and Atiyarathu Narayani Amma, and was a schoolteacher at Ramakrishna Mission School at Kozhikode.

USHA MEHTA is a well-known social and literary figure in Maharashtra. She has worked in the field of education for thirty-five years and has published three books for children—*Salim Sarancha Sameer*, which received the Sandipani Award by the Bal Kumar Sahitya Sammelan, *Juchiya Goshti*, a collection of short stories, and a book of poems, *Survantrao Ani Itar Kavita*. She has also published three volumes of poetry and has co-authored a biography of social worker and cancer survivor Dr Arun Limaye.

MUTHALAPPURAM MOHANDAS is a senior lecturer at the District Institute of Education and Training in the Idukki district of Kerala. He has written five collections of poems for children.

BAUDDHAYAN MUKHERJI was born in Kolkata in 1973 and is an Economics graduate from St Xavier's College. Today, Bauddhayan is an award-winning ad film-maker with Black Magic Motion Pictures. Based in Mumbai with his wife Mona, Bauddhayan writes for fun and is currently working on a script for a feature film.

M.D. MUTHUKUMARASWAMY is a well-known Tamil academic, folklorist, playwright and writer. His publications include collections of short stories written under the pen-name 'Sylvia', plays, several essays of literary criticism and a novel written under his own name. He has also written a Tamil book on post-structuralism and semiotics and translated postmodern writings from English to Tamil. He is currently editor of the quarterly *Indian Folklife* and the annual *Indian Folklore Research Journal*.

SANT NAMDEV (1270?–1350?) was born in Narasi, to a low-caste family of tailors. He married at age eleven, not uncommon at the time, and had four or five children. He was a follower of the Bhakti poet-saint

Jnanadev, and travelled for many years as a wandering minstrel of sorts, singing his spiritual devotion. He eventually settled down, became a revered poet-saint in medieval India and gathered his own following.

MANGESH PADGAVKAR is a prolific writer for children in Marathi. Padgavkar has published volumes of verse and nonsense and has invented a new nonsense form called *vaatratika*. His books include *Aata Khela Naacha* (1993), *Vedamkokru* (2000) and *Chandomama* (2000).

SARITA PADKI's first poem was published in a school magazine some sixty-five years ago. She has had a long and distinguished career as a writer, in Marathi, of short stories, poems, plays and of several translations from English. She is best known for her writings for children. She has won several awards at the national and state levels.

K. AYYAPPA PANIKER (1930–2006) was a poet, scholar, professor and critic in English and Malayalam and has been a pioneer of modernism in Kerala. He received a Ph.D from Indiana University and did post-doctoral research at Yale and Harvard. He has received numerous awards, including several Sahitya Akademi awards, the International Man of the Year (IBC, Cambridge, UK, 1997) and the Indira Gandhi Memorial Fellowship.

SRI PRASAD was born in Parna, a village in Agra. He has a Master's and Ph.D in Hindi and specialized in children's literature. He took to writing for children in 1950. He taught at Sanskrit University in Varanasi. His books of children's rhymes include *Meri Saathi Ghoda*, for which he won the Sahitya Akademi Award, and *Tak Dhina Dhin*.

S. RAMAKRISHNAN is a fiction writer, essayist and playwright in Tamil. He has written five collections of short stories, two novels, three collections of essays and one book on Jorge Luis Borges. One of his plays was chosen for the National Theatre Festival. His novel *Nedumkuruthi* was selected as the Best Tamil Novel of 2003. He is the editor of the literary magazine, *Atcharam*. He is thirty-nine years old and lives in Chennai with his wife, R. Chandra Prabha, and two sons.

TENALI RAMALINGA (1500–1580?) was a major intellectual figure in the court of Sri Krishnadeva Raya, king of Vijayanagara. Possibly from the town of Tenali, now in Andhra Pradesh, he was a royal jester and a master poet of the Prabandha Age. Many stories in Kannada, Tamil and Telugu are told of this man, variously known as Tenali Rama, Tenali Ramakrishna, Ramalingudu and Tenali Raman.

ANNADA SANKAR RAY (1904–2002) was a prolific and iconic Bengali poet, novelist, essayist, travelogue writer and political activist. Born in Orissa, Ray chose early on to explore his roots and write in Bengali. He won many literary awards, including the Sahitya Akademi Award.

SUKUMAR RAY (1887–1923) was the second son of Upendrakishore Ray and Bidhumukhi Debi. As a student at Presidency College, he created the Nonsense Club, a platform for acting, literature and general absurdity. From 1911 to 1914 he went to England on a scholarship to study photography and printing. He married Suprabha Das, and their son, Satyajit, was born in 1921. Upon his father's death in 1915, Sukumar Ray took over editorship of *Sandesh*, the high-quality children's publication, while continuing to be active in literary circles. Besides children's literature, he also wrote plays, essays and short stories. He is usually considered to be the pre-eminent writer of nonsense in India. All his books were published posthumously, with *Abol Tabol* appearing just nine days after his death.

SARVESHWAR DAYAL SAXENA (1927–1983) was Hindi poet who belonged to the Nayi Kavita tradition. He was born in a mufassil town in Uttar Pradesh, and studied at Queen's College, Varanasi, and Allahabad University. He began as a short-story writer and went on to be a well-known poet and was on the editorial board of the Hindi paper *Dinman*. He won the Sahitya Akademi Award in 1983 (posthumously) for *People Hung on Pegs*.

SHANTA SHELKE (1922–2002) is a renowned Marathi poetess, writer and columnist. While writing for children was her favourite occupation, she became known and received many awards for her lyrical compositions for Marathi film songs. In her lifetime she penned lyrics for close to 300 songs, some of which have been made immortal by the voices of Lata Mangeshkar, Asha Bhosle and Kishori Amonkar. In 2001, Shanta Shelke was awarded the Yashvantrao Chawan Pratishan Award for her contribution to Marathi literature.

SRI SRI (Srirangam Srinivasa Rao) (1910–1983) was born in Visakhapatnam, Andhra Pradesh. He is considered the first modern Telugu poet. His poetry, such as the volume *Maha Prasthanam* (1950), changed the face of Telugu poetry through a unique fusion of Western and Eastern modern and postmodern ideas. He also composed lyrics for many songs in Telugu films.

RABINDRANATH TAGORE (1861–1941) was born in Calcutta to a prominent family and was home-schooled, except for one year at University College, London. In 1883 Tagore married Mrinalini Devi Raichaudhuri, with whom he had five children. Tagore wrote volumes of poetry, novels, plays, musical dramas, essays, historical texts, textbooks, travel books, and was a pioneer in short-story writing. He also wrote a substantial amount of children's literature and was a composer and musician. He won the Nobel Prize in literature in 1913.

SHREEKUMAR VARMA is a journalist, editor, publisher, radio broadcaster, entrepreneur, college lecturer and regular Sunday columnist for two newspapers. His award-winning plays include *The Dark Lord* and *Bow of Rama*. His debut novel was *Lament of Mohini* (2000). His book for children, *The Royal Rebel*, is about the freedom fighter Pazhassi Raja. He was awarded the Charles Wallace (India) Trust Fellowship and was Writer-in-Residence at the University of Stirling in the UK in 2004.

Copyright Acknowledgements

Grateful acknowledgement is made to the following for permission to reprint copyright material:

Banishilpa, Kolkata, for 'Meye Kemon Shikchhen', 'Dilli Cholo' and 'Clerihew' by Annada Sankar Ray from *Chhoda Samagra*, Annada Sankar Ray, Kolkota: Banishilpa, 1985, published here in translation by Sampurna Chattarji

Prof. Pradeep Acharya for 'Naugao' by Navakanta Barua from *The Complete Children's Literature of Navakanta Barua*, Vol.1, Guwahati: Anwesha, 2003, published here in translation by Dileep Chandan, and 'O Flower: A Lullaby', 'The duck chased off the civet' and 'Lullaby', trans. Navakanta Barua, from *Cradle Songs & Playtime Verses of Assam*, Guwahati: Anundoram Borooah Institute of Language, Art & Culture, 1999

Anushka Ravishankar and Tara Books for extracts from *Excuse Me Is This India?*, Chennai: Tara Books, 2001, and *Wish You Were Here*, Chennai: Tara Books, 2003

Vinda Karandikar and Popular Prakashan Pvt. Ltd, Mumbai, for 'Untavarcha Shahana', 'Mejwani', 'Pishi Mavshiche Parasu', 'Pishi Mavshiche Yatra' and 'Ranichi Baag' by Vinda Karandikar from *Ajabkhana*, Mumbai: Popular Prakashan Pvt. Ltd, 1974, published here in translation by Anita Vachharajani

Mangesh Padgavkar for 'Gull' from *Aataa Khela Naacha*, Mumbai: Mauj Prakashan Griha, 1993; 'Bichari Chimni' and 'Khara Ki Kaay?' from *Vedamkokru*, Mumbai: Mauj Prakashan Griha, 2000; extracts from *Vaatratika*, Mumbai: Mauj Prakashan Griha, 2002; 'Gharta' and 'Aasa ek manoos' from *Chandomama*, Mumbai: Mauj Prakashan Griha, 2000; 'Nasail' from *Vatdivasachi Bhet*, Mumbai: Mauj Prakashan Griha, 2000; and 'Nakoba' from *Sutti Eke Sutti*, Mumbai: Mauj Prakashan Griha, 2000, all published here in translation by Anita Vachharajani and Anushka Ravishankar

Sarita Padki for 'Gulte Aanne', and Sarita Padki and Popular Prakashan Pvt. Ltd, Mumbai, for 'Aanghol Stotra' by Sarita Padki from *Guttargoo Guttargoo*, Mumbai: Popular Prakashan Pvt. Ltd, 1998, published here in translation by Anushka Ravishankar

Usha Khadilkar and Navneet Publications (India) Ltd for 'Jhadavarun amba padla' by Usha Khadilkar from *Navneet Baalgite*, Mumbai: Navneet Publications, 2003, published here in translation by Anita Vachharajani

Anant Bhave for 'Kele, Kele' by Anant Bhave from *Jhim Jhim Sari*, Pune: Rohan Prakashan, 2001, and 'Jehva-tehva' by Anant Bhave from Haso Haso, Mumbai: Akshar Prakashan, 2001, all published here in translation by Anita Vachharajani

Navneet Publications (India) Ltd for 'Ekda' by Shanta Shelke and 'Aapdi thapdi' from *Navneet Baalgite*, Mumbai: Navneet Publications, 2003, published here in translation by Anita Vachharajani

National Book Trust, India, for 'Jamoon' by Sri Prasad from *Mehke Sari Gali Gali*, eds. N.D. Sewak and Krishan Kumar, New Delhi: National Book Trust, 1996, published here in translation by Sumanyu Satpathy

Meena Kumari for 'Kula Patakam' by K. Ayyappa Paniker, published here in translation by J. Devika

D.C. Books for 'Two Sad Souls' by Muthalappuram Mohandas from *Paatam Rasikaam*, compiled by M.R. Gopalakrishnan and Jose Nanjilethu, ed. Prof. S. Sivadas, Kottayam: D.C. Books, 2001, and 'Padippum Theetayum', 'Kondaavaam' and 'Katha Parayu' by Kunjunni from *Kunjunni Krithikal*, Vol. 1 & 2, Kottayam: D.C. Books, 2006

Prof. R.E. Asher for the extract from *Me Grandad 'ad an Elephant!: Three Stories of Muslim Life in South India* by Vaikom Muhammad Basheer, trans. R.E. Asher and Achamma Coilparampil Chandrasekaran, UNESCO Indian Translation Series, Edinburgh: University of Edinburgh Press, 1980

Manoj Das for 'Haladia Bhalu' from *Tumagan o Anyana Kabita*, Cuttack: Friends Publishers, 1992, published here in translation by Sumanyu Satpathy

J.P. Das for 'Poda Kapala', 'Bhagrathi Bhaina', 'Professor Kara', 'Sadananda Satpathy', 'Uda Khabar' and 'Dara' by J.P. Das from *Ali Malika*, New Delhi: Publication Division, Information and Broadcasting Ministry, Government of India, 1993

M.D. Muthukumaraswamy for 'Marma Naaval' by M.D. Muthukumaraswamy, published here in translation by Latha Ramakrishnan

S. Ramakrishnan for 'Ramasamigalin Vamsa Saritram: Sila Maraikkapatta Unnmaigal' from *Thavarangalin Uraiyadal*, Chennai: Tamarai Selvi Publications, 1997, published here in translation by Latha Ramakrishnan

Romu Sippy and Allied Pictures Pvt Ltd. for '*Nani ki Nao*' from the film *Aashirwad*

Prakash Mehra for the extracts from the script of the film *Namak Halaal*

Hirawat Jain & Co. for the extracts from 'My *Name is Anthony Gonsalves*' from the film *Amar Akbar Anthony*

Sahitya Akademi and Laltungliana Khiangte for 'Folk Song I' and 'Folk Song II' from *Mizo Songs and Folk Tales*, edited and translated by Laltungliana Khiangte, New Delhi: Sahitya Akademi, 2002

Sahitya Akademi for 'Hoote-maate' and 'To ve totarheya' from *Punjabi Lok Geet*, compiled by Devendra Satyarthi and Mohinder Singh Randhawa, New Delhi: Sahitya Akademi, published here in translation by Nirupama Dutt

Orissa Sahitya Akademi for 'Kathara Katha, Bhai Maharatha' from *Lokagulpa Sanchayana*, edited by Dash Kunjabihari, Bhubaneswar: Orissa Sahitya Akademi, 1964, published here in translation by Sumanyu Satpathy

Vidyapuri Publishers, Orissa, for 'Interlude from an Oriya Opera i' by K.C. Pattnaik from *Oriya Loko Sahitya o Loko Sanskriti*, ed. K.C. Pradhan, Cuttack: Vidyapuri, 1995, published here in translation by Sumanyu Satpathy

READ MORE IN PENGUIN

The Panchatantra
Visnu Sarma
Translated by Chanda Rajan

The Panchatantra is one of the earliest books of fables and its influence can be seen in *The Arabian Nights*, the *Decameron*, the *Canterbury Tales* and most notably in *The Fables of La Fontaine*.

Tradition ascribes this fabulous work to Visnu Sarma whose existence has not been conclusively established. Faced with the challenge of educating three unlettered princes, to awaken their intelligence, Visnu Sarma evolved a unique pedagogy—for his aim was to teach the princes how to think, not what to think—and it was thus that these entertaining and edifying stories came to be composed.

The Panchatantra started travelling from the land of its origin before AD 570, as a version in Pehelvi. Since then more than 200 versions have been executed in more than fifty languages.

Chandra Rajan, a noted Sanskrit scholar, has based her translation on the Purnabhadra recension (AD 1199). While remaining faithful to the original, she breathes new life into the stories, skillfully combining prose and verse to give us an eminently readable translation.

Classics
India Rs 250

READ MORE IN PENGUIN

Simhasana Dvatrimsika: Thirty-Two Tales of the Throne of Vikramaditya

Translated by A.N.D. Haksar

The fabled monarch Vikramaditya is considered a model of kingly virtues, and his reign a golden age. These famous stories narrated by the thirty-two statuettes of nymphs supporting the magic throne of Vikramaditya extol his courage, compassion and extraordinary magnanimity. They are set in a framework recounting the myths of his birth, accession, adventures and death in battle, after which the throne remained concealed till its discovery in a later age. A fascinating mix of marvellous happenings, proverbial wisdom and sage precepts, these popular tales are designed to entertain as well as instruct. Many have passed into folk literature.

The original author of the *Simhasana Dvatrimsika* is unknown. The present text is dated to the thirteenth century AD. It exists in four main recensions, from which extracts have been compiled together for the first time, in this lively and faithful translation of this celebrated classic by a renowned Sanskritist.

Classics
India Rs 200

READ MORE IN PENGUIN

Selected Stories
Parashuram
Translated by Sukanta Chaudhuri and Palash Baran Pal

Parashuram, or Rajshekhar Bose (1880–1960), was one of the most eminent and versatile figures of twentieth-century Bengal. Best known for his comic and satirical writing, he was the author of the popular Bengali dictionary *Chalantika*, played an innovative role in Bengali printing technology, and was awarded the Padma Bhushan in 1956.

This book is a selection of Parashuram's best comic tales: most of the classic pieces from his earlier volumes, as well as his later, more fanciful work. While some present biting social satire, others reflect a lighter view of human folly or eccentricity. There are also stories in a rare vein of philosophic critique and speculation. Collectively, they reveal the changing patterns of Bengali society, thought and attitude over a span of about forty years. Parashuram worked closely with the artist Jatindrakumar Sen, and the earlier stories are inseparably linked with Sen's delightful illustrations, some of which have been reproduced in this edition.

This is the first time that the range and variety of Parashuram's comic genius have been presented in English within the covers of a single volume.

Modern Classics
India Rs 295